Of Angels

and

Rolling Pins

๛

Jackie Gould

Acacia Publishing
1366 East Thomas Rd. Suite 305
Phoenix, Arizona 85014
www.acaciapublishing.com

ISBN 978-0-9814629-2-9
LCCN 2008920530

Cover design by Jason Crye

Printed and bound in the United States of America.

Also by Jackie Gould

Letters to Allie

Beyond Forever

Foreword

The inspiration for writing often comes from unusual or distant places. Sometimes it comes from fleeting thoughts that dart across one's mind, or from a photograph, a newspaper article, or perhaps a snippet of a movie or TV drama, or even from an obituary.

However, the inspiration for this story came from right underneath my nose. It originated from my collection of 170 rolling pins. Why collect rolling pins? One might ask. I am not sure how it began, but there is a certain intrigue to see the different rollers shaped from wood, ceramic, plastic, marble, and metal.

As I browsed through antique stores searching for unusual rolling pins, the question most often entering my mind was, "who had previously owned this pin?" and "what were the circumstances going on in his or her life?" Yes, I have a couple of pins that have charred marks on their barrels, and two have nail head indentations, as you will read.

But perhaps the one that is my prize is the cobalt blue glass souvenir pin with fading paint that says "Remember Me." When I discovered it nestled among other old treasures at the antique store, the tag on it said, "A parting gift from a sailor to his sweetheart—circa 1890." Now THAT had a story behind it for sure! So BESSIE'S story was born.

The inspiration for ANDREW came from a diary and letters lent to me by my dear friend, written by one of his ancestors during the Civil War. So the facts and locations mentioned were from the eyes of a firsthand witness.

As for TIMOTHY — his story was one I lived through, and I called upon my memory of how life was during WWII. The entire country was galvanized together as one people — to work toward the war effort. Every factory stopped producing consumer goods to manufacture tanks, planes, weapons, and uniforms. Ordinary citizens gladly put up with rationing of goods, shortages of meat, butter, flour, sugar, shoes, and automobile tires, just to mention a few things. "Fix it, mend it, or do without!" became the motto of the day. Anything to help "our boys." Finally, it became "we lived through it, and we won!"

The story still has to be written about my favorite rolling pin. It resides in my kitchen drawer and I use it all the time. A simple, wooden pin with orange handles which was a wedding shower gift to me some ____ years ago. If I told you how many, you would be surprised!

J.G.

Chapter 1

It seemed innocent enough, just a short, casual trip—a Good Samaritan sort of thing that Jennifer was happy to perform for her aging aunt. Jennifer knew that she, herself, needed the break now more than anybody. More than Aunt Bessie needed her. Even more than Don needed her. Parting from him had not been what one could call cordial. On the contrary, it had been heartbreakingly painful, full of hurt and bitter words, tying Jennifer's stomach into knots.

Oh, she needed space now, all right. Space and a new perspective. And this trip was just the opportunity that would put distance between her and the troubles she attempted to leave behind. Thank God Aunt Bessie could use her help! But how could Jennifer have known what a profound effect this simple homecoming would have on the rest of her life? How could she have foretold that a reunion in the days to come was about to turn her life upside down once more?

Now, as she peered out the bus window, the young woman watched low gray clouds scud just above the rows of tall corn stalks across fields that never seemed to quit in this quiet countryside of southern Wisconsin. The very scene she gazed upon slammed memories back into her mind... memories that she thought had long ago been abandoned.

Home again. Jennifer had come home once more to where she had been born and raised. The familiarity of it all rushed back to her in an instant, and it was as if she had never left, in the fall of 1950, eleven years ago.

Eleven years. Was it possible for that many years to creep by already? To glide away silently, like a leaf floating down a placid river? *How do you measure time anyway?* Jennifer wondered. There was her life in Arizona, and there was her life as she had lived it in Wisconsin. Somehow the two lives did not want to mesh.

As she looked at the rolling fields, now green with summer, dotted here and there by neat farm buildings and giant trees spreading their umbrellas of shade, Jennifer thought of the extreme contrast to the dry Arizona landscape which she had grown to love these past eleven years. Lush green everywhere now seemed a bit gaudy to her, and she smiled, reminding herself she had better not voice that opinion when she met her cousin, for Patty would never understand.

The bus shifted down as it entered the outskirts of Waterville, an old college town of ambiguous population, set in the middle of the fertile farming area of southern Wisconsin. Jennifer craned her neck, looking at the aging brownstone and brick buildings as the bus maneuvered through the town streets. She hoped Patty would be at the bus depot to meet her. Her cousin would have driven over from Iowa that day and, if all went as planned, the two would meet here. In her letter, Jennifer had clearly explained her scheduled flight into Chicago, and the resulting bus link that would bring her to her final destination, arriving at about four in the afternoon, August 10, 1961.

The bus gears ground down as the driver slowed almost to a stop, easing the groaning conveyance up over the edge of the driveway. He parked on the pad in front of "The Dairyland," a busy local restaurant with a few motel cabins in the rear. Jennifer retrieved her small bag from overhead, followed her fellow passengers out the doorway, and stood waiting as the driver unloaded suitcases from the cargo hold in the lower part of the sleek silver bus.

A sudden squeal, a rush of padding feet, and Jennifer found herself crushed in Patty's arms.

"Jenny! Oh, how great to see you!"

"Patty... let me look at you. You look super!"

Jennifer stood back at arms length, admiring Patty's long, slim, shapely legs showing beneath her white shorts. She wore a pale green cotton top that clung nicely to her small bust, and complimented her dark, curly hair.

3

"Jenny... my gosh! I almost didn't recognize you. You are so tanned."

"It's that Arizona sun," Jennifer grinned, running her fingers through her short, sunbleached hair. Already the humidity was wilting the slacks that she wore, and she could feel the cloth clinging to her body. The dampness was heavy, and Jennifer found she had to take deeper breaths to fill her lungs. She had forgotten how different it was here, after living in the desert southwest for so many years.

Patty linked her arm through Jennifer's and picked up her cousin's bag, steering her to the '58 Ford Station Wagon where she placed the bags in the back.

"Let's go in and get a Coke," Patty suggested.

"Oh, that would be great. I feel clammy and want to wash my hands, anyway."

After they had settled themselves into a booth and ordered burgers and Cokes, the two cousins chatted non-stop until their food came.

"It's been too long, Patty," Jennifer said between bites. "I really miss being able to talk to you."

"Same here. Gosh, but the years just go by so fast!"

"And, now here we are, together again to help Aunt Bessie move into her retirement apartment. Have you seen her lately?" Jennifer queried.

Patty shook her head. "No, not since I moved to Iowa with Jim five years ago. I don't get back over here very often."

"How are the boys and Jim?"

"Oh, they're fine... fine," Patty uttered quietly, but did not directly meet Jennifer's eyes. "And Don? How is he doing? How is the business?"

"We're struggling as usual," Jennifer said with a big sigh, thinking how her husband was trying to deal with business reverses, among other things, and trying to forget their latest quarrel. "But, at least the girls are in college now," referring to Don's two grown daughters from a previous marriage.

They finished their burgers and got a refill on their Cokes.

"So Aunt Bessie has finally decided to give up the house?"

Patty nodded, "It's about time, wouldn't you think? I mean, she's 89 years old, and she insists on doing everything herself. I hear that she even shovels her own walks in the winter, for heaven's sake!"

Jennifer shook her head. "That lady is amazing. I guess she lives right. I should be so lucky to live anywhere near that age. But I guess it runs in the family. Weren't there several who lived well into their eighties and nineties?"

"I think I heard years ago that one couple lived to celebrate their son and daughter-in-law's 50th wedding anniversary, while they celebrated their 75th!" Patty added.

"Good grief! Can you imagine being married to anyone that long? Living with someone all those years, without killing each other?" Jennifer blurted.

Patty glanced at Jennifer, detecting a slight tone of discontent, or was she imagining something that was not there? "Well, I think we'd better get on to the house. Aunt Bessie will be expecting us. I telephoned her this morning and told her we would be there late afternoon but not to fix supper for us."

Jennifer paid the check and followed Patty out into the late cloudy afternoon, settling herself in the front seat of the station wagon. It only took a few mintues for them to drive the short distance to Aunt Bessie's place, pulling into the driveway beside a magnificent old gray stone house with a "SOLD" sign on the front lawn. A huge covered porch circled half-way around the three story building, accessed by a wide bank of cement steps. A round turret reached up the full three stories, flanking the left side of the front door; its curved glass windows shining clean, even in the darkness of the overcast sky.

A maple tree spread giant branches across the greater part of the lawn, and snowball hydrangea bushes crouched at the foundation of the porch, forming a backdrop for geraniums and dusty miller, which had been planted in a graceful curve around the house. More red geraniums tumbled from white wicker baskets suspended from the porch beams.

"My word!" Jennifer breathed, "Who takes care of all this?" admiring the neatly trimmed lawn and carefully edged flower beds.

"Three guesses," Patty uttered, starting up the front steps.

"Land o' Goshen! Look who's here!" Bessie Herrington cried out as she scurried through the screen door to meet the pair at the top step. She was a slim woman, who, even at 89, stood tall and straight. Silver white hair was piled atop her head, and she wore bifocal glasses which slipped on her nose. Her face was almost smooth, and so soft, hardly a wrinkle could be detected. The woman spread her arms wide to encircle both her nieces and immediately ushered them into the parlor.

"Sit. Sit. You must be tired from your travels. You sit right there where I can look at you. Jenny— Oh, Jenny—it has been such a long time! And Patty, I haven't seen you in a coon's age."

It had not been but a minute when the older woman sprang up on her way to the kitchen. "I've got lemonade. I'll be right back," she flung over her shoulder.

The younger women protested, but to no avail. Soon Bessie returned with glasses of iced, sweet lemonade, clinking on a tray as she bustled back into the room. A plate of homemade gingersnap cookies accompanied the beverage, the crackled tops sugared just perfectly.

"Oh, you two are sure a sight for sore eyes," Bessie fussed and babbled, firing question after question, not waiting to hear an answer before she posed another inquiry. Her smooth oval face erupted into easy smiles as she chatted, and the laugh lines crinkled around her eyes, which were amazingly clear and bright blue.

"You sure you have eaten, now? I would gladly whip up something for you to eat," Bessie pressed the issue. "You two are naughty not to have let me fix you supper after your long trips."

"We would not think of putting you to that much trouble, Aunt Bessie," Jennifer said. "It will be hard enough just coping with the two of us while we are here."

"Nonsense! I'll love every minute of it. I'm only sad that you girls will have so much work to do. There's a lot of sorting and packing that needs to be done. The auction is scheduled for a week from Saturday. Now, I want to be perfectly clear. If you girls want any of this, just speak up before we sell it."

Jennifer looked around at the Victorian furniture in the room and stifled a negative response she was about to make. The curved settee, upholstered in burgundy mohair, and matching chairs with their carved mahogany wood trim did absolutely nothing for the young woman, whose taste ran more to the sleek lines of Danish Modern. *This stuff is old,* Jennifer thought. *Who would even want to buy it?*

Patty assured her aunt that there would, indeed, be possibilities she would like to consider. Unlike Jennifer, Patty appreciated antiques and was herself a collector of sorts, spending her weekends prowling garage sales and flea markets, every now and then finding a treasure she could not resist.

"Well, now, you girls just settle in and get comfortable in your rooms. Towels are in the bathroom," Bessie said later as she prepared to retire. "If you don't mind, I think I will call it a day." She moved off to the downstairs room she had converted into a bedroom. "See you in the morning."

"Good night, Aunt Bessie," both girls chimed in unison.

Jennifer gathered the empty glasses and tray and carried them to the kitchen, halting in the doorway, surprised that she had not remembered the 1920's ivory and green enamel gas stove sitting against the wall. A whole array of ivory and green enamel cookware was neatly stacked on open shelves along another wall. A long, high shelf held at least a dozen teapots of various designs and vintages, and along the windowsill, above the high-backed sink, little pots of African violets and ivy lent cheery color to the room. On the counter in one corner was a tall old iron wine rack which was filled with rolling pins.

"Patty, come here."

Patty followed Jennifer into the kitchen.

"Look at this!" Jennifer pointed to the pile of rolling pins. "Ye Gads! Have you ever seen so many rolling pins?"

"There must be fifty or more," Patty said as she walked closer to inspect a white ceramic pin with red handles, which was cradled in a twisted wire hanger. "And look, there are even some on hangers on the walls."

"What in the world is Aunt Bessie doing with so many rolling pins?" Jennifer shook her head as she inspected the stack of wooden pins, noting the variety of shapes and sizes.

"I guess she likes to bake." Patty shrugged.

Later, the two women went onto the porch and sat in comfortable, high-backed, white wicker rocking chairs which were adorned with well-worn, faded yellow and green cushions. A misty rain fell gently outside the screened walls of the enclosure, bringing a cooling relief to the humid day. Jenny leaned her head against the cushion and closed her eyes, soaking up the refreshing evening air. Then she dared to let memories of years long past slip back into her mind of the time she had made the decision to move to Arizona.

I wonder if he is still in this area? She thought, referring to the person who had once devastated her life, and caused her to quickly change her plans many years ago.

Patty's voice broke Jennifer's reverie, making some kind of remark that Jennifer had to ask her to repeat.

"I was saying, I wish Jim could have come along, but he is teaching summer school."

Jennifer nodded. "Too bad, I'm sure we could have used his help."

"I'm just lucky that the boys are off to the YMCA camp for two weeks." Patty paused, and then immediately regretted her next thought as soon as it left her mouth, "I don't like leaving Jim alone, but maybe the separation will be good for both of us."

Jennifer was suddenly alert. "Troubles, Patty?"

Patty averted her face from the soft light that spilled out from the window so that Jenny would not see her eyes tear up.

"It's nothing," Patty lied.

But Jenny sensed that Patty was holding back and looked closely at her profile in the semi-light. "Hey, tell me about it, if you would like. I'm here, and I am a good listener."

Patty shook her head, and in a voice that was strained from a constriction in her throat, managed to utter, "No—no. Not now. It will be okay."

Jennifer continued to rock back and forth and put a reassuring hand on Patty's arm, giving it a squeeze, as she thought, *Oh, poor Patty. Your life seems so perfect. Now there must be trouble in paradise.* Jennifer often admired her cousin's seemingly comfortable life as the ideal housewife and mother. Everytime she thought of Patty, Jennifer pictured her in a happy household, with a loving and devoted husband, and their two well mannered boys excelling in school, living the American Dream in a well-kept home. The proverbial cottage with the white picket fence held a vision that Jennifer admired, and longed for, and sometimes coveted, so it surprised her that there could possibly be anything to mar that tranquil scene.

Jennifer mulled over this news and contemplated how much they now had in common. *Troubles between Patty and Jim?* And now it seemed to mesh with her own marital discord with Don. They seemed to fight about everything these days. Money, sex, even what TV program to watch. How could this be happening to both of them? All the while, Jennifer still held on to the fairy tale belief that once she married, she would live happily ever after. Wasn't that the way it was supposed to be?

Jackie Gould

Chapter 2

Jennifer woke to the fragrance of coffee as it wafted up the stairwell into her bedroom. Sunlight dappled the ivory colored shade drawn at the window, casting shadows of tree leaves that danced in the breeze like a painter's brush on canvas. For a moment, she lay there, watching the patterns move and change, and daydreamed, just as she had done hundreds of times as a child in her own bed. The songs of morning birds greeted her ears, and she relished the lively exchange of calls, detecting a cardinal's whistle somewhere near.

At that moment, a clawing, cold hand seemed to grip her stomach with the realization that she was no longer that child, but now a grown woman, and would never again be able to skip down the stairs to greet her mother with a warm smile and hug. Never again be able to have that carefree exuberance of youth, to enjoy endless days of freedom from responsibilities. Her mother was gone, passing seven years ago. Yet Jennifer's insides cried out to bring it all back. *Mom!,* the depths of her seemed to cry. And so she rose to face the day with an emptiness aching inside that took its place beside a sudden homesick feeling that she could not explain.

After a quick shower in Aunt Bessie's cast iron, claw footed bathtub, Jennifer fluffed her short, blond curls. Swiftly, she donned a pair of olive colored Capri pants and a yellow shirt, buttoned in the front. She tied the long shirttails together at her waist, and rolled the sleeves up above her elbows. A touch of lipstick was all she needed for make-up, since her face was well tanned. She wet the edge of her index finger, brushed her eyelashes to make them curl up a little, and stared at the hazel eyes peering back at her from the mirror. With a nod of approval, she descended the stairs and joined Aunt Bessie in the kitchen, following the sounds of a whisk beating eggs in a bowl and the rich aroma of freshly brewed coffee.

"Ah, there you are, Dearie. Come sit right here and pour yourself a cup of coffee. Did you sleep well last night?"

Jennifer nodded and took a sip of coffee from the mug she had poured before answering, "Very well, Aunt Bessie."

Everyone called the woman Aunt Bessie, even though in reality, she was Jennifer's and Patty's great-aunt. Jennifer's mother had been the older woman's niece. Now she and Patty were the only surviving relatives, Patty being the only daughter of Aunt Bessie's late nephew. Aunt Bessie's siblings had died years ago.

Many times over the years, Jennifer had wondered why Aunt Bessie had never married. It dawned on her now that this tall, strong, capable woman standing before her, was alone. There were no relatives to whom to turn. No husband, no children—just alone—an old woman all by herself, nearing the end of her years. A tinge of compassion began to build in Jennifer's heart, and she forgot the empty feeling that had assailed her earlier.

Patty skipped down the stairs and joined the two in the kitchen, her face bright and cheerful, shining from the scrubbing she had given her skin. Her lips were tinted pink and complemented the natural glow of her complexion.

"Good morning! Gee, I guess I'm the lazy one this morning. Sorry. You been up long?"

"Just got here, Patty. You haven't missed a thing."

"Now, you two just sit down. The eggs will be ready in a jiffy," Aunt Bessie directed, a happy smile on her face.

"Aunt Bessie, can't we help?" Jennifer was insistent.

"Okay. You pour the juice and get out a new jar of preserves from the pantry for our toast. It's so nice to have someone to cook for."

Aunt Bessie seemed animated this morning, inspired by her house guests, with spry movements belying her advanced age. Indeed, there appeared to be an extra spring in Bessie's step today.

"Where do you suggest we start, Aunt Bessie?" Jennifer asked, between bites of golden toast, slathered with her great-aunt's homemade elderberry jam.

Without hesitation, Bessie replied, "First of all, I think we should take a look at my apartment. That way, you can see what I should take there and how much room there will be. You two can help me decide just which things to take. Patricia, perhaps you can drive us after breakfast?"

Within an hour the trio was inspecting a neat, two bedroom, ground floor apartment. It looked painfully small compared to the large, antique-filled house that the older woman now occupied. Jennifer made measurements of each room and drew a rough floor plan on a large note pad. The kitchen was small, but laid out efficiently, and had its own stove and refrigerator.

Jennifer was determined to make it cozy for the woman.

"See this little area in front by the porch?" Aunt Bessie was referring to a postage stamp sized rectangle of earth that hugged the small, covered porch. "I'll be able to plant some flowers.

Oh, I searched a long time to find a place where I could walk out and be able to get my hands in the soil. I have to do that, you know. I have to be able to connect with the earth. You don't know how much that means to my soul—to be able to dig down and plant the flowers I love, to have the moist earth sift through my fingers. Do either of you girls do a lot of gardening?"

Patty nodded. "Yes, in fact we have a rather large vegetable garden. I do enjoy gardening, just like you, Aunt Bessie."

"It's different in the desert," Jennifer said wistfully. "I miss being able to grow certain things. I was frustrated at first, when I moved to Phoenix, like not being able to grow tuberous begonias. I used to love those the most. Down there, we have to do our planting in October, and the flowers are at their peak in February and March. April is the most gorgeous month, though, as all the petunias and roses are just spectacular. By the time May comes, it starts getting too hot, and from then on we don't garden much. We just do a lot of swimming in the pool."

"You've got your own pool?" Aunt Bessie was impressed.

Jennifer nodded. "But everyone there has their own pool. That doesn't mean we are rich, it's just a necessity to help survive the 110 degree days we have from June through September."

Bessie shook her head, unable to comprehend such high temperatures, wondering how anyone could possibly endure such a place. Jennifer attempted to explain how the low humidity and air conditioning in Arizona made the heat tolerable, but knew that the older woman could not relate to something she had never experienced.

Back at the house, Aunt Bessie stood in the parlor, her hands on her hips in a total daze.

"How can I give up anything?" she mused.

Jennifer was busy sketching out the floor plan and measuring sofas, chairs, the bed, and bookcases. She and Patty huddled together, each suggesting certain pieces of furniture and the exact location on the floor plan where they would be placed. Aunt Bessie would nod in agreement at times and at other times vehemently reject the girls' ideas.

"But I must take that corner lamp table. It has been in the family for over one hundred years," Bessie pleaded, gesturing to a marble topped mahogany twist-leg table.

Jennifer studied the plan and said, "There we are! We can use it in the bedroom as one of the night stands."

Aunt Bessie frowned as she squinted at the rough layout, then nodded her head in agreement. Room by room, the three women strolled, eyeing each piece of furniture until they were satisfied with what Aunt Bessie would use. Other pieces were tagged to be sold in the auction.

Afternoon brought a new direction of focus after the major furniture pieces had been decided upon. Jennifer could plainly see that the task of sorting, boxing and arranging was going to be monumental, considering the vast amounts of knickknacks and decorative things that cluttered the parlor, sitting room, and dining room. The very thought of the job ahead was mind boggling and there seemed to be no way to find a starting point.

The porch swing beckoned Jennifer when Aunt Bessie suggested they take a break mid-afternoon for refreshments on the wide, shaded porch. The young woman drank in the view of the sun-dappled expanse of green lawn, sprinkled here and there with patches of flowers, as she lazily pushed the wooden slat swing back and forth with her foot. She could not help but feel that the scene she was witnessing would be perfect to publish in *House Beautiful*, or *Better Homes and Gardens*. Mentally, she composed just the angles she would shoot the pictures from, if she were a photographer for such magazines.

A soft breeze blew across the porch in near perfection, and Jennifer wished she could stop that moment in time and wrap it in a box to keep forever. A more perfect summer day could not be imagined. The sun shown brightly without a cloud in the blue, blue sky. It reminded her of the perfect summer day many years earlier, when she had strolled along the river trail, hand-in-hand with a dark haired young man. Just like today, that summer day was perfect, and was made even more perfect because she had been madly in love with the man at her side.

Now, in a rush, the delicious feeling of being in love for the first time stirred Jennifer. Suddenly she was transported back in time eleven years, to the carefree, innocent summer of 1950. She had just completed her junior year at Waterville College. Everything seemed perfect then. Her studies had gone well, and she had a part-time job at the drive-in. She had met Ralph Warren, a handsome Air Force Veteran of World War II, who was completing his education through the GI Bill of Rights.

Jennifer distinctly remembered how the air had felt that summer day so long ago. How the breeze had rustled through the maple and oak leaves, sending them shimmering in the clear sun light, and how patches of blue sky peeked between the branches, without even a wisp of a cloud in sight.

A perfect day it was—perfect in every way. The young college girl's spirits had risen to exhilarating heights, as exciting waves of love danced over her with ever increasing intensity.

Along the walk, Ralph had drawn Jennifer off the trail they were hiking, into a well shaded spot where soft moss covered the ground. They had been surrounded by ferns and wild grapevines, which provided a dense screen from everything except the birds that flitted overhead, from tree top to tree top.

Even now, Jennifer remembered the way Ralph's arms had encircled her. She could still feel his lips enclosing her mouth, his tongue caressing hers. She recalled the very masculinity about him, his muscular arms, his broad shoulders, and how firm his body felt against hers. She remembered how excruciatingly delicious the moment had been. How perfect the union had felt on that perfect summer day long ago.

Jennifer jerked back to reality when Aunt Bessie repeated a question she should have heard.

"I was asking if you and Patty would mind going to the grocery store to see if they might have some boxes we could use. Are you all right, Jennifer? You seem a little far away."

Jennifer's daydream snapped, and she blinked into the present.

"Of course, Aunt Bessie, we will be happy to get some boxes."

Patty rose. "Come on, Jenny, let's see what we can find. I can fit a lot in the station wagon."

Patty sent an inquiring glance at her cousin, and knew the young woman was upset about something. Perhaps not upset, but rather bothered, would be the word, and Patty determined sooner or later she would find out what Jennifer was holding back from her.

Chapter 3

The next morning while in the kitchen for breakfast, it was Patty whose curiosity could no longer be contained, and she finally asked Aunt Bessie about the vast array of rolling pins the woman had collected.

"Are you going to keep all these rolling pins, Aunt Bessie?"

Without a moment's hesitation, Bessie exclaimed "Of course!"

"But how come you have so many? Certainly you can't use them all?"

"Oh, girls," Bessie patiently started to explain. "Every one of these pins represents a love story."

The two girls both frowned and glanced at each other, shrugging their shoulders in a helpless gesture.

"Of course, you could not possibly know the stories that these rolling pins represent. You see, almost all of these..." here, the older woman rose from the table and stood beside the counter where the pins rested, placing a gentle hand on top of the stack. "...all these rolling pins once belonged to our family or a dear friend, and what stories they could tell, if they could talk."

"What do you mean, Aunt Bessie? What do you mean they are love stories?"

"I mean that every one of these pins were at one time in the hands of someone who lived, and loved, and cooked, and baked for their own loved ones. Now they have passed on. Members of our family— going way back before the Revolutionary War!"

Suddenly perked with interest, Patty and Jennifer sat a little straighter in their chairs. Aunt Bessie searched a moment, and then, carefully, with loving hands, picked out a wooden rolling pin, obviously very old, about sixteen inches long. The pin was crude by modern standards, and was dark with age.

"Look at this," Bessie said, thrusting the rolling pin into Patty's hands. "See, it was carved out of a single piece of wood. Hard maple, I think, though it might be hickory. I doubt it's oak. The grain is too smooth to be oak."

Patty fingered the rolling pin, noticing how old the bit of wood seemed. The handles were not well defined, but rather, the pin tapered off, and there were only crude bumps at the ends. There were flat nicks and rough edges, now well worn, which clearly were not what a machine lathe would have produced. The wood itself was very old and dark. There was a suggestion of a crack in the main shaft in a couple of areas due to its extreme age.

"This one was handed down by the Herringtons, and was found along with an old long-rifle next to baby John Herrington. It is told that his parents ran with him in their arms to the safety of a fort when he was but eighteen months old. That was in 1761, before the Revolutionary War."

"I never knew that!" Jennifer looked at her great-aunt in amazement.

Aunt Bessie nodded. "The story is that both parents died from exhaustion after running with the baby to escape from renegade Indians. All they were able to tell their rescuers before they expired was that the baby's name was John Herrington. No one seems to know the first names of those young parents. All we know is that the family name is Herrington. John is as far back as the family tree can be traced."

"But where did the rolling pin come in?" By now Jennifer was totally intrigued by the sketchy story that Aunt Bessie was relating.

The older woman shrugged her shoulders and raised her eyebrows. "Story has it that this rolling pin and a rifle were found with the dead parents. I'm only guessing, but perhaps the mother carried it as a weapon or club of some kind as she was running from the Indians. If you look closely, you will see some initials carved in one handle. What do you make them out to be?"

Jennifer held the seemingly worthless bit of wood in her fingers, gently turning the pin over and over, examining every inch of the crude implement

"It looks like E or F-H, and the one below is really weird. A strange N-H, but the N has a fishhook on the left side at the bottom as if it started to be a J."

Patty peered closely to see the faint mark and shook her head, unable to decipher the letters.

"But think, girls," Bessie's voice was now an intensely hushed whisper. "Think of the love those parents must have had for that child. To run, perhaps miles, with him in their arms. To speed to safety, to be sure the wee one could be saved. That's love, girls. That's love."

It was Jennifer who picked up on the mystery. "But those two parents... they must have loved each other too. There must have been a love story even before the baby was born."

Patty was in awe. "Two hundred years! Do you realize this piece of wood is probably over two hundred years old? Wow! What do you know about that baby John, Aunt Bessie?"

"Well, by all known accounts of family history, John Herrington was estimated to have been born January 1, 1759, somewhere in what is now western Pennsylvania. He served in the Revolutionary War."

Bessie returned to the table with a fresh cup of coffee, and her voice was soft, almost reverent.

"He fathered eleven children and homesteaded several farms in Ohio. You know, he lived to be 103 years old! I have got a lot of letters and things tucked away from cousins and relatives scattered all over the United States. After I settle down in the apartment, I intend to write all the genealogy down so you girls will have a copy and know about your Herrington roots."

"Is that a promise, Aunt Bessie? I never knew about John, or any of our ancestors, for that matter. Promise you will write down as much as you know."

There was an urgency in Jennifer's tone, and suddenly she was intrigued and absorbed in the prospect of learning a lot about her family history. For the remainder of the day, Jennifer could not shake the notion of the dramatic run to save baby John. She began to imagine what the parents of that little one were like. *Were they blond or dark haired? Blue eyed or brown? Had they immigrated to America, or were they descendants of the earliest Colonists? What were their names? Who were they?*

Later that evening, while retrieving a snack in the kitchen, Jennifer removed baby John's rolling pin from its nest among the others. Suddenly, it had become precious to her, more than just a cylinder of random wood shaped into some utilitarian utensil. It had a life and story of its own. It was almost a spiritual experience for the young woman just to hold it in the palms of her hands. To know that this item had been used by that unknown mother, that far distant relative, some two hundred years before. Jennifer felt a chill and goose bumps rose on her arms.

"What tale do you hold within the very depths and pores of your cells?" Jennifer whispered. "Whose delicate hands held you and used you? Whose strong hands shaped you from an inert bit of a tree?"

She clasped the rolling pin in both hands and brought it to her chest, squeezing the wood as if to wring the very life out of it. A bit shaken and surprised at the emotion she was feeling over a silly piece of wood, the young woman moved under the kitchen light to look again at the crude letters carved into the end so long ago. With her index finger, she traced the tiny E-H and mused at the strange N with the J fishhook on the front leg.

If she could have had a magical sixth sense, Jennifer would have been able to determine that this crude bit of wood belonged to an English woman named Elizabeth. It had been roughly carved by her husband, Nathan Herrington, in 1760. Had the story been able to be told, Jennifer would have discovered that it was not Nathan, but actually his twin brother, Jonathan, the real brother who had survived the horrible massacre in 1755, known as Braddock's Defeat. And when Jonathan, who had married Nathan's sweetheart without her knowledge of his real identity, carved the rolling pin for his lovely wife, he inadvertently started to carve a J, for his own name, but changed it quickly to an N for Nathan. Thus, the strange looking fishhook letter remained for those in the twentieth century to ponder.

The story of blooming love, mistaken identity, Indian wars, captures, and rescues before the Revolutionary War would forever remain a mystery, locked within the core of this nondescript piece of wood. It was a rolling pin that had survived with its secret for over two hundred years. Just a piece of inert maple that could never tell about the dark haired frontiersman who fashioned it, nor the lovely blond-tressed wife who treasured the gift and carried it as she ran when she and her husband saved their infant son. It could never relate how the couple expired from exhaustion after that great race.

No one would ever know that three angels, Nathan, Jonathan, and Elizabeth, looked after the baby John all his long life. They hovered over and looked after his many children and their prolific offspring with a love so strong as to fairly shake the gates of heaven, itself. Oh, if only the rolling pin could talk. What a tale it would tell.

Chapter 4

"And this roller was brought from New York State, across the country in a covered wagon! It belonged to my Grandmother." Aunt Bessie remarked as she showed off yet another rolling pin carved from a single piece of wood. The dark wood was well seasoned with years of working with lard-infused dough. Bessie explained that in the early 1830's, immigrant families followed the Indian trails across Ohio, Indiana, and Illinois, passing along the south shore of Lake Michigan. They stopped for a while in Chicago, which was but a small village at the time.

"She was a young bride when she came to Wisconsin. This rolling pin tells a tale of the trails—see the burn marks on the pin?"

The girls examined the wooden cylinder and saw charred marks in a couple of areas.

"I guess it got too close to the camp fire," Bessie chuckled. "I never knew my Grandmother. She passed away before I was born, but my mother told me stories about her. How she and Grandpa pioneered the farm and raised their children. Mama told me how it was with Grandma in the early days. How the prairie was so beautiful... all grassland and filled with wildflowers, a riot of color," she said.

"I remember Mama telling how there were so many doves that the sky would be black as they flew. Oh, they had dealings with the Indians, too. Once Grandma was alone with the babies when a group of Indians came to the cabin demanding whiskey. Well, there was no whiskey in that house! So she tried to convince them she had none, all the while her knees were knocking in fright. It ended up she gave them two pies she had baked with this very rolling pin, and they seemed satisfied. I guess they were taken back by the sweet treat, even licking their fingers, Mama learned years later when Grandma related the incident."

Bessie paused for breath. "I can't imagine how difficult it must have been at first, with scarcely any neighbors, very little of the creature comforts, trying to cook and bake on an old iron stove."

Jennifer and Patty murmured in agreement, all the while turning the rolling pin in their hands as they tried to imagine the young mother whose hands had used it, riding all that way in a covered wagon, pioneering new land. It was a humbling experience to know of the life that this bit of charred wood represented. To know that it had belonged to Aunt Bessie's grandmother sent chills up their spines.

"This little toy rolling pin was made by my grandpa." Bessie showed the girls a miniature wooden pin about five inches long with graceful rounded handles. Again, the pin was extremely old. "My mother gave it to me when I was a child. It is one she played with when she was a little girl."

Jennifer thought she saw a tear swell in Aunt Bessie's eyes as she seemed taken back in time. Ah, the memories she must have of 80 years ago. Of play times and cozy days in the kitchen at her mother's elbow.

They all giggled at another pin Bessie showed them. It was obviously a much lighter wood, probably soft pine. Bessie pointed out the round indentation marks of distinct nail heads on the barrel.

"I think this housewife used it for a hammer. See the nail marks?"

"I'll bet she was trying to hang up the kitchen curtain rod," Patty offered, a grin on her face a mile wide. "Can't you just see her now, standing on tiptoe on an old kitchen chair, hammering away?"

"Who would have known there were so many different kinds of rolling pins?" Jennifer marveled.

Bessie nodded. "There are marble, glass, ceramic, plastic, and wood, of course. Every conceivable thing that might get the job done. Green handles, red handles, metal handles... long, short, fat, skinny. I've got them all!"

Two days later, the packing and sorting was progressing at a satisfactory pace, pleasing both Jennifer and Patty, and Aunt Bessie as well. So well, that one evening the two younger women decided to attend the County Fair which was being held at the Fairgrounds for the entire week.

"Oh, you two gals go on, have a good time! You deserve it for all the hard work you have been doing," Aunt Bessie urged, "but you will forgive me for not going... it would be just a little too much for me."

"Are you sure you will be all right? I mean we don't want to leave you alone, Aunt Bessie." Patty was concerned that it would appear rude for the two of them to go off for an evening of entertainment and not invite their host to come along.

"Nonsense! I am used to being alone, and I will be perfectly fine to just stay here at home and catch up on some reading. Now you two run along. Have a fun time!"

The evening turned out hot and humid with the promise of a late night thunderstorm brewing. Heat lightning signaled a storm somewhere on the distant horizon, reflecting faint flashes far off.

"Do you know how many years it's been since I attended the County Fair?"

Patty shook her head. "Gosh, Jenny, I have no idea."

"Ever since moving to Arizona. It's just not the same there. We usually go to rodeos instead. Gee, I almost forgot what an exciting thing it is—especially for the little kids."

Jennifer was watching families with little children line up for the kiddie rides. A wistful expression fell over her face, and she could not disguise the envy she felt as she studied the cherubic faces of the little ones. A pang of loneliness and longing waved through her, and her heart reached out to the children with an emptiness that was unmeasureable. So great was her yearning, that despite her efforts to stop it, her eyes misted, and a lump rose in her throat.

"What is it, Jenny? Are you all right?"

Jennifer nodded and quickly turned away. "Let's go to the animal barn," she said, blinking away the tears, hoping Patty had not seen them. She took a deep breath and put on a happy face, but she couldn't fool Patty.

"I'm not going one step farther until you tell me what is wrong! You've been acting strangely ever since you got here, Jenny, and I know you well enough to know when something is bothering you."

Patty found a bench and pulled Jennifer down to sit upon it. "Now, tell me. What in the world is wrong?"

Jennifer blinked, swallowing hard. "It's just—it's just that I want to have a baby of my own so much!"

"But you and Don still have lots of time to have a family of your own, don't you think?"

Jennifer stifled a sob that rose from her depths. "But... but Don doesn't want any more children. His two girls are all he wants!"

"Oh, surely that cannot be true, Jenny. He must want to have a baby with you."

Jennifer shook her head. "No... no, he has made it very clear that he does not want me to get pregnant. You see, his first wife died in childbirth when she had Melissa, and Don never forgave himself for that."

"Oh, Jenny!" Patty did not know what to say.

Jennifer was silent for a long moment, locked in her own self-pity. "I thought I would be able to change his mind after we were married, but I guess I was wrong. They say you can't change a man, but I thought our love was strong enough to prove 'them' wrong. They were right, after all. I can't change his mind."

"Then you knew of his feeling about not wanting children before you married him?"

"Yes, but you know the old saying—love is blind. In this case, it was not only blind, but deaf and dumb, too."

"Oh, Jenny, how sad. I am so sorry. You are a wonderful mother to Don's two daughters I'm sure."

"But Patty, Colleen, the oldest, is only ten years younger than I am, and Melissa is twelve years younger. I feel like their sister, not their mother."

"I never stopped to think of it like that," Patty said.

"Come on." She grabbed Jennifer's hand. "Let's do something wild and fun. Let's pretend we are just two young girls out for a lark. Let's buy cotton candy, and go on the Tilt-a-Whirl, the Whip, and the Ferris Wheel!"

Jennifer held back, reluctantly allowing Patty to pull her toward the cotton candy booth. However, she started to giggle when she faced the big mound of air blown, pink confection. Soon she was laughing like an adolescent, and being silly, like someone half her age, and it made her feel better.

It was while they were on the Ferris Wheel that Jennifer caught a glimpse of him. The huge wheel had stopped when the two young women were almost at the top and let a new group of riders onto the chairs. Jennifer happened to casually glance down at the couple boarding, and a shock wave shot through her as she saw his familiar figure. She had not been prepared to see him, but there he was, that same tall, lanky frame, easing with graceful control into the seat. His dark hair was slicked back perfectly, the part as straight as an arrow. The very shape of his head and how he cocked it just so sent a second shock wave through her. It was Ralph Warren, all right, no mistake.

There was a child, a girl with golden curls, about four or five years old who sat between him and the woman with him. Ralph had his arm across the back of the seat, his hand resting protectively on the woman's shoulder. Each time the Ferris Wheel swept around in its arc, Jennifer could see them as their chair swayed, and she could see how tenderly Ralph touched his companion. She saw how he leaned his head close to the child between them, talking to the little girl as she looked up at him and smiled.

Jennifer imagined Ralph's grin and could almost detect the dimples in his tanned face. She tried to stifle the small thrill that waved through her when he threw his head back and she heard the deep rumble of his laugh.

There was a sting in Jennifer's heart as she remembered Ralph's touch, and how, eleven years ago, she had been the young woman sitting on his right in the swaying Ferris Wheel car at this very same place. She had been the one who had screamed delightedly when he playfully leaned over the restraining bar, tipping the seat forward, threatening to toss them both out.

Now, Jennifer remembered how bittersweet those carefree days had been. How exciting the new found, innocent, delicious feeling of being in love had thrilled through her, those many years ago. She had felt at the top of the world then, just like the exhilarating feeling of the rushing wind blowing past her face as the wheel catapulted them to the apex of its revolution.

There had been no cares then, no worries, only the pure innocence of youth, with the promise of all the future looming ahead, bright and exciting, stretching on forever. Everything lay ahead of her back then; marriage, a home, family, the fairy-tale perfect dream... Cinderella and the Prince.

The ride ended, and as the wheel stopped at each seat to dislodge its load of passengers, Jennifer's heart started thumping. She became nervous, her mouth suddenly as dry as that cotton candy had been. She and Patty disembarked four cars ahead of Ralph's. Part of Jennifer wanted to hold back, to turn and come face to face with the man who had devastated her life years ago, but she was afraid. Afraid of her own reactions. How would she face him? What would she say? He with his smooth Country Club swagger... would he even remember the girl who had fallen head over heels in love with him eleven years ago?

Jennifer glanced back over her shoulder as she and Patty headed down the crowded midway, hoping to catch a glimpse of Ralph, and at one point thought she saw the top of his head above the throng of people.

"Come on, Jenny, let's do the penny toss." Patty was pulling on her arm.

Jennifer laughed. "Patty, I didn't know you were such a kid at heart."

"Didn't anyone tell you that I never grew up?"

"I can see that now!" Jennifer retorted, giggling again.

Thirty minutes later, when Patty's arms were loaded with two huge stuffed animals, so large that she could hardly see around them, the two young women headed for the exit gate.

"Just where do you expect to keep these? Your boys are a little too old for stuffed animals, don't you think?"

"Oh, these will go to the Children's Hospital. I volunteer some of my time there. The kids will be thrilled with these big guys." Patty squeezed the huge white-faced panda bear and the tall, gangly giraffe which she held in each arm.

"Let me carry one," Jennifer offered, tucking the giraffe under one arm, letting the legs straddle her hip. They had hardly gone a few yards around the end of the last building when they bumped into a couple coming in the opposite direction.

"Whoa there! Sorry!" a deep voice boomed, and Jennifer felt two strong hands grab her arms above the elbows to steady her. She closed her eyes tightly, recognizing the voice instantly, and color rose up her neck to her face. When she opened her eyes again, she was staring directly into Ralph Warren's face.

The man peered closely down at her, recognition slowly igniting in his clear blue eyes, which shown like beacons out of the depth of a tan that had turned his face to bronze.

"Jenny? Jenny Foster?" He cocked his fine head a little to one side, a quizzical expression on his face, as he tried to connect the memory. He attempted to mask how this encounter had startled him as the full recognition of the girl in front of him sailed in.

Jennifer was tongue-tied, and could only stare stupidly, helplessly, back into his devastatingly handsome face. She nodded dumbly, and clutched the giraffe even tighter, knowing that she would melt if he touched her again.

"Hello, Ralph." Her voice was weak, and she hoped he could not detect the trembling that suddenly shook her body. There was an awkward moment when neither one spoke.

Finally, Ralph, always smooth and suave, never shirking the polite manners of the proverbial sophisticate, introduced the woman at his side.

"This is my sister, Karen, and her daughter, Lindsey."

Jennifer murmered a greeting and moved to pass around the trio, but Ralph spun her around with his hand on her arm.

"Are you back for good?"

Jennifer shook her head negatively, now agitated at the delay.

"No, just visiting. And my name is Adams now." Her words were short and clipped.

"How long will you be in town?"

"Just a few days."

"Perhaps I'll see you again before you leave. Where are you staying?"

Jennifer hesitated, reluctant to give him a clue as to where he could find her. When she had come back to Waterville, she had both desperately wanted to see him, yet dreaded the moment at the same time.

"We're at Bessie Herrington's place," Patty burst out. "By the way, I am Patty Peterson, Jenny's cousin." Patty extended her hand.

Ralph returned her greeting, his smiling eyes briefly scanning Patty's form from top to bottom with an admiring glance before returning his gaze to Jennifer.

"Maybe I'll see you around." Ralph's voice held a tone that Jennifer knew was meant especially for her, and a thrill went through her despite the hot night that choked close.

She gave a half-hearted smile, ducked her head, then left with Patty through the exit. Jennifer was glad the area was in half darkness, because she did not want Patty to see how much that brief encounter with Ralph was affecting her, for now her face was burning and her heart beating rapidly.

Jackie Gould

Chapter 5

It wasn't the crashing sound of a thunderstorm that kept Jennifer awake that night, it was the disturbing result of the chance meeting with Ralph Warren, once again, which had her fitfully tossing in her bed. Every emotion she had experienced eleven long years ago: love, desire, passion, and especially guilt, flooded the young woman like a giant wave. She found herself riding the crest of that emotional wave, seeing the smooth downward slope in her mind's eye, and she fought to keep from tumbling down.

Jennifer did not want to relive those painful times; yet, just like a surfer who catches the curl of the big wave and starts the downward glide, the distraught young woman was powerless to prevent the inevitable pull, so down she slid, into the abyss of memory.

The enormous energy of the violent thunderstorm outside was nothing compared to the turmoil roiling inside Jennifer. Each brilliant flash of lightning that illuminated the bedroom window only served to sear the image of Ralph deeper and deeper into her mind, until, with a little gasp, she allowed the full memory to crash back into her. She could not hold back any longer. What had taken almost eleven years to bury deeply now only took a scant few minutes to completely uncover.

Damn him! she thought, fighting the sting of tears that welled from deep inside. *Damn the way he has of cocking his head just so. Damn the way his smoldering blue eyes pierce into my very soul! Damn the way his perfect teeth gleam white when he smiles, and the deep-lined dimples crease his cheeks at each corner of his mouth. Damn the way the planes of his face form such handsome features.*

Jennifer realized in an instant that she was still madly in love with him. *Damn! Damn! Damn!*

The thunderstorm cracked and boomed outside the house, but Jennifer was oblivious to the torrents that lashed the summer night. The torrent of memories crashing in her mind became even stronger.

"Don't tease me like that," Ralph had whispered to her that summer day long ago. "You know how it affects me."

His lips were next to her ear, and she could feel the heat of his breath against her face.

"You drive me crazy," he groaned as if in agony, sending Jennifer thrilling as she loved the newly found feeling of power she had over him when she flirted dangerously, knowing she could bring him to a mindless frenzy.

His lips began to brush across her cheek, edging slowly, slowly down to her mouth. Jennifer's lips quivered in anticipation, and she felt limp when Ralph's warm, wet mouth enclosed hers in a sensuous kiss that sent her senses reeling. His hands were everywhere, roving across her back, then lowering so his palms pressed her hips into him.

He loosened one hand and slipped it skillfully beneath the folds of her blouse as he lowered them both to the ground. Jennifer was helpless, straining her body to cling to his, allowing his tongue to search her mouth, sending erotic waves shooting through her body. Then his hand moved smoothly down across her belly, his fingers inching slowly downward. Momentarily Jennifer resisted, trying to pull away, but her efforts were useless. Ralph's kisses were setting her on fire. Those kisses blocked out everything except the delicious sensation that threatened to explode inside. No— no, she must not let this happen! No, this was wrong. She should stop—stop. She must not allow— she must not...

Jennifer did not remember how it happened, but nothing mattered at that point, for she was reeling in sensations never before experienced. She was washed again and again with feelings of warm love. She clasped her arms about his body, pulling him closer to her, letting him grind his kisses until her lips were bruised.

Suddenly it was over, and Ralph panted as he lay on his back beside her, a lock of his dark hair clinging to his forehead, now beaded with perspiration. Jennifer slowly, awkwardly redressed, too shy to meet his gaze. He pulled her over onto his chest, ran his fingers through her hair, and kissed her, more gently this time.

"You were great, but I didn't know it was your first time."

She nodded, her face buried in the crook of his neck, glad that he could not see the embarrassment she was unable to hide. Jennifer was trembling in the aftermath of passion as the glow slowly ebbed from her body. She could not deny that is was her first time. Her physical body had told him so, yet she fought to be nonchalant, trying to make believe she was not totally naive and inexperienced.

"I love you," she whispered hoarsely, desperately needing to hear him say he loved her, too.

"You're something else, you know?" his voice was low and husky, and Ralph leaned on one elbow, tracing a finger across her cheek as he gazed down at her, his blue eyes smiling into hers.

Then he reached down and kissed her again, softer this time, laying a familiar hand on top of one of her breasts. His kiss never stopped, but became more intense, and Jennifer moved to press closer to him. It did not take much urging to arouse him once more, and they coupled again.

Jennifer lost track of how many times they made love that afternoon in the woods beside the river. For the remainder of that summer, every day was the same. They were almost always together, and made love as often as circumstances allowed. They were inseparable, it seemed, when she was not working at the drive-in, and he was not working on his Chevy.

Jennifer never seemed to catch on to the fact that sometimes, when Ralph failed to come around for days at a time, he was off at the Club tennis courts.

Jennifer had been too naive to realize that Ralph never took her to meet any of this friends or family, nor did he involve her in any of his social activities. She did not come from the same social class as he, therefore, was never exposed to the Country Club life. She was too much in love with him to recognize that Ralph was using her for his own purposes. That thought never occurred to her until years later.

Jennifer was positive that the handsome ex-Air Force pilot, the Veteran of World War II, was in love with her. He had to be. If he were not, then

Jackie Gould

how could he be so convincing when he made love to her? However, later, as she had looked back upon those summer weeks of 1950, it struck her like a blow. He had never once uttered the words she longed to hear—that he was in love with her.

Then, the unthinkable happened. She missed her period. But she was young and inexperienced, naive, and trusting, in the throes of full blown love. It was not until Jennifer missed her second period and was feeling queasy and strange, that she became terrified. *Pregnant! Oh, no!* Her parents would be mortified. She would not be able to face them, could not possibly face the wrath of her father, nor bear to see the terrible hurt that would be on her mother's face.

When she confronted Ralph with the awful truth, his shocking response had sent her into the depths of despair.

"Pregnant? You are in the family way?" He seemed highly agitated, his voice rising to an unusual pitch, one which Jennifer had never heard before.

"Yes, Ralph. I'm going to have your baby."

"How did that happen? I thought you were taking care of yourself!"

Jennifer was stunned at the tone of his voice.

"I guess... I guess that means we should get married," she blurted out, sure that he would sweep her into his arms, agreeing eagerly that their wedding day should be tomorrow. She would be utterly disappointed.

Ralph turned so his profile was toward her, reached into his shirt pocket and pulled out a Camel cigarette. He took a big drag on the lite and let the smoke out of his nostrils in a long breath. Then he took two more drags before turning once more to Jennifer.

"You don't have to stay pregnant, you know. There is a friend of mine at the Club... a physician... he could help you end this."

Jennifer sat down suddenly, shocked beyond belief. This was not what she wanted nor expected to hear from Ralph. She had expected that her knight-in-shining-armor would have swung her around in a jubilant celebration, and kissed her tenderly. She had thought that he would have tilted her face up to him and gazed at her with love melting in his eyes. She thought that the man she loved would have wrapped his arms around her, lifted her off the ground, and carried her off into the sunset.

"But,—I love you, Ralph, I love you!" Her voice was trembling. She ached with love for him, and now tried to calm the panic that was threatening to engulf her. "You don't mean that... you really don't mean that I should have... have... get rid of the baby?"

Jennifer stifled a sob.

"Look, Jenny," he took hold of her hand. "This is not a good time right now. Our country is going to war in Korea, and I am being called back into service. I was going to tell you. I leave next week. I'm going back into active duty, probably go overseas and fight in the war. I don't know when—"here he paused dramatically, "or *if* I will come back."

Jennifer remained silent. Tears burned her eyes and brimmed over, splashing onto the hands with which she tried to cover her face. She was shaking uncontrollably, attempting to stem the hysteria that leaped within her.

"But, we could get married before you go!"

Ralph shook his head, his mind racing, trying to extricate himself from this most unpleasant situation.

"Look, Jenny, this is what we will do." He reached into his billfold, extracted three one hundred dollar bills and forced them into Jennifer's hands. He then scribbled a name on a scrap of paper. "You contact this doctor. He will end your situation. But be sure not to mention my name. It would get all over the Club, you know."

Jennifer shook her head. "I can't... I can't do that." she sobbed, bitterness burning inside, choking her words.

"Take this! Take the money!"

"No... no. Oh, Ralph, don't you understand? Don't you love me too? You must love me—you must!"

"Look, you are a great gal, and a super piece of ass, but I am not ready to settle down. It would not be a good time right now with me going back into service. Maybe, when I come back from the war... then we'll talk about it."

That's how it ended, with a thud, a dagger in her heart. Ralph Warren walked out of Jennifer's life that night and left her heartbroken and pregnant. She sobbed for days in between bouts of morning-sickness and tried to conceal her puffy eyes from her mother's inquiring gaze. That is when the young girl made the decision to go to Arizona, to finish her senior year, she told her parents. She had saved enough money from her drive-in job, and along with the three hundred dollars that Ralph insisted she keep, the distraught, depressed girl fled to the southwest, enrolling in the University of Arizona in Tucson.

It was there in the lonely, harsh desert city, that she bore a son the following March, and without ever getting so much as to hold the tiny infant once, watched as the nurse whisked him away. The baby was put up for adoption, just as she had wished, and Jennifer felt as if her heart had been ripped from her body.

This was the secret Jennifer had kept to herself. The bit of her life that could never be revealed. She had even used a fake name on the birth certificate. Her family would have been humiliated beyond belief had they ever known that she had a child out of wedlock.

She moved to Phoenix after graduation, where she tried to pick up the pieces of her life. From that time on, she had returned to Wisconsin only once, to attend the funeral of her parents when they died in an auto accident. Eventually she met Don, a widower with two daughters, whom she married several years later.

"Oh, Donald," she cried out to him now. "I never want to hurt you, and I shall do everything in my power to prevent you from ever knowing, but I want to have a baby of my own! I need to have a baby all mine, to cuddle, to care for, to love. I'm aching, Donald. Don't you understand? I'm hurting, aching, dying inside." Jennifer moaned outloud, sobbing into her pillow. And the storm raged outside her window.

Chapter 6

"Did you girls have a good time last night? Come, sit, and tell me all about it." Aunt Bessie said as she cheerfully poured the morning coffee, anxious to hear all the news about the fair. "I used to go to the fair every year, and oh, my! How I loved to take in all the sights."

"Gosh, Aunt Bessie, you should have gone with us," Patty exclaimed, now saddened that the two girls had not insisted she come along with them last night.

"No, really, girls, my arthritis is acting up a little, and I would not have been able to keep up with you two. Besides, I was too busy this year to enter my cookies and pies. I always used to take a ribbon in one category or another."

Patty grinned. "I'm sorry, Aunt Bessie, but the two of us did act kind of foolish. We went on all the wild rides just as if we were kids out of school. It was fun, wasn't it, Jenny?"

Patty glanced closely at her cousin and was immediately shocked to see that she was obviously distressed. Jennifer, her eyes puffy and with dark circles etched under them, could only nod dully as she gripped the coffee mug with both hands, bringing it to her lips, letting the warm liquid trickle down her throat. She had scarcely slept, her mind had been so tortured with memories that even now threatened to explode right here in front of Patty and Aunt Bessie.

Jennifer desperately wanted to talk about those long forgotten events, which she had locked away so carefully, for they were here with her now as if it had all happened yesterday. She felt raw, like a fresh wound had ripped open her flesh. Raw and irritable. Every sound and sight felt like another electric jolt stabbing into her.

"Jennifer, dear, the storm must have kept you awake last night. You look as if you didn't get much sleep. You poor thing!" Aunt Bessie murmured.

Jennifer tried to brighten and blinked her eyes, shaking off the horrible aftermath the memories had dredged up from the deepest, darkest recesses of her mind.

"I'll be all right, Aunt Bessie—," her voice trailed off into a whisper.

"Jenny, what is it?"

Patty placed her hand on her cousin's arm, concern clouding her face.

Jennifer hesitated, ready to blurt out the whole tale of her long lost love, the whole story of the baby she had given up, and about how her heart was breaking for the lost child. She wanted to tell how deep her yearning was for that which she could never have now. The young woman found herself filled with guilt and rage. Guilt for the agonizing decision she had been forced to make to give up her baby, and rage that Donald would not allow her to become pregnant. Double rage now, because Donald was considering having the new treatment, a vasectomy, to be sure she would not conceive.

There was a sharp rap at the back door, interrupting Jennifer's thoughts, and a jolly, "Hello, Bessie!" rang out. It was Mrs. Wilbur, one of Aunt Bessie's neighbors, who stood holding a large cardboard box, almost as wide as she was. Her round dimpled face shown with cheeks as rosy as polished apples, beneath wire-rimmed spectacles that perched on her nose. The woman's dappled gray hair was smoothly pulled back into a bun, except for one stray strand that refused to stay in place. A yellow apron covering her flowered house dress was tied around her ample waist with a large bow.

"My gracious, Fanny, what have you here? Come right in."

Aunt Bessie held the door open for her friend. "Let me help you."

"I brought a casserole and a homemade pie. I thought with you being so busy packing and all, that you wouldn't have time to cook."

"Well, now, isn't that sweet of you! You are always so thoughtful, Fanny. Here, I'd like you to meet my nieces. This is Jennifer and Patty... Mrs. Wilbur."

Aunt Bessie put an affectionate arm around the other woman's shoulder.

"Fanny, here, makes the best pies in town, next to mine, of course!"

The two older women burst out laughing.

"Oh, pshaw! Bessie, you always were such a flatterer."

"Nonsense, Fanny. Your pies are delicious. In fact, everything you cook is excellent. This is such a nice thing for you to do for us. Thank you very much."

Aunt Bessie removed a high, sugar-crusted, delicately browned apple pie from the box. The apple-cinnamon aroma wafting from the still warm pie spilled into the room, and Patty's taste buds did a quick twinge.

"Aren't you a good neighbor!" Patty smiled. "That is really nice of you, Mrs. Wilbur. Mm-mmm, I can hardly wait to taste this."

She turned the pie plate slowly around to admire the flaky crust and resisted the temptation to pull a crumb off the edge and pop it in to her mouth.

Aunt Bessie ushered her friend to the kitchen table and poured a cup of coffee for the new arrival.

"How is it going, Bessie?"

"Well, the girls, God bless them, are doing a very good job of sorting things out. We pretty well know just what we are going to take to the apartment, and we're gathering things for the sale."

There was a long silence as Fanny Wilbur blinked back a mist that had suddenly formed in her eyes, and she tried to squash the thickening she felt in her throat.

"I sure am going to miss having you for a neighbor, Bessie."

"Oh, Fanny, I'm going to miss you, too. That's the hardest part of this whole thing... to pull up and leave all my friends of so many years."

Aunt Bessie was a little emotional, herself, as it was starting to dawn on her that she actually was going to be leaving her old neighborhood for good. A big change in her life was on the horizon, but she would face it as she faced everything, with confidence, hope, and enthusiasm.

"But, you know, I'll only be a couple of miles away. We'll have to get together often. Especially when we do our volunteer work at the church and all."

"Oh, I know, Bessie, but hang it all, I won't be able to pop in your door anytime, like now, to have a cup of coffee and gab like we do so often."

"You two will just have to make sure you get together for lunch or something every week. You can manage that, can't you Aunt Bessie?" Patty peered closely at her aunt, hoping to insure that the obviously close friendship could endure the upcoming separation.

Bessie nodded. "Of course, Fanny! I'll just crank up the old Plymouth and come get you so we can have lunch at The Dairyland."

"It's times like these I wish I'd have learned how to drive an automobile. But Mr. Wilbur, God rest his soul, never would trust me behind the wheel. Said I'd for sure drive everyone off the sidewalks in the whole town if ever I was to take the wheel. Maybe he was right. It always seemed so complicated, with all those levers and pedals. Doesn't it bother you to drive in all that traffic, Bessie?" Fanny patted the stray lock of hair back in to place and wiped her glasses with the edge of her apron.

Bessie shook her head. "Lord, no, Fanny! I just get in and GO! Besides, with no lawn to mow or sidewalk to shovel, I'll have plenty of time on my hands. Which reminds me, I promised I would help bake for the church suppers and I volunteered to be a substitute House Mother at the college if they need me."

Jennifer and Patty exchanged astonished glances, each wondering how this remarkable woman, at the advanced age she had attained, could even think about such an ambitious schedule. The very thought about her energy made both of them feel guilty when they allowed themselves the luxury of feeling even a little bit tired.

"It must be something she drinks," Jennifer whispered to Patty, and they smiled at each other over their private joke.

Fanny Wilbur rose and took the casserole dish out of the cardboard box. "Here, this should go in the ice-box. It's a ham and scalloped potato thing you can heat up, whenever."

Aunt Bessie and the girls thanked Fanny profusely for her thoughtfulness. Patty and Jennifer had both taken a liking to Mrs. Wilbur immediately, and were happy that she was such a good friend. It eased their minds that Aunt Bessie had people like Fanny to keep an eye on her.

Fanny reached into the cardboard box one last time and brought out something wrapped in a kitchen towel.

"Bessie, I want you to have this," she said, handing the bundle to her friend. "I'm sure it will fit into your collection."

Puzzled, Bessie unwrapped the towel, and with a start, looked down at a white ceramic rolling pin with wooden handles peeking out from beneath the folds of the red and white checkered dish towel. She looked up to meet her friend's eyes.

"What's this, Fanny?"

Fanny Wilbur dropped her eyes and tried to cover up the momentary flicker of pain that crossed her face, which did not go unnoticed by the keen eyes of Jennifer and Patty.

"Oh, you know, Bessie, this is the rolling pin that... that... you know... when Timothy was... " Her voice trailed off in a strange crackle. "I could... I could never use it... again." The last was just a whisper.

"Oh, Fanny!"

"I want you to have it"

"Are you sure, my dear?"

"Yes... yes, Bessie you keep it... and remember Timothy."

"It's really a beautiful gift, Fanny," Bessie was truly moved. "It will take a special spot in my collection. I shall treasure it always."

She put her arms around her friend and hugged her close, sensing the sobs she knew Fanny was trying to suppress.

That evening, as Patty and Jennifer knew she would, Aunt Bessie told the story of Timothy. It almost seemed as though they were reliving it as it happened.

Legend 1
"Timothy"
Part 1

"Mom! Dad!" Timothy called, coming down the stair steps two at a time, his close cropped light brown hair tousled haphazardly across his brow. "We're in it! We're in the war! The Japs bombed Pearl Harbor!"

Excitement quavered in his voice, and the boy was almost breathless when he reached the living room where his father, who was puffing on his favorite pipe, sat reading the Sunday paper.

"It's on the radio! I just heard it!"

Fanny Wilbur hustled out from the kitchen, drying her hands upon her apron, as she heard the commotion caused by her teenage son.

"What is it, Timothy?"

"We're in the war, Mom! They bombed a place called Pearl Harbor in Hawaii." The boy's chest heaved under his favorite green and white knit sweater, his brown eyes glistening with excitement.

"Who?"

"The Japs! They bombed us!"

"Oh, mercy me! What does that mean?"

"That means we will have to go to war now, Mother," Herman Wilbur said somberly, clenching the pipe between this teeth, as he folded the Sunday newspaper neatly in his lap. He noted the date on the paper, December 7, 1941, and tucked that fragment of information away in the corner of his mind.

Fanny sat down suddenly, as if the air had been let out of a balloon, and her fingers clenched and unclenched nervously in her lap. Her eyes clung hungrily upon Timothy's face. Seventeen. He was just seventeen. His eighteenth birthday was only a scant three months away. A chill ran through her, for in the back of her mind, without actually forming a thought, she already knew that her son would be in that war. The chill deepened within her, and suddenly, the safe, secure world she had known all her life turned upside down.

"I've got to go see Spud," Timothy uttered, excitement still raging, as he dashed up the stairs to his room, grabbed his coat, and barely said good-bye when he slammed out the back door. The sound of the old '32 Ford engine's roar rumbled into the house, and he was gone.

"Oh, dear, oh, dear," Fanny's worried voice exclaimed, distress clearly visible on her face.

"Now, calm down, Mother, calm down. Don't get upset. It won't help anything."

A muffled sob coming from the stair landing whipped both parents back to reality, and it dawned on them that they had completely forgotten about their eleven year old daughter, Barbara.

"Oh, Sweetheart, what's the matter?" Fanny said from the bottom step. "Come here, dear, come down."

The gangly girl, her pencil-stick legs showing white between her socks and the hem of her dress, slowly approached her mother, brushing tears from her eyes as she shyly descended the last few steps. Fanny put her arms around the girl, brushed stray hair back from her face, and tried to calm her own fears as she guided Barbara into the kitchen.

"What does it all mean Mama?" the little one barely whispered, tears still dampening her cheeks.

"Come, sit down, darling, I'll make you some hot chocolate." Fanny tried to put a lilt of reassurance into her voice, knowing how sensitive and fragile her daughter had been of late.

"Are we in war, Mama? Are we going to get bombed? Are the bad soldiers going to come and lock us up? Is there going to be shooting?"

Fanny busied herself at the stove. "Oh, Barbara, Heavens no! Our army will just take care of us, and go fight the enemy overseas. Everything will be just fine, you'll see. Don't worry your pretty little head about those things."

Barbara, in her pre-adolescent way, shy, and unsure of how to talk out loud about the fears she held inside, struggled to find answers to questions she did not even know how to ask.

"Is Timmy going to have to go to war and be a soldier?" she finally asked, hoping that her mother would be able to convince her that what she feared most would not come true.

Fanny poured the hot cocoa into a mug and set it in front of her daughter along with a plate of oatmeal cookies.

"Why, Timothy is too young! He is still in school. He's not going to war, Barbara, don't you fret about that, dear."

As much as Barbara wanted to believe her mother, she could not help the feeling of despair that engulfed her when she had heard Timothy's excited disclosure. At her tender age, the little girl, already struggling with the new, conflicting emotions emerging in her effort to grow up, was confused, and wanted desperately to believe that everything would be okay. But the nagging doubts refused to go away.

At the same time, Fanny struggled to remain calm even in the face of her own anxiety. She tried to mask her own fears so that Barbara would not become unduly upset. Her heart rate had increased, and her hands shook slightly, as she turned her back, and proceeded to make a pot of hot tea for Mr. Wilbur.

"Finish your cocoa, Babs, it's almost bedtime. School tomorrow, you know."

Barbara nodded, and brightened suddenly, "Can I wear my new gray sweater and skirt? The ones you gave me for my birthday?"

Momentarily Fanny frowned. "That's for good, dear. Don't you think you should keep it for special occasions?"

She saw the disappointment flash in her daughter's face, and noticed a decided slump in the girl's shoulders, and so she relented.

"Oh, all right, just this once. Now off to bed."

Later that night, in the quiet of their darkened bedroom, Fanny and Herman lay side by side in the double bed, caught up in their own thoughts. Neither one was able to talk about the fears and the uncertainty that lay deep within their hearts. They both heard the boy's footsteps on the stairs, and heard his bedroom door close, and each, without the other knowing, wondered how long their son would remain under their roof. How long would it be before the adventure of war would lure him away from the security of the Wilbur household? From the warmth of their grasp?

The following day, the entire high school body gathered in the assembly hall to listen to the radio address President Franklin Roosevelt gave, asking Congress for a declaration of war against Japan. It was a somber group that sat in silence while the loudspeakers cracked the historic news. The customary boisterous behavior of the student body was now subdued in the seriousness of the moment. None assembled there on that December Monday morning could possibly imagine what suffering, sacrifices, and hardships lay ahead for all of America. They were young, eager, and obviously unaware of what ramifications would be caused by Japan's attack.

Timothy Wilbur, clean cut as always, his handsome face bearing a suggestion of a somber frown, on a whim passed a note up the row he was sitting in to a red-headed girl wearing a yellow dress. "Meet me at the malt shop after, OK?" the note read. He had written the message on a lark, at the urging of Spud, who poked Timothy in the ribs and winked, a broad smile on his lips. The girl leaned forward so she could look at the writer of the note, and shyly smiled at him, nodding imperceptibly, a rosy tint starting to color her cheeks.

Wow! An invitation from Timothy Wilbur! He was a big man on the high school campus. A good-looking senior who was the dream-boat of many of the girls, including practically every underclass female in school. To get a special invite from him was an honor not taken lightly, for he only needed to cock his head, and crook his finger to have the girls flock to his side.

Virginia McClusky scarcely heard the rest of the assembly, for her thoughts were racing as fast as her heart was pounding. She was only a junior, and to be asked to join Timothy was something the girl had dreamed about ever since the school year had begun. Now she fidgeted in her seat, crossing and uncrossing her saddle-shoed feet, fiddling with the buttons on the brown cardigan she wore. She glanced at the big clock on the back wall, and wondered how she would live for the next four hours until the final bell would ring, and she could dash to the malt shop.

The juke-box was blaring Glenn Miller's "In The Mood," as excited teenagers converged in Adamson's Malt Shop later that afternoon, piling into the red leather booths, slamming their school books down on the tables. Timothy, Spud, and their friends, Mike and Jamie, squeezed into a booth at the rear of the shop, and huddled their heads close together, discussing the news of the war.

"The Marines, that's what I want to join!" burly Mike Matson declared, fresh off a successful football season where he had been a star linebacker for the high school Varsity team.

"It's the Navy for me. How about you, Spud?" Timothy's eyes sparkled as he looked at his friend.

"Yup! The Navy, never any doubt."

Jamie remained quiet, not at all surprised that those two would prefer the Navy, for they were already members of the local Sea Scouts troop. Pictures and models of sailing ships and big battleships covered every inch of their respective bedroom walls. For him, slim and of small stature, Jamie had no desire to enter the military. He wanted to become a veterinarian. The boy was extremely sensitive, and abhorred violence in any fashion. Animals, and the love and compassion he felt for them were the only things Jamie was interested in.

Virginia McClusky shyly approached the booth where the boys were sitting, clutching her arms around a stack of school books, feeling very much like a stuffed bear in her heavy winter coat. Timothy moved over, and motioned for her to sit beside him. She sat down quickly, barely able to hang onto the edge of the bench, because the booth was now over crowded.

"What do you think, Ginny? The Navy or the Marines?" Timothy asked, turning his gaze toward the flustered girl.

She shrugged, lifting her eyebrows, and in a little voice uttered, "I don't know."

"Come on, Ginny," Timothy demanded. "You have to make a choice. Navy or Marines?"

"What's the difference?"

"The difference is—" Timothy quickly searched his mind. "The difference is, if you make the right choice, I'll take you to the Christmas Formal!"

Timothy surprised even himself at that bold statement. He already had plans to ask Rosemary Brown, his frequent date, to the dance. Now, what had he done? He was already kicking himself.

Virginia gulped. Had she really heard him right? A few hours ago, she was merely an ordinary junior, walking the hallways of Waterville High, daydreaming girlish dreams of dating the senior. Not just any old senior, but the *catch* of the class. The one person whom all the other girls drooled over. The very young man whose ears must burn all the time, for he was the constant subject of every girl in the school from freshmen on up. Now, hardly believing her ears, Virginia was on the brink of having a real date with her idol.

Jackie Gould

Four pair of eyes intently studied her face, which she suddenly felt grow hot, and knew the flush was rising from her neck up. In desperation, she gave pleading glances to each of the other three, hoping to get a clue from them, but their eyes were unreadable.

"What about it, Ginny? Navy or Marines? Which one should I join?"

Again, Timothy demanded she make a choice.

What an excruciating decision faced the young girl. Her eyes traveled to the pea coat Timothy was wearing, and she noticed the anchors etched into the black buttons.

"Navy—?" she barely whispered.

Timothy cocked an ear forward. "Say again?"

Virginia looked Timothy squarely in his brown eyes, melting just to be able to gaze into them, and said louder, "Navy," and held her breath.

There was a long silence, which felt like her death-blow, before a snicker erupted from Spud Weaver's lips, and he clapped Timothy on the shoulder.

"Looks like you got a date for the Christmas Formal, Tim, old man!"

PART II

"As soon as you finish putting stamps on those Christmas cards, come help me bake the Christmas cookies," Fanny called out from the kitchen. She was rolling out sugar cookie dough with her favorite rolling pin, a white, opaque ceramic cylinder with smooth, worn oak handles, which Timothy had given her as a gift one Mother's Day. He had used the very first money he had ever earned on his paper route to buy the pin. Even though Fanny had an all wood rolling pin tucked away in a drawer, she preferred the ceramic one to all others she had ever used. It was smooth, and the dough rarely ever stuck to the utensil, no matter what the recipe.

Proceeding to cut the thinly rolled dough into festive holiday shapes, with her own mother's large collection of old tin cookie cutters, Fanny's thoughts drifted to the many years she had made the same cookies, following methods she had been taught by her grandmother. Now Fanny could hear the radio softly playing Christmas music in the living room where Barbara was finishing licking the envelopes.

Fanny thought how strange this Christmas season was going to be, knowing the country was at war. It was hard to get into the Christmas spirit, for the news from the Pacific already told of places named Guam and Wake Island, which had surrendered to the Japanese. On the other side of the world, Germany and Italy had declared war on the United States.

Bad news seemed to bombard everyone from all sides, and indeed, things looked dark and foreboding. There seemed little to be cheerful about this year. Gamely, Fanny tried to maintain a little sense of balance by continuing the family traditions surrounding the season. Tomorrow Timothy would take his new girl friend to the Christmas Formal, and there still remained so much to be done.

The fine shaped Christmas tree that she and Mr. Wilbur had taken such a long time to decide upon the other day, leaned in a corner of the cold garage, awaiting the time when her husband could build the wooden tree holder. He's got to do that tonight, Fanny mused, as she whisked a hot tray of cookies out of the oven, mentally tallying up all the projects she needed to accomplish before tomorrow night. Timothy would be bringing a carload of young friends over after the dance for a post-formal midnight supper. Of course, Fanny would outdo herself, as usual, in preparing the spread for her son.

The tree needed decorating, and food needed to be prepared. How had she let Timothy talk her into this, anyway? Then her heart warmed at the thought of her son's breathless urging, and she could still feel the wet kiss he had planted on her cheek when she had agreed to prepare the midnight buffet. "You're my Sweetheart, Mom!" he had said, as he grabbed one of her homemade doughnuts and disappeared out the door.

That evening, Fanny heard cursing coming from the basement as Herman struggled to build the tree standard. Sounds of sawing and hammering came from the stairwell, and Fanny worried the process along. No, it leaned too far to the right—that branch was too crooked—can't you fill in that blank space by splicing in another branch? And so the annual argument about the tree took its usual course, until finally, puffing with effort, Herman struggled up the basement steps with the prize tree, as it shed needles all the way.

Triumphantly, Herman set the tree in the usual spot beside the fireplace, and turned it slowly to Fanny's satisfaction, where it stood tall, bare, and dark. Untangling the strings of lights was another frustrating matter, and though Herman never uttered a word, Fanny could tell by how hard he clamped his pipe in his teeth when his patience had worn thin. Barbara helped put the fragile but colorful glass ornaments on the branches, and at last topped off the decorating by loading every branch with silver tinsel, which danced in shimmering waves at every movement of air.

The young girl stood back in awe, as she always did, and admired the decorated tree, now transformed before her. Fanny turned off all the lights in the room until the only illumination came from the tree itself. Barbara, whose eyes were wide with amazement, watched as the colored bulbs threw red, green, and yellow reflections on the ceiling, interweaving shapes and shadows into a wonderland of colored fantasy.

"Oh," she said softly, "it's beautiful!"

"I think it is the most beautiful tree we have ever had," Fanny uttered in awed silence, just as she did every year.

Later that evening, after Barbara had gone to bed, Timothy came into the house to find his parents sitting in the living room by only the lights of the tree. Mr. Wilbur was puffing contently on his pipe, emitting a small cloud of smoke every so often, which drifted in a lazy dance upward, stretching into a surreal shape to disappear like magic. The boy was startled to find the two sitting there, for it was unusual for his parents to sit in semi-darkness doing nothing. He always knew them to have some kind of project in their hands, such as needlework painstakingly done by his mother, or a book being read by his father. This scene struck him as so strange, that instead of bolting up to his room like always, Timothy slowly approached their chairs.

"Everything all right?"

"Yes, son, we were just sitting here remembering every Christmas we have enjoyed in this house."

What Fanny did not tell him was the worry and concern each of them felt about the future, and how they wondered if this would be their last Christmas together.

"Come, sit awhile." Mr. Wilbur motioned to another chair, as he made room, drawing it close to the tree.

"It's really pretty, Mom. A pretty tree."

Fanny nodded in silent agreement. There was an awkward moment, then Mr. Wilbur cleared his throat and proceeded to knock the ashes out of his pipe.

"We, your Mother and I, were wondering, son, what your plans might be. You know, after your graduation next spring." Mr. Wilbur was wary of what his son might be thinking.

Timothy answered with no attempt to disguise his excitement. "I want to enlist, Dad. Enlist before

I get drafted. I want to enlist in the Navy. Mike is going into the Marines right after Christmas."

"Oh, but Timmy, wait to graduate first. Please do that much, dear." Fanny said, alarmed, but not totally surprised.

"But some of the guys are going in right away, and I want to go with them."

"Please think about it, son. You would do better to graduate before you go off enlisting," Mr. Wilbur's calm voice seemed unruffled, and only Fanny, who knew him so well, recognized that her husband was upset, too.

"But, Dad!"

"We'll talk about it later, Tim, but in the meantime, I don't want you spoiling our Christmas with talk about enlisting. You know how much this time of year means to your Mother."

"OK, but I want the Navy, remember that."

The big gymnasium at the "Y" was decorated with evergreen garlands and colored lights the Saturday night before Christmas. A huge decorated tree stood in the lobby, setting the mood for the evening as couples tramped in from the heavy snow that was falling outside. Coats and boots were tossed aside in the cloak room, and soon strains of a live orchestra echoed through the hall, beckoning the dancers to the floor.

All the girls were beautiful in their long dresses, swooping and twirling in folds of rainbow colors. The young men, a few of whom were in formal jackets, for the most part wore suits. Some looked a little awkward and uncomfortable, not used to being so dressed up.

Timothy had dutifully picked Virginia up at her home, and had presented her with a corsage. A thousand times since his spur-of-the-moment invitation to her the boy wondered why he had gone through with this date. Everybody knew he was dating Rosemary Brown, and that on a dare he had gotten himself into this pickle.

When Rosemary found out that he had another date for the dance, she was furious, and threw a tantrum. Timothy soon learned about the wrath of a woman scorned, and it did not take long for the lesson to be hammered home. Rosemary refused to talk to him or see him, no matter how hard he tried to explain that the date with little Virginia, a lowly junior, was just the result of what he perceived to be a thoughtless joke. The hapless young man was very sensitive, and inside, it hurt him deeply to know that in turn he had hurt someone else.

But Timothy was honor-bound, and had been taught throughout his life to always honor his commitments. So he found himself now with his arms around this little mite of a junior, who had her hair in some kind of a weird "do" on top of her head, as they danced. He wished that she would stop looking at him with such soulful eyes. It reminded him of a deer he once shot while hunting with his father. It had looked at him in the same way as it lay dying, with eyes that were accusing and painfully hurt. He could never get that sight out of his mind, and had never hunted since. But Virginia's gaze was one of worship, not pain, although there did not seem to be much difference to Tim.

A commotion at the entry door drew everyone's attention to the couple just coming through the archway of green garland. The male voice was loud and a bit slurred, causing everyone in the gym to turn when they heard him speak.

"Well, hello, children——nice party!" The author of that voice stumbled slightly, and may have fallen, had it not been that his companion momentarily held him up until he could regain his balance. His charming young date was adorned in a stunning, flaming red, strapless gown that showed almost like neon in the dimly lit hall. On the arm of a tall, dark haired, very handsome man, the girl in question walked through the throng of dancers with her blond head held high.

Timothy felt as if he had been struck in the stomach, in fact even lower than that! *Rosemary!*

Rosemary Brown, how could you? How could you come with HIM? How could you dare come to the dance with Ralph Warren, the devil-may-care, social ladder climbing college student? How dare you come with a man at least four years older, and light-years away from everyone else at this high school dance? You know the rules, only high school students were supposed to be at this dance. All these thoughts were swirling in Timothy's head.

He saw Rosemary's eyes search the dancers until she found Timothy's, and a smirk crossed her face, causing him to want to sink through the floor. She turned a haughty nose up and away, but not before Timothy could detect that she, too had been drinking.

"Well, come on, men, letsch have shum music. We want to dansh!" Ralph slurred loudly at the orchestra, leaning heavily across Rosemary's shoulders as she snuggled her face against the man's neck.

The music started again, and startled dancers slowly began to fill the floor once more, although the previous sound of merry chatter was substantially reduced. Timothy's face burned bright red, and he was thankful that the lights were so dim that perhaps no one noticed the chagrin that tormented him at that moment. Poor little innocent Virginia, she hadn't the faintest idea of the agony Timothy was in, and timidly followed his lead as he whirled her away from the offending couple.

Chaperones, discreetly positioned in the darkened area underneath the balcony, watched with careful obedience, ready to step in if there was the slightest possibility of a disturbance. They whispered among themselves, wondering if they should already intervene, knowing that the young man in question had obviously been drinking, and was too old to rightfully be there anyway. The consensus was to watch and wait.

"Man, I guess he's really trying to show you up," Spud Weaver breathed quietly under his breath to Timothy as they convened in a corner while Virginia and Spud's date excused themselves and went to the ladies room.

"She is making an embarrassing spectacle of herself, and she's clearly ignoring the rules by bringing a guy so much older. She knows good and well that this is only for seniors and underclassmen," Timothy said fiercely through his teeth. He glanced at the chaperones. "Why don't they kick him out?"

"They're gutless, that's why."

Timothy could not help but feel guilty that he was the one who had put Rosemary into this situation. She would be safe with him now, if he had not asked the little girl from the junior class to the dance on that whim a couple of weeks ago.

"Look!—Look, Spud, he's trying to reach into her dress!" Timothy hissed, rage rising in his body, as he saw Ralph Warren's hand slyly edging into the top of Rosemary's strapless gown.

The couple was turned away from the chaperone area, and it seemed only those two senior classmates could see what the college man was doing. Ralph had his lips at Rosemary's cheek, slowly brushing them toward her mouth while the two were locked in a close dance embrace. Ralph's fingers were between his chest and her bosom, and Timothy could see his hand suddenly reach inside.

"Spud! He's feeling her up! God! Spud, what should I do?" Timothy was in agony.

It turned out, he could do nothing, for at that moment, Virginia and Spud's date returned, and Timothy had to turn his attention once more to the girl he had brought to the dance. As the evening wore on, he only glimpsed Rosemary and Ralph one more time, and that was in a dark corner of the cloak room where by chance, he witnessed Ralph offering Rosemary a drink from a flask retrieved from the his overcoat pocket.

Toward the end of the evening, as Timothy was finishing in the men's room, Ralph staggered in, his eyes bleary, and proceeded to fumble with his zipper in front of the urinal. Ralph weaved as he stood, obviously inebriated, and took what seemed like an eternity to empty his bladder.

"Sweet li'l Rosemary Brown," Ralph mumbled, "you'll have this big thing tonight, you li'l shit."

Although Timothy was only of average height, and certainly no match for the bigger, more mature college student, he had only one chance. Without even thinking of the consequences, young Timothy swiftly reached around Ralph Warren's body, grabbed the zipper and yanked up hard, catching the man's flesh in an excruciating burst of pain. Ralph whirled and staggered toward Timothy yelping, his glazed eyes unable to focus.

"Not tonight, Mr. Warren, not tonight," Timothy said smoothly, and with a well aimed kick at the man's groin, sent him reeling to the floor, writhing in agony.

Timothy bolted out the door, and grabbed Spud's arm.

"Come on, we've got to get out of here! Get the girls, now! I'll explain later."

Timothy, swallowing his pride, sought out Rosemary, and with a firm hand on her elbow, quickly shoved her to the cloakroom. He fiercely whispered in her ear, "Mr. Warren isn't feeling well. He asked me to take you home. Get your coat."

At first, Rosemary resisted, trying to pull away from Timothy. Even though her senses were clouded by the booze she had consumed, she could tell that Timothy was far more agitated than she had ever seen him before. At that point, she allowed him to bundle her into her coat, and hurry her out the door. Poor little Virginia, completely innocent of any of the things which were happening behind the scenes, was understandably bewildered.

When the group reached the Wilbur household, Timothy, Spud, Mike, their dates, and now Rosemary all gathered around the dining room table where Fanny had assembled a lovely midnight buffet. Timothy was urging Rosemary to eat something, plying her with hot coffee and sandwiches. He was nervous, trying to sober her up before he took her home. *Thank God Mom and Dad are in bed,* he thought. *They won't see how tipsy Rosie is.* Then with a maturity beyond his years, he proceeded to act the perfect host, and never let on about the events that had taken place back at the Christmas Formal.

The next day, Spud and Mike could hardly stop laughing while they slapped their buddy on his back when Timothy was finally able to explain how he had taken care of Ralph Warren. They repeatedly clapped him on the shoulder, and shook his hand, pumping his arm with renewed respect and vigor.

"That's our Buddy!" they exclaimed, and Timothy felt inches taller and very mature. Inside, he was thankful he had been the one to rescue Rosemary's honor that winter evening. He was the hero of the hour, so it seemed.

PART III

Barbara Wilbur thought that her brother, Timmy, was the most handsome man she ever had seen, dressed as he was in his Navy Summer Whites. In the young girl's preadolescent stirrings of sexual awareness, the very sight of men in uniform thrilled and excited her. She was watching the boot camp graduation ceremonies at Great Lakes Naval Training Center, near Chicago, where she and her parents had come by train for Timothy's graduation ceremony.

Waterville was only a three hour train ride away from where Timothy had taken his basic training, and there was no way Fanny was going to miss this special event. So this day found the whole family sitting in the bleachers, observing the parade ground of the Naval Center.

Fanny and Mr. Wilbur swelled with pride at the sight of their son on that late summer day of

1942. They were impressed how their first born had grown and filled out in the few weeks he had been at basic training. Timothy's tanned face glistened bronze in the August sun, and he had his white sailor cap at a jaunty angle when he hurried toward them.

"Mom! Dad!" his voice had even deepened since he had left them six weeks ago, "and Babs! Look at you!"

He swept his young sister into a heady hug, kissed Fanny on the cheek, and shook Herman's hand with a firm grip. They all tried to talk at once, while the foursome headed away from the parade grounds toward the train station. Barbara was asking rapid-fire questions, and Fanny was beside herself with joy. Herman Wilbur walked proudly beside his son, standing as tall as he could, and squared his shoulders back, beaming from every inch. The train ride was so quick they could hardly believe it when they reached Waterville and home, for they had all talked nonstop.

It was so good to have Timothy under their own roof again, even if it were only for a few days. As usual, Fanny was busy in the kitchen, rolling out pie crust dough with her favorite rolling pin, the white ceramic gift from her only son, and her thoughts were tumbling in rapid succession, one on top of the other. To think her boy had graduated from high school a scant two months ago, and now he was a seaman, headed to Virginia for training in the Seabees. It made Fanny fairly burst with pride, and she could hardly contain the exuberance she felt. For a brief moment in her life, Fanny was ecstatically happy. Her face softened, and she hummed a tune as she rolled out the dough.

Everywhere throughout the United States, the populace was galvanized to the war effort, and the bond holding everyone together was the patriotic effort to help "the boys." They were eager fighting young men, who were now manning guns, piloting planes, and sailing the seas to stop the enemy. Young men—very young men—eighteen and nineteen year olds, some barely learning how to shave. Now they proudly wore the uniforms of Army, Navy, and Marines.

Timothy had gotten his wish. He and his best friend, Spud, had joined the Navy, both assigned to the Seabees, the Construction Battalion. They would now be off to Virginia for further training, then would await orders, which most likely would take them half a world away into adventures and dangers unknown.

Timothy stopped at the kitchen doorway, knowing that his mother had not heard him, and listened to the lilting hum of her wordless song as she rolled the ceramic pin back and forth, ever shaping the crust that would top a mound of freshly sliced apples in the deep pie tin. Strangely, the boy felt his heart lurch, and an unnamed feeling darted through his body. Just a momentary shadow of darkness like the shutter of a camera, click-on, click-off. A twinge, a little pang, and a sudden realization dawned on him that it was all different now. He could not recapture the carefree days of his childhood, skipping into the warmth of his mother's kitchen, with only thoughts of the playground racing in his mind. No, not now, for everything was different. Presently, there was an underlying seriousness, a rush to grow up, to be an adult, to go out into the world, to be somebody, to fight in the war!

With a deep sigh, Seaman Timothy Arthur Wilbur knew then that he could never really go back home, not in the way he remembered. Those innocent years, so recent, yet so far distant, could never be recaptured. The pang of that realization struck hard, and he suddenly felt a lump in his throat, as he watched Fanny studiously working at the kitchen counter.

When had her hair started to turn gray? He had never noticed before. *When had she started to stoop just a little? Were her movements slightly slower than he remembered? No!* Not his mother. *She couldn't, mustn't change.* She should remain always the way he remembered her from his childhood. *Mom!* Timothy agonized silently. "Mom, dear Mom!"

He sneaked up behind Fanny, and put his arms around her waist, giving her a smack on the cheek.

"How's my Sweetheart?"

"Oh, Timmy, you surprised me! It's so good to have you back home. Just like the old times. The cookies are in the cookie jar, and the milk is in the ice box. You haven't forgotten where the glasses are, have you?"

"Gosh, Mom, I've only been gone six weeks!"

Fanny nodded, "But it already seems like a lifetime."

Dinner that evening was at the picnic table in the back yard, in plain view of the neighbors, whose yards all met in one carpet of unbroken green grass. Fanny passed heaping dishes of potato salad, and deep fried chicken, secret pride welling inside her. She knew her recipes were the best in town. Timothy was keeping one eye on the apple pie, as he wolfed down the good old fashioned home cooking. He tried not to dwell on how long it might be before he would be able to enjoy his mother's cooking again, once he returned back to base.

A shimmer of excitement tickled through Timothy's middle when he thought about his uncertain future, and where he might be stationed. He was eager and anxious to be on his way, to join in the fighting for his country, and to help protect his homeland.

Friendly neighbors waved and called greetings across the lawns, causing Fanny and Herman to puff with pride at their son, who was the first on their street to don a uniform. Barbara sat close to her brother, gazing up at his profile with awe and affection, excitement, and pride. The young girl was thrilled to her toes whenever he turned and winked at her, and gave her a secret smile. She vowed to herself that she could never love anyone more than she loved her brother at that moment.

Twilight lingered in the hush before nightfall, and a quietness settled on the neighborhood, while the first of the fireflies blinked secret codes in the darkest corner under the raspberry bushes. Fanny and Barbara had retired to the kitchen, and Timothy sat fidgeting on the picnic bench, anxious to be off with his friends for the evening. Herman drew a deep puff from his pipe, slowly blowing the smoke sideways, away from his son, and cleared his throat. It was always hard for the man to talk about his emotions. He never did have many words to say, regardless, and it pained him to the core to say out loud what he was feeling. Tonight, he wished there was some profound and sage advice he could impart to his oldest child, his only son. The son who might never know how dear he was to the older man, and who would soon embark on the adventure of his lifetime.

"A-hem." Herman cleared his throat once more. "I'm mighty proud of you, son." He paused and took another drag on the pipe which he clenched in his teeth. Tilting back his head, he blew a cloud of smoke toward the heavens, and noticed a single star twinkle in the darkening velvet sky, the first star to shine in the deepening twilight.

"Have you any idea where they might send you?"

"No, Pop, it could be anywhere. You know, the Seabees is a brand new unit for the Navy, and they are just getting started. All I know is that we will be off building air strips, or a hundred other projects. CB—Construction Battalion, Seabees for short. They say we will be the first ones in, even before the marines, so we can build the landing areas and support facilities."

"It's a good thing you had all that experience helping build the Scout camp last summer. I'm sure that was a factor in you being selected for the Seabees."

Timothy nodded, squirming in his seat, anxious to be off to meet Rosemary at the park on the riverbank.

"You will write to your mother often, won't you, son?"

"Of course, Dad."

"You'll be very careful Tim?"

"Gee, Dad I want to come back just as much as you want me to. I'll be OK, really I will."

Herman sat in silence for a moment more. Timothy recognized that his father was, in his own way, trying to tell him how much he loved him. *Why can't he just come out and say it?* His father suddenly appeared older, and even a bit frail, and Timothy longed to take him in his arms to comfort and reassure him. In the semi-darkness, the young boy strained to see the features of the older man's face, to study them, and capture the image in his memory so he would be able to carry it with him wherever the future might take him.

Herman sat for a long time in the darkened summer night, lost in thought, struggling to find the words that refused to come. There were all kinds of dangers he wished to warn his son about. Loose women, booze, cigarettes, all sorts of things he could not put into words. The profound words of wisdom that any father should proclaim to a son going off to war were buried deep in the older man's heart. To be able to translate them into the spoken word escaped him, much to his dismay. Finally, sensing that Timothy was impatient to be gone, Herman sighed deeply, rose, and placed a gentle hand upon his son's shoulder.

"Go, have a good time with your friends."

"Thanks, Pop."

Timothy put his hand on top of the one that grasped his shoulder, gave it a squeeze, and disappeared into the night.

PART IV

Rosemary was there, just as Timothy knew she would be, waiting at the river dock underneath the faint light of a single bulb that shown above the ticket stand. Spud and his date were already aboard the "River Queen," a flat, open barge-like vessel which carried party goers up and down the river in the summer months. During the day, it was a sightseeing boat, but at night, it became a romantic, floating dance hall. A string of colored lights outlined the perimeter, making it look like a floating circus wagon as it plied up and down the river.

Music from a juke-box was piped into speakers at the far end of the "River Queen's" open dance floor, echoing and re-echoing across the water. It reached the ears of those who chose to snuggle on blankets along the edge of the river in the long, narrow city park. Picnic tables and shuffleboard courts were prominently disbursed in the recreation areas, and the park became a meeting place on hot summer nights. Those residents who were fortunate enough to have built riverside homes were treated nightly to the music and merrymaking coming from the boat, which many considered the pride of Waterville.

It was the highlight for many a family in that small mid-western community to take a Sunday excursion on the "River Queen," to relish the cool breezes wafting off the river, and sip a soft drink, or an occasional beer aboard the slow moving craft.

"Hi, Timmy," Rosemary smiled, tiptoeing to accept his light kiss, then clung to his arm as he bought the tickets for the ride. Then they hurried on board.

"I almost thought you were not coming."

"Got hung up with the family dinner. I wanted to leave earlier, but you know how it is. Mom— Dad—they were hard to get away from."

The two young people found Spud and Lorraine sitting on one of the benches that rimmed the outside rail, and squeezed in beside them. Spud and Timothy exchanged light punches on each other's arms. Both were decked out in their summer uniforms, and were secretly pleased that all the others on board seemed to give them wide, patriotic respect. The two sailors were almost treated like celebrities, with older men tipping their hats to the boys, making them stand tall and proud.

Not long after arriving, lively jitterbug music blared from the loudspeakers, and Spud and Lorraine began putting on a regular clinic of fancy Swing dance steps. The young sailor swung his partner first over one hip, then the other, down through his legs, up over his back, to land once again on her saddle-shoed feet. All the dancers were wildly swinging to the rapid beat of a Tommy Dorsey song. Rosemary tried to urge Timothy onto the dance floor, but he reluctantly shook his head.

"Rosie, you know I can't dance to those fast songs."

"Oh, come on, Timmy, all you have to do is move with the beat of the music. Like this."

She grabbed his hand, stood in front of him and proceeded to swing her hips in wild gyrations in time with the music. Her saddle shoes appeared to wiggle in a virtual blur, and Timothy feared she would actually drag him onto the dance floor, where he knew he would make a complete fool of himself. His preference was to dance to the slow, romantic ballads, where he could wrap his arms around her, pull her body close to his, and feel all of her warm curves against his chest.

All evening, young couples laughed, danced and necked. They drank beers when their dates were able to convince the concessionaire to sell it to them. It was an unforgettable warm summer evening, and only the lights of the River Queen and stars overhead blinked in the inky blackness, their reflections skipping along in the silky smoothness of the river. As the night grew later and darker, the river boat Captain cut half of the decorative lights on board, and all the young couples took advantage of the semi-darkness to snuggle, kiss, and clutch each other.

At that time, the music switched to more soft, melodic ballads, and Timothy swept Rosemary close, easily swaying in a smooth foxtrot rhythm. He tingled at the feel of her softness pressing against the front part of him, and inched a hand beneath her sweater to feel the flesh of her back. The young sailor leaned to kiss her as they danced, and could not surpress the feelings that began in his groin. He pulled her even closer, feeling her thighs against his own as they moved as one to the music, and he wished the evening would never end.

Without warning, there was a scream, a deep splash, and all dancers stopped in their tracks. Timothy rushed to the rail where the sound had come from, and could barely detect a form in the water off the starboard side of the River Queen. With no hesitation, shucking his shoes, in one step he dove off the rail and swam furiously toward the sound of the thrashing water ahead. His uniform was dragging him down, but he kicked with powerful strokes, finally reaching a frantic young girl, who thrashed wildly about, sputtering and choking.

While the Captain reversed engines, and switched on the spotlight, Timothy was already swimming back to the craft with one arm wrapped around the girl in the classic lifesaving grip. Dance patrons lined the railing and cheered as he drew near with his embarrassed cargo. It was Spud who threw him the life preserver, and many hands helped the pair over the side to safety.

Once on deck, young men clapped him on the back, congratulating Timothy on his lightning speed rescue. With shining eyes of pride, Rosemary stood by her boyfriend's side, admiring him even as he stood dripping wet. He looked even more handsome than ever, now with his damp hair disheveled, the short, curly locks clinging to his tanned forehead. Quickly, a blanket was thrown about his shoulders, and another for the girl, and the Captain turned the craft around, heading down river toward the boat landing. He made a special effort to shake Timothy's hand, then announced that there would be free drinks for everybody.

"Man, you'll do anything to attract attention, won't you, Pal?" Spud teased.

Timothy chuckled, ignoring the attempted dig, and tried to dry out his clothing with the blanket.

"How did she fall in? Anyone know who she is?" Timothy asked as he squeezed water out of his socks.

"It was whispered that the guy she came with shoved her overboard. He's had a few too many beers. I think he is now sitting right where the Captain can keep an eye on him," Spud sneered.

Rosemary fluttered about, patting Timothy with the blanket to help him dry out. Her eyes were big with wonder and admiration.

"You were wonderful the way you just jumped right in, Timmy."

Timothy shrugged. "Oh, it was nothing special. Anybody would have done the same thing."

"Well, you were magnificent! My hero!"

Rosemary tiptoed to kiss him on the lips.

This embarrassed him, and he could feel a blush start to burn his cheeks.

"I guess that's one way to impress the girls," Spud joked.

"Cut it out, Spud! You would have done the same thing."

"And get my uniform all wet and wrinkled? Not on your life, Pal."

"Oh, you would, too, and you know it."

""No, Pal, not me. You were the lifeguard all those summers, remember?"

The music resumed, and Spud and Lorraine drifted off by themselves, leaving Rosemary and Timothy alone at the stern of the River Queen.

"You are my hero, you know, Timmy?"

"Don't make such a big thing out of it, Rosie."

"But it is a big thing. You saved that girl's life, and I love you for it. I do love you, Timmy. You know that. I am so much in love with you."

Timothy was flattered, yet he struggled to determine exactly what his feelings were toward Rosemary. Certainly he was fond of her, and she could raise him to a fever pitch of passion in an instant, yet, somehow, he felt empty. As close as he was to her, in the back of his mind, he felt that perhaps she was not the girl for him. Somewhere, out there, another girl waited with whom he would be able to spend his whole life. Besides, he was far too young to even think about settling down with one girl right now. *Doesn't Rosemary realize that? Can't she see that we are far too young to think of such serious things? Then why is she always trying to pressure to go farther than we should?*

Rosemary cuddled close to Timothy, and tears started flowing from her eyes.

"I missed you so much when you were away," she sobbed "and now there's only a couple of days and you will be gone again."

"Oh, Rosie, I know. I will miss you too. But you will write to me often, won't you?"

He pulled her close into the curve of his arm, and she leaned her head upon his chest.

"Of course, Sweetie, every day!" she uttered between sobs.

"And I will think of you wherever I am stationed. In fact," Timothy nodded to the music now playing as he pulled the girl onto the dance floor. "I'll see you in my dreams," he murmured.

That was the last song playing on the juke box as the River Queen neared the landing dock.

"I'll see you in my dreams—hold you in my arms,—" Timothy sang softly into Rosemary's ear as they danced. Her tears flowed freely, and she clung to him, sobbing and missing him already.

PART V

"What will it be for you today, Mrs. Wilbur?" the kindly voice of old Mr. Bobkin, the neighborhood grocer, sounded from behind the counter.

"I've been saving up my ration stamps for extra flour and sugar. With the holidays coming, there's a lot of baking to do, you know," Fanny uttered as she searched her purse for the little folder of stamps.

Mr. Bobkin nodded. "What do you hear from overseas? Any word from Timothy?"

"Oh, yes. He writes quite frequently," Fanny said proudly. "He's somewhere in the Pacific. He can't say just where. 'A slip of the lip will sink a ship,' as they say."

"How long has he been gone this time?"

"It's been fourteen months since his last leave home."

Mr. Bobkin shook his gray head, removed his glasses and cleaned them on his white grocer's apron.

"Seems just like only yesterday that little Timmy was running in here to peek over the counter and buy candy with his pennies. I can remember how his big brown eyes would sparkle when he was trying to decide which flavor he wanted to buy. He always ended up with orange slices, every time."

Fanny smiled, fondly recalling her tousle-haired child scampering from one place to another. He was never still, it seemed, but always running on to the next adventure.

"Did I ever tell you about the time he came in with a nickel, and a poor little fella came in the door, pushed his nose against the glass, and dreamed about having a piece of candy? Well, Timmy saw that the little fella did not have a penny, and when he saw tears start in the little guy's eyes, Timmy gave the lad his only nickel, and smiled the biggest grin I ever saw, when he realized how that gesture lit up the little boy's dirty face. That's the Timmy I remember."

Fanny was moved by the story. How like Timothy to help out one not so fortunate, she thought. It reminded her of the time when Timothy was in junior high school, riding the bus home, when he saw a strange young boy in tears reach inside a paper bag, obviously having just purchased a phonograph record from the local music store. It turned out, the boy had somehow broken the record, and was crying in despair. It was Timothy who escorted the lad back to the record store, paid for a new Frank Sinatra record to replace the broken one, and got the boy back on a bus for home. It had been all the money that Timothy had saved up from his paper route at the time, but joyfully, and willingly, as her son had later related the story to her, he walked home, his heart soaring.

"Timmy always did like his sweets," Fanny said, "that's why I want to bake a box of cookies and goodies to send to him. He enjoys the packages we send from home so much. The deadline for sending Christmas packages is next week, so I need to get busy."

"Well, all you mothers sure take care of the boys overseas. Nothing is too good for our fighting men."

Fanny finished her list, and paid her bill.

"You want Calvin to deliver these for you, Mrs. Wilbur?"

"No, I brought Timothy's old coaster wagon to take the groceries home in. I knew the load would be more than I could carry, what with the extra flour and sugar."

"By the way," Mr. Bobkin said thoughtfully, "did you hear about the Fisher boy?"

His tone was so serious that Fanny stopped and turned, suddenly alarmed. She almost knew before the old man spoke that there was tragedy.

"Yup, the telegram came this morning, I heard. He was killed in the war in Europe."

Fanny's hand went to her throat, and she stifled a cry. "Oh, poor Ellen Fisher! Oh, the poor, poor woman. Her only son! Thank you for telling me."

Fanny hurried out the door, and while she pulled the coaster wagon the two blocks to home, her mind was in a whirl. That would be Jamie Fisher, Timothy's school friend. And she tried to imagine the sadness and anguish that must be going on in the Fisher household this very moment. As she passed house after house, Fanny noted the small flags that were so proudly displayed in the windows of those families who had a loved one in service. One blue star on a field of white, bordered in red, represented one service man, two stars, two, and so forth. One house had three stars. And one house had a gold star. That was home to the young soldier-son who had been killed a year ago.

Now, sadly, Mrs. Fisher would have to post a gold star in her window, too, Fanny mused. How tragic, how unthinkable, to lose a son, a child. She could not begin to comprehend the agony. As she neared her own home, and saw the blue-starred flag hanging in her own front window, her heart warmed. Timothy! it shouted to her, and she felt a great sense of pride at what the simple, small square of fabric represented.

Later in the afternoon, when Barbara came home from school and plunked down in her usual place at the kitchen table, Fanny noted the girl was in a strangely somber mood. The woman was putting the finishing touches to a layer cake she intended to take to the Fisher house later. She was so engrossed in her project that she did not notice how quiet her daughter was. One more dab of frosting completed the cake, and Fanny rotated the plate, making sure that everything looked perfect.

"Is that for us?" Barbara asked quietly.

"No, dear, it is for the Fishers. Word just came today that Jamie was killed in Europe."

"Oh," Barbara suddenly let out her breath, and looked crushed.

"What's the matter, dear? You look so downhearted. You didn't know Jamie very well, did you? Are you upset hearing about him?"

Barbara shook her head no.

Fanny persisted. "Something happen at school?"

"No."

Fanny wiped her hands on her apron and sat down across from her daughter.

"What is it, dear?"

Again, Barbara hung her head.

"It's all right to feel sad about Timothy's friend. That's normal. I feel sad, too. I feel very sad for Mrs. Fisher. I'm sure she is heartbroken. I know I would be, if it were my son."

Tears welled in the young girl's eyes, and Fanny frowned. Surely something was bothering the school girl, and Fanny wanted to get to the bottom of it.

"Tell me, dear, what in the world is troubling you?"

"Tim—Timmy is dead!"

"Oh, Barbara, what a foolish thought. Whatever makes you think that?"

Barbara swallowed hard, attempting to dislodge the lump in her throat, and struggled with the thought she had been having all day.

"Timmy was in my room last night," she managed to whisper.

Fanny grabbed Barbara's arm. "What in God's world are you talking about, Barbara?"

"Timmy was in my room. He woke me up in the middle of the night, and sat on my bed."

"Oh, my dearest, I'm sure you must have had one of those very real dreams. It was just a dream, darling, just a dream."

Barbara shook her head. "No, Mother, he really was there! He told me to do well in school, and to always make you and Daddy proud of me."

Now Fanny was very perplexed. She came around the table and laid her arm across her daughter's shoulders, trying to think of how to best deal with Barbara's insistence that Timothy had actually visited her. Surely the girl must know that it would have been impossible, for her brother was thousands of miles away across the ocean.

"It was a dream dear, just a dream. Sometimes we all have dreams that seem so real, that the next day, we can't get them out of our minds. It just means that you are thinking about him so strongly, and that you love him so very much."

Barbara, her eyes still misty, looked up at her mother. "Do you think so?" she asked hesitantly, her voice small and worried.

Fanny nodded her head, and gave the girl a squeeze. "I know so, dear. Now have some milk and cookies while I take this cake to the Fishers."

That same evening, after Fanny and Barbara had done the supper dishes, the three Wilburs gathered around the piano in the living room, as was their nightly ritual. Fanny played as she and Barbara sang, while Mr. Wilbur, in his most melodious trilling, whistled "My Sweet Little Alice Blue Gown," and "My Blue Heaven." The trio rendered song after familiar song, until it was Barbara's bedtime. Then, while Fanny sat quietly beside her husband, Herman was enjoying his last pipe full of tobacco before going down into the basement to bank the furnace for the night. The late November night had grown colder, and when the wind came up, there was a promise of snow in the air.

Herman peered out the front window to look toward the streetlight shining on the corner.

"No snow yet, but I'll bet before morning, we'll have some on the ground," he grunted, clenching the pipe in his teeth.

Fanny nodded in agreement, and set aside the mending she had been doing, ready to go upstairs to bed, herself.

"Oh," Herman said, turning to his wife. "I forgot to tell you about a strange thing that happened today."

He walked over to knock ashes from his pipe into the ashtray atop the smoking stand beside his favorite chair. Fanny paused, one foot on the stair step, waiting for him to continue. She was mildly surprised that Herman wanted to talk, normally he was so quiet, he had very little to say. Though always observant, he was reluctant to carry on much of a conversation, and Fanny knew it was the shyness which prevented him from voicing an opinion other than a soft "yes" or "no."

Herman continued, "I was changing a flat tire on the car, and had it up on the jack. I was trying to get the wheel off. It was stuck—had a real tussle with the darned thing." Herman paused, remembering. "Anyhow, there I was, way out on Mineral Point Avenue, where I was going to deliver something to old Mrs. Curtis. Her son was at work, and he couldn't get in to town, so I offered to take out the part she needed for her furnace and fix it for her."

Fanny sighed. When he did have a story to tell, Herman always took such a long time to get to the point.

"Well, the tire went flat, right on top of the hill outside town, just before you get to the Curtis place. So, there I was, kind of off the road, with this darned flat tire. The road is gravel there, you know. Anyhow, I jacked up the car, and was trying to pull that wheel off so I could get the tire off the rim. That stubborn wheel just wouldn't come, so I had to crawl under the car and give it a whack from the inside with my feet."

Fanny waited while her husband carefully scraped out the bowl of his pipe, and placed it neatly beside his other pipes in the smoking stand.

"Well, I was foolish, and I knew better, but, suddenly, the jack slipped, and there I was, pinned. The wheel went flying off, and the undercarriage came down on my chest. I bet I'll have a big black and blue mark on my chest tonight."

"Oh, Herman, my dear, are you okay?"

The man nodded his head. "I'm fine, Fanny, just fine. But to get back to the story, there I was, trapped by the car, and had little hope that another auto would come along that road soon.

It's not a very busy place, you know. But then the strangest thing happened—I can't explain it."

Again, Herman paused, driving Fanny crazy with his slow, methodical recital.

"What was it?" she urged.

"This—this person just appeared suddenly out of nowhere. He lifted up the side of the car enough so I could roll over and crawl out. Well, by the time I got to my feet to look around and thank him, there was no one there! Just no one... nothing. No other auto, no vehicle—no one on the road—just no one!" He shook his head in bewilderment.

Fanny was stunned. Had her husband suffered from some kind of "spell" that made him imagine this strange event, or did it really occur as he related?

"Some Good Samaritan must have just happened along at the right time," she said, putting a tentative hand on Herman's arm. "Perhaps it was a hunter out in the woods that came to your rescue. Or maybe you blacked out for a little bit."

Herman frowned, shaking his head. "No, the woods were a long way off from where I was, and I would have seen somebody walking away. He couldn't have gotten away without my seeing him. This person just appeared, then disappeared all of a sudden—just like magic. I can't explain it."

Goose bumps rose on Fanny's arms, and as they climbed the stairs to their bedroom, they were both mute, lost in thought. At the time, Fanny did not connect Barbara's dream to the extraordinary event involving her husband.

Thanksgiving came and went, celebrated quietly at the Wilbur household that year. It was the second time the family marked the holiday with one empty chair at the table, and just around the corner, it would be the second Christmas season without Timothy's boisterous presence. The boy's enthusiastic joy for life had been contagious, and never failed to give those around him a lift.

"We sure could use him around here again," Fanny mused. The war news in the papers and on the radio was grim and full of graphic details of battles both in Europe and the Pacific Theatres. They anxiously went to the movie theater often to see the latest newsreels showing the fighting. Fanny felt proud of the way all Americans pitched in to help in the war effort. There was never a reluctance from any citizen about sacrificing their own comforts in the face of shortages of goods and food so that the commodities could go to the troops. Every one did their best to help those brave fathers, sons, and brothers who were fighting and dying to save the country's freedom. They all took the inconvenience of having to deal with rationing, limiting the amounts of certain items so everyone could share equally, with enough butter, meats, flour, and sugar to go around.

The scrap heap of metal collecting at the school ground was getting to be huge, with every household contributing any spare bits of old, useless, worn out iron or steel they could lay their hands on. Even old Model T cars, and worn out, rusty farm machines were hauled to the area to add to the scrap metal heap, later to be loaded onto railroad cars and shipped to the steel mills. There it would be re-melted and turned into tanks, battleships, shell casings, and jeeps. Adults were buying war bonds to help finance the military effort, and every school child bought the ten cent Liberty Stamps which they proudly pasted into a booklet every week. When the booklet was filled, it could be turned into a War Bond.

All these thoughts ran through Fanny's mind one December morning as she went through the routine of housework. Barbara was off to school, and Herman had gone early to the hardware store. Outside, a blanket of new snow wrapped everything in layers of white, as if someone had wound bats of cotton on every tree branch and bush. Inside, the house was warm and cozy, giving Fanny a sense of contentment, and put her in such a Christmas mood that she resolved to do baking today. But first, she ought to put another couple of shovels of coal into the furnace, even though Herman had a good fire going earlier, it was time to stoke the "beast" again.

At the top of the basement stairs, she failed to see the scrub bucket which someone had inadvertently placed in the wrong spot, and as she descended the stairwell, she tripped, and felt herself pitch forward. Down, down, in slow motion, she went, her arms and legs splaying out in a desperate effort to break the fall. Fanny could see the darkened landing below, and instantly pictured herself lying there, broken and lifeless. Incredibly, the next thing she knew, she felt herself being lifted up by a strong pair of arms, and set upright and steady upon her feet at the landing. Stunned, Fanny looked around, back up the stairwell, only to find herself utterly alone.

Had she dreamed she had fallen? Had she momentarily blacked out? She had no idea how she had arrived unhurt at the bottom of the stairs. She only remembered the sensation of arms beneath her, holding her up. Cautiously, she tested her arms and legs, fearing she may have twisted or broken something, however, she felt fine. Nothing hurt. She could walk and move just as always.

Fanny bit her lip and frowned. *I must have imagined the whole thing*, she thought. *My mind was on other things, and I was not paying attention to what I was doing. Just walking down the stairs, that's all. It was my imagination that I fell, it must have been, otherwise how could I be here, standing up, all okay? I must have been daydreaming.*

Returning to the kitchen, Fanny assembled flour, sugar, and butter to make her famous holiday cut-out cookies. When she had mixed the dough, she reached for the rolling pin that Timothy had so proudly given her one Mother's Day. It was the white ceramic pin with smooth oak handles. As she floured the cutting board, and flattened out the first mound of rich cookie dough, she fondly remembered how proud her son had been the day she unwrapped the present he had so carefully purchased with the very first money he ever earned from his paper route. Now, she smiled, recalling how Timothy's youthful excitement lit up his eyes until they sparkled like shiny buttons in his grinning face, as he watched her unwrap the rolling pin. His chest had fairly heaved with pride when he saw how much the gift had pleased her.

While she rolled the dough, Fanny allowed her mind to drift to memories of Timothy's growing up years. Back and forth she rolled the pin, flattening the dough thinner and thinner. She recalled the boyish enthusiasm with which her son tackled life. Everything he experienced was with wild anticipation. It seemed he had always wanted to be on to the next thing, barely relishing each new accomplishment before he wanted to extend himself to the next level. When he was an infant, he was not content to just gradually learn to sit and walk, but was in such a rush to grow up, that each phase flew by in record time. It was as if there was some kind of internal hourglass that was running out of sand, and he felt compelled to accomplish it all before the last grain had fallen.

Back and forth, back and forth, Fanny pushed the rolling pin, automatically performing the task she had done for so many years. The kitchen was warm and inviting, and steam gathered at the window panes. Outside, the snow was falling again. Inside, the fragrance of baked cookies filled the house. She was rolling out the third batch of cookies, when she heard a knock at the front door. Carefully laying the ceramic rolling pin aside, she wiped her flour-dusted hands upon her apron, patted a loose lock of hair away from her face, and proceeded to open the door. A blast of cold air brushed past, chilling her arms.

"Telegram for Mr. and Mrs. Wilbur."

Fanny felt her heart skip a beat, and she stood awkwardly, holding the door open, unable to speak. All the blood drained from her face as she reached with trembling hands for the pale yellow envelope.

"Mrs. Wilbur? Sign here, please."

Numbly, Fanny scrawled her name, closed the door, and with wooden motions, slowly made her way to the nearest chair. She stared at the envelope in her hands, carefully turning it over and over, afraid to open it, wishing that the news it surely must contain would go away. Bad news. Telegrams always held bad news. Hardly breathing she slowly opened the envelope, and unfolded the page which was shaking so hard in her hand, she could barely read the words.

"WE REGRET TO INFORM YOU... YOUR SON TIMOTHY... KILLED IN ACTION"

Fanny slipped from the chair, unconscious.

It was months later, when the terrible shock had worn off, and Fanny had time for retrospective thought, that she started to put the pieces together. *Barbara's dream about Timothy, the unexplained stranger who lifted the car from Herman that day just before Thanksgiving, and the loving arms she had felt surround her on the basement stairs—it was Timothy! It had to be have been!*

Confirmation came in the form of a letter from the boy's best friend, Spud, who was with Timothy the day he was killed. It happened a few days before Thanksgiving, according to Spud's letter, and it was Timothy who threw himself in harms way, pushing others to safety as a crane they were working on toppled over. *That was so much like him,* Fanny thought.

"Tim saved my life, Mrs. Wilbur," Spud's letter continued. "Not once, but twice! Because a few weeks later as we were pinned down by Jap sniper fire, I was hit, and lay wounded out in the open. I was an easy target for the Japs, yet bullets whipped around me and never touched me. Then, this GI appeared beside me, lifted me up, and carried me to safety. Nobody from our outfit recognized him, and he just disappeared! Everyone swore they did not know who pulled me out of danger. It must have been my guardian angel, they said. And then I knew it was Tim!"

Fanny knew, too, as she sadly, yet proudly hung the gold starred flag in the front window, fingering the gold fringe that laced the bottom. Memories were now all that sustained the family. Bittersweet memories of Timothy's zest for life, his sense of humor, and capacity for wild fun. His youthful enthusiasm sometimes led to exasperation, but always ended with complete and total endearment. Perhaps because their son had lived life to the extremes was the reason he gave so much to those who knew him. His goodness could not be contained, and for that reason, Fanny was confident somewhere in God's realm, an angel named Timothy roamed. A free Spirit soaring, dashing to the aid of those in peril. Fanny was finally at peace.

Jackie Gould

Chapter 7

"It makes me mighty proud to have this special rolling pin, knowing how much it must have meant to dear Fanny," Bessie said, turning the pin in her hads, feeling the coolness of the white milk glass against her palms. All three women were sitting on the screened in porch, where the girls had been mesmerized by Bessie's story of Timothy.

"Do you believe in angels?" Patty asked, tracing the rim of her iced tea glass with her index finger.

"Oh, without a doubt, dear, without a doubt." Bessie's expression grew soft and pensive as she lay her head back against the rocking chair cushion. "Some day I'll tell you girls about my angel," she said, almost as an after thought.

Somehow, Aunt Bessie always seemed to have an aura of mystery about her, of things from the past, a narrative unsaid, a thought not shared, stirring Jennifer's curiosity. Silently, she vowed to find out what mystery lay in Aunt Bessie's past before she would leave for home.

Patty sighed. "I sure need an angel right now," she mumbled under her breath, but not soft enough to prevent Jennifer from overhearing.

"Well, girls, sweet dreams. I'm off to bed. You girls go out and have a good time if you want. The night is still young." Bessie called out as she rose from the porch chair and disappeared into the house.

Somewhere a cricket was singing in the garden, and way off in the distance faint music from the fair grounds drifted across the quiet night air.

"Want to go back to the fair?"

Patty shook her head. "No, last night was enough for me."

Jennifer felt compelled to get Patty away from the house. Obviously, something was bothering her cousin, and a good talk was in order. The kind of talk that neither one had enjoyed in a long, long time.

"Let's go down to the park and see if the River Queen is still running. It's been at least fourteen or fifteen years since I've seen the darned thing. I wonder if the old scow still floats?" Jennifer grinned, as she pulled Patty up from her seat.

They found the boat landing was still there, and that the River Queen was on its first evening excursion. There was at least an hour before the next run, pleasing Jennifer, for this would give her a good opportunity to have a private talk with Patty. Finding a comfortable bench beside the river, where the soft night breeze coming off the water was refreshing, the two sat down to await the craft's return.

After some general chit-chat, Jennifer coyly steered the conversation around to Patty's boys, then to Jim, sure that her cousin wanted to confide something that was not going smoothly. Patty had referenced some discord the first day they were together, and again earlier tonight. Jennifer knew instinctively that Patty's usual cheerful smile and bubbly enthusiasm, not to mention lilting laugh, were only a well practiced cover up, a facade, to mask some hurt or worry.

"Have you talked to Jim lately?"

Patty blinked and stared straight ahead at the blackness of the water.

"I tried calling a little while ago, but there was no answer."

"Maybe he was out for a late dinner."

"That's not like Jim. He likes to eat at six on the dot, and he should be home doing his lesson plans." Patty choked slightly. "I'm afraid, Jenny," she finally blurted out. "Afraid Jim is interested in another woman."

"Oh, Patty! That's not like Jim. He's too much of a family man to fool around. And you two love each other so much."

"But he has changed."

"How?"

"Well, he's so much more quiet. He tends to spend more time by himself. We used to enjoy doing things together so much... enjoying music, and reading, browsing in old book stores. But lately, he has lost interest in all those things. Especially when it comes to doing things together."

Patty poured out her fears, trying to rationalize all the little nuances, reading more into Jim's actions than was probably actually there.

"I should not have left him alone these two weeks. It gives him a perfect time to go to her."

"Who would that be?"

"The woman he is probably having an affair with."

Jennifer sighed deeply. This could not be happening to Patty. *She is so sweet and pure, filled with so much unconditional love. How could Jim hurt her like this? And the boys!*

"Have you confronted Jim?"

Patty shook her head no.

"Then why don't you come right out and ask him?"

"I couldn't do that, Jenny! Why, what if I am wrong? That would start such a rift that Jim would never forgive me for doubting him."

"But you already suspect some kind of hanky-panky going on."

"What if I'm wrong? What if I only suspect there is some else? How else am I supposed to believe? He is drawing away, spending more time at work, so he says. There are meetings he is supposedly attending that go on late into the night. He's never home on Saturdays any more. It must be someone else."

Though she tried to be compassionate, Jennifer was growing impatient with her cousin.

"Patty, if you still love him, then fight for him, don't just give up. Fight!"

Patty burst into tears at that point, feeling miserable in her disappointment and grief. At that moment, the River Queen came into view, its motors burbling softly, propelling the craft to the landing where the captain threw it into reverse and effortlessly brought the boat broadside against the mooring dock.

"Come on, Patty, let's get on board. The ride will do you good."

As they glided along up river, Jennifer could not help but recall the story of Timothy Wilbur's rescue of the young girl who fell overboard, almost twenty years ago. Aunt Bessie is a good narrator she decided, able to bring to life in vivid detail the events of Fanny Wilbur's rolling pin story. Her

Aunt had made it seem so real, it had almost been like watching a movie. The two girls sat in the stern, watching the wake of the boat as it broke up the reflection of a nearly full moon into silver shards, which darted V-shaped outward to each bank of the river. There was almost a hypnotic rhythm to the swells that lapped away from the propellers, keeping time with the dull throb of the engine that churned the vessel upstream.

The tranquillity of the easy excursion was suddenly shattered by the high-pitched whine of a speedboat, growing rapidly closer and closer. Everyone strained their necks to see a faint white object hurtling toward the River Queen. Quickly, the Captain yanked on the boat whistle cord, giving three sharp blasts of the horn, while he swore under his breath. At the same time, with his other hand, he spun the rudder wheel hard to starboard. The speedboat, piloted by a blond young woman, swerved slightly, then sped around the big craft and across its wake, waves slapping hard against the hull.

Two other young women in the speedboat, with their hair streaming in the wind, threw back their heads, screaming with delight. Those on board gasped as they saw a water skier behind the boat skillfully maneuver across the wake, close enough to throw a spray of water upon some of those on board.

"Damn your hide, Ralph Warren!" the Captain muttered. "I'll get the Sheriff after you!" He recognized the muscular figure even in the moonlight, and he shook his fist after the skier. "Sorry about that, folks," the Captain came on the PA system. "Some idiots don't have the brains they were born with!"

Jennifer's face burned. She had overheard. Ralph Warren! Why wasn't she surprised? It would be just like him to flaunt his dare-devil, devil-may-care self into everyone's face. She, too, had recognized his dark head and deeply tanned body in the moonlight as he sped past, even if the glimpse she got was nothing more than a flash. The sound coming from the speedboat of the three women's hilarious screams had even drowned out the whine of the engine, as the small craft hurtled down the river into the darkness.

Jennifer knew they were headed for the landing at the park where there would be sure to be a large audience to witness whatever antics Ralph had up his sleeve.

"Why can't I get away from him? Why must he pop up like some kind of Genie every time I turn around?" Jennifer lamented to herself.

"Idiot!" Patty spat, brushing some water beadlets off her blouse, she being one of the recipients of Ralph Warren's slashing moves. "They ought to put someone like that in jail. He could have been killed, skiing at that speed in the dark. What if those bimbos driving the boat had hit a log or something? They didn't even have running lights, for God's sake!"

Jennifer was thankful that Patty did not recall meeting Ralph at the Fair. In fact, she doubted Patty had even heard the Captain utter his name. Just as well.

An hour later, after the river excursion ended, Jennifer and Patty stopped for coffee at the ever popular, always open Dairyland Cafe. It was the meeting place for all the locals, and was usually crowded, no matter what time of day or night. Tonight, the place was jumping, even at eleven o'clock, so the two girls had to settle for seats at the counter. Patty allowed Jennifer to talk her into having a gooey, hot fudge sundae along with her coffee, and even though she protested the selection, it did not take her long to demolish the treat.

"Gosh, Patty, I guess you enjoyed that! Next thing we know, you will be licking the bowl!"

Patty laughed, which made Jennifer happy to see that she was in a little better mood. She hoped Patty would be able to sort things out, and with the weekend coming, perhaps she would be in contact with Jim. It was hard for Jennifer to believe that Jim was having an affair. He seemed too quiet, too straight-laced a person. Serious all the time, that's how she remembered him. And Patty was so sweet, how could he pull that on her?

The hum of busy conversation around them lulled Jennifer into ignoring her surroundings, but her ear picked up a snatch of conversation which made her jerk alert.

"Ya, so here comes the big airline pilot, swaggering into the emergency room, dripping wet in his bathing suit, no less!" a male voice was saying in the booth behind her.

"You mean Ralphie-boy broke his arm?"

"Yup... says he was water skiing in the dark and missed the boat ramp."

A group of male hospital orderlies were discussing the evening events in the ER. Now, Jennifer's ears were burning. A big, hoarse laugh erupted from the group, and she could have died when she heard the snickers and snide remarks.

"You should have seen the blond doll who brought him in! Wow! What a broad! That guy is so lucky. She had boobs out to HERE!"

"*I* should be so lucky!" another said.

"Well, airline pilots have their pick of the lot, don't you think?"

"That fly-boy always has a stunner on his arm, and never the same one twice, so I hear."

"Yeah, how would you know? You don't belong to the Country Club."

"Word gets around."

"Well, fast cars, fast women, now fast boats. It's bound to catch up to him sooner or later."

The conversation turned to whispers, more raucous laughter, and the sound of hands slapping their knees, then more snickering. Jennifer wanted to sink into the floor, but did not dare to let on to Patty how this overheard conversation was disturbing her.

Damn Ralph Warren! Why does he keep intruding on my life? Why am I letting him into my thoughts, and letting these things disrupt me? Jennifer thought. *I should never have come back to Waterville. He is everywhere.*

"Let's go home, Patty."

Chapter 8

It was hot and humid on Saturday, the air hanging oppressively heavy, as if to crush the very breath out of anyone who attempted even the most simple of tasks. It made it that much more miserable for Jennifer and Patty as they struggled bringing heavy loads down from the attic. Boxes, trunks, old magazines and papers now cluttered the downstairs.

"There! That's the last of the attic. Everything is cleared out from there now." Jennifer puffed, beads of perspiration rolling down her face. She resorted to putting a sweat band around her forehead. Patty had a tennis visor holding back her damp, dark curls, and looked pert and cute in shorts and a tee shirt. An electric fan hummed in the hallway, blowing a stream of air their way. It helped a little.

"Anybody home?" A male voice boomed in the front door screen, at the same time rapping his knuckles on the door frame, startling the young women.

"Well, my stars! James! Come in, come in. What a surprise!" Aunt Bessie exclaimed.

She held the screen open, and a tall, sandy-haired man stepped into the hallway, accepted

Bessie's embrace, and planted a kiss on the woman's smooth cheek. His eyes searched quickly, finally locking onto Patty's startled stare, and softened as he met her gaze.

"Jim!" Patty whispered. "How did you get here?"

Jim Peterson's face cracked a smile. "In the Volkswagon, of course."

"I mean... I mean, we didn't expect you," Patty stammered, frozen to the spot, not knowing how she should greet him, reticent and unsure.

"I thought you girls could use some help. Besides," his eyes again locked onto Patty's and she felt herself tingle inside. "I missed you!"

"Oh, Jim, you silly!" Patty squealed as she ran across the room to him and threw herself into his arms, accepting his bear-hug with a big smile.

"It's so good to see you again, Jim," Jennifer smiled, noting that there certainly did not appear to be a problem between these two. Patty must have been imaginning trouble. Whatever the perception, it was not even remotely evident now.

"Jenny! My, it's been too long," he gave her a hug.

The years had been kind to him, Jennifer thought. His face was a little more craggy, lines a little deeper, hair thinning just a bit, but he was the same Jim Peterson she had known years ago.

Even though Patty seemed flustered, Jennifer could see by the sparkle in her eyes that she was pleased, almost to the point of speechlessness.

"Well, now you're here, let's put you to work," Patty blurted out, grabbing his hand, and pulling him to the trunks.

"Okay. Just tell me what you want me to do."

With another pair of hands, and strong ones at that, soon the boxes and trunks were sorted in no time, putting all items for next weekend's auction aside. Aunt Bessie busied herself marking tags and doing a certain amount of reminiscing. She poured over newspaper clippings and old magazines, smiling and remembering as the memories flashed back to her.

After Jim had learned the details of Aunt Bessie's move to the apartment and when he came to a good stopping point, he volunteered to go rent a truck and get her moved that very weekend.

"Oh, bless your heart, James, that is so nice of you, but you understand, I can't make the move until after the sale. You know, we just don't know how much will go."

Jim nodded in agreement, as he leaned against the hallway door, mopping his brow. It was mid-afternoon and still sultry.

"You all go onto the porch. I'm going to make some lemonade," Bessie insisted, and shooed the three out on to the great porch, where a slight breeze rustled the geranium baskets.

Jim and Patty sat on the swing, and Jennifer noticed Jim's big hand reach to grasp Patty's as they slowly swung back and forth. Both were silent, and the only sound was the metallic squeak of the porch swing as the rings holding the chains groaned in protest.

"How is school going, Jim?" Jennifer tried to end the awkward silence.

He nodded. "Fine," pulling a pipe out of his pocket, and loading it with fresh tobacco. He lit the bowl and blew a ring of smoke toward the ceiling before continuing. "In fact," and he gave a long sideways glance at Patty, "I came to tell Patty that I am resigning."

"Resigning?" Patty stared at her husband.

"Yup! After summer school is over, I will not be renewing my contract."

Patty's mouth dropped open. "Now, wait a minute, Jim. What are you talking about?"

"I'm going to start my own business."

"You're what?"

"Start a business."

"Jim!" Patty stumbled over her words, shocked to say the least. "Why, we haven't discussed this. I mean, I can't... we can't just start a business!"

"Sorry, Patty, but that's what I want to do."

Jennifer and Bessie sat holding their breath, the news coming as a shock to them.

"But, Jim!"

"Patty, the deal's already been made."

"Doing what? What kind of business?"

"It's a bookstore, Patty. I've bought a bookstore. Oh, Patty, I've been dying to tell you for months! I've been working out the details for a long time, and finally it all came together this week."

Patty was stunned. "But, how come you never once mentioned a word?"

"I wanted to surprise you, Hon, and I guess I did. I've got a lot of ideas, like maybe having a little refreshment bar, starting reader's groups, and just lots of ideas! Oh, Patty, I'm so excited!"

She could see how enthused he was, his eyes sparkled and his words came in a rush. Patty dared not reprimand him in front of Jenny and Aunt Bessie for not including her in his planning. But she was hurt that he had not confided in her long ago. *Shouldn't this have been a joint decision? Shouldn't this have been a thing we both could have worked on together?* Thoughts tumbled into Patty's mind.

Jim continued, "I've been studying nights and weekends, taking some business courses, and I know we can do it, Patty! I'm positive!"

"So that's where you have been spending your time. And all the while I thought... I thought... "

Jackie Gould

"What, Patty?"

"Never mind."

Jennifer jumped in, knowing what Patty meant. "It sounds great, Jim! I know how you both love literature."

Jim continued talking as the afternoon slipped by, and their glasses of lemonade emptied. "I really came to beg Patty to come back home early. I've got so much to show her. How about it, Aunt Bessie? Do you think you can spare her?"

"Of course, James. We're actually in pretty good shape. Jennifer and I can do all that is left. You are welcome to stay here the night. It's up to you, but in any case, we should have dinner. How about going out to eat? It will be my treat."

They all protested, of course, but in the end, Aunt Bessie won out. "We'll celebrate your new venture in style!"

After Jim and Patty's departure the following morning, and Aunt Bessie had gone off to church, Jenny strolled through the house by herself, a mug of coffee clutched in her hand. It was strangely quiet in the big old house, which no longer looked lived in. Boxes and crates, trunks and furniture were shoved into corners and against the walls, in cluttered chaos. Aunt Bessie's personal touch was already missing, packed into boxes she would take to her new apartment. Jennifer browsed absentmindedly through the empty rooms, wondering more and more about Aunt Bessie's life, especially when she had been a young woman.

"She must have seen a lot," Jennifer mused aloud. She knew her aunt had been born a few years after the Civil War ended, and she was vaguely aware that Bessie Herrington had lived in, or at least traveled in the west as a young woman. Taking advantage of her Aunt's absence, Jennifer stepped into her Aunt's downstairs bedroom. Up to now, she had not invaded the area more than to peek in the door to see the bed and dresser which were to go to the new apartment.

Jennifer had time to gaze at the pictures on the walls, and was immediately drawn to a large, hand-tinted portrait. The image of a lovely, in fact, beautiful dark haired young woman glowed from an ornate frame. The image wore a huge, very pink feathered hat, perched a bit askew on her head, allowing her dark hair to escape around her face. The whole hat, full of feathers, lace, and mammoth silk roses, all in the same shade of vibrant pink, framed the young woman's head, complimenting her porcelain-ivory complexion. It seemed to match the faint pink of her cheeks.

It was so striking, Jennifer gasped out loud as she gazed at the figure in the portrait. She studied the incredible face, from the pert nose, above full, slightly parted lips, to the dark brows which framed startlingly blue eyes. In the portrait, the young woman wore a white lace dress with a high collar encasing the most exquisitely slender neck Jennifer had ever seen. Though the colors had faded slightly, Jennifer was struck by the haunting look in the girl's eyes. There was a depth there that could not be measured, and it stirred an emotion in Jennifer which she could not recognize. A longing—a yearning for something lost.

Aunt Bessie! It had to be Aunt Bessie, when she was a young woman, for there was the same straight back, the head held at that familiar tilt, shoulders squared and capable.

"Oh, how perfectly lovely!" Jennifer said out loud, immersed in the beauty of the young woman's likeness. *I wonder what story this portrays? Was it heartbreak? Surely the haunting look conveys something dramatic.* "Aunt Bessie, I'll not rest until you tell me about this portrait. When,—how—what did this represent?"

Jennifer jumped at a sudden knock on the front door and pulled back to the present. She glided quietly to the entrance hall, her tennis shoes padding softly on the oriental runner in the hallway. She could make out the outline of a figure through the stained glass door, though she was totally unprepared for the visitor when she swung the door open.

"Hi, Jenny," a deep voice said softly, with the hint of a smile buried cleverly in the words.

She took a step back, and a gasp escaped her lips as she sucked in her breath. Standing before her was none other that Ralph Warren, his left arm in a cast, cradled in a very medical looking sling.

"What are you doing here?" was all she could think to say, and felt very stupid doing so.

"I came to see you."

"How—?"

"Your cousin told me, remember? And by the way, I happen to own this house now. Bought it from Bessie Herrington. Are you going to let me in?"

Her knees turned to rubber, and Jennifer stood aside dumbly, holding the door open for him as Ralph squeezed past her, brushing her lightly as he entered. Her mind was racing, but she could not focus, and her heart pounded so loudly, she thought he would surely be able to hear. He must be able to see the color that rose to her face. Shakily, she motioned for him to sit.

"I was intending to help Miss Bessie move until this happened." He raised his broken arm. "Guess I can't be of much help this way."

There was an awkward silence before he spoke again. "It's really good to see you again, Jenny."

"I heard about your accident," was all she could utter.

"Really? So soon? It just happened night before last."

"Word gets around."

Ralph continued to press her as to how long she would be staying, and when she was scheduled to return home. He did not ask about her marriage, nor seem to be interested in her new life. The conversation seemed to swirl around him and his accomplishments. Jennifer found out that when he had returned from the Korean War, a decorated hero, he reminded her, he was immediately sought by some of the major airlines, and became a pilot for one of the big carriers. At 37, he was at the height of his career. Now, because of his injury, he would be off work until his arm healed.

"But this gives us a chance to be together," he said as he smiled a white-toothed grin at her.

"Ralph, I told you before, I'm a happily married woman."

"But he is in Arizona, and you are here now."

At that moment, Aunt Bessie returned from church. "Ah, Mr. Warren! How delighted I am to see you. I see you have met my grand-niece." She fluttered about, asking after his well being. "Do stay for dinner. It's my Sunday Special, you know."

Jennifer groaned internally, wishing Aunt Bessie had not made such an offer. She wanted Ralph Warren gone, out of her life. Like a trapped doe, she wondered how she could wiggle out of the next couple of hours.

"I'd be delighted," Ralph said, and glanced at Jennifer with a look that disturbed her in more than one way, for she was trying valiantly to resist the emotions that rose up within her. Reluctantly, she recognized that she was still very much attracted to him. That realization angered her, and she was furious with herself for her weakness, and furious at Ralph for exposing those long lost emotions. She felt herself fill with turmoil and rage, and tried to suppress any outward sign so Aunt Bessie would not suspect anything was wrong.

"Tell me how you broke your arm, Mr. Warren." Bessie's question was solicitous.

Ralph looked at Jenny as he replied, "I had an accident while water skiing."

"My, how unfortunate."

Jennifer hoped that her face did not give away the fact that she knew the bone-truth about the "accident." Good thing Aunt Bessie didn't know the real story, that Ralph's own recklessness was the culprit.

Bessie chatted on, offering a continuous stream of conversation in which Ralph was also animatedly engaged. All the while, Jennifer quietly observed how Ralph had Aunt Bessie charmed in an almost school-girl-like crush. It was easy to see how he drew people to him. His easy going self assurance would please even the most cantankerous, cynical person alive. He smiled as he talked, the lines around his eyes crinkling in pure pleasure, and those deep dimple lines on each side of his mouth brought back vivid memories to Jennifer.

She felt herself helplessly spiraling down, powerless to stop the rush of buried emotions, until she knew in her heart that she still loved him. The sudden realization somehow did not surprise her one bit, and she was as positive of her love at this moment as she had been a few nights ago in the thunderstorm. After all, how could any girl ever really get over her first love? Hadn't the bittersweet affection always been there, hidden just under the surface, waiting for a simple strike of a match to rekindle the ember until it burst into flame once more?

She tried to suppress this emergence of feeling, but found it was already too late. Just seeing the tilt of his head, his dark wavy hair, gave her a little tickle inside. When his clear blue eyes met hers, she seemed to come undone. His gaze burned into her until she felt her stomach do a flip-flop, and she melted, furious at him for being here. More furious at herself for falling once more for his charm.

"Damn you, Ralph, damn you," she whispered to herself.

Jackie Gould

Chapter 9

That evening, totally drained emotionally, Jennifer sat with Aunt Bessie on the great porch exchanging small talk. It was a relief when a cool breeze ruffled the hanging baskets, and brushed her cheeks like the kiss of an angel.

"I didn't know Ralph Warren was the one who bought your house, Aunt Bessie."

"Oh, then did you know Mr. Warren before?"

"Yes, I knew him years ago when I lived here."

Bessie nodded. "That's right, he would have been roughly your age. He's quite a successful young man. I understand he was an ace pilot in World War II, not to mention the Korean War. And now he is one of the best pilots in the airlines. He commutes to Chicago in his own plane when he is scheduled for duty, I hear. I'm surprised he still wants to live in Waterville, such a little town, instead of living in Chicago where there are so many more cultural things to do."

Jennifer was only half listening, imagining Ralph in an airline uniform. *He must be devastatingly handsome,* she thought, and felt a twinge within her.

"Mr. Warren is also a smart businessman. He owns several properties here, both commercial and residential."

"What do you think he will do with this magnificent old house, Aunt Bessie?"

The older woman shrugged. "I hope he keeps it restored. I would hate to think it would go to ruin."

"Do you think he intends to live here?"

"I have no idea. Why don't you ask him?"

Jennifer shook her head. "It really makes no difference to me, I was just curious."

Aunt Bessie became pensive as she pondered the thought of leaving the old homestead. "You know, Jennifer, I'm trying hard not to think too much about leaving the old place. It was built the year I was born, you know, 1872. That was after Pa came back from the Civil War. I was the last baby. Three girls and two boys were already in school. Mama lost two babies in between. After Pa came back I was a surprise, I guess. Papa built this house after recovering from the ravages of what he saw in the war."

This tidbit of information stirred Jennifer's interest.

Bessie continued. "He was on Sherman's March to the Sea. I have some old letters and parts of a journal where Papa tells of the awful events. I even have the rolling pin he used to bake pies with. He sold the pies to the soldiers to earn extra money to send to Mama. Things were awfully tight then, and Mama had to support five little ones all the while he was gone. Seems as though the paychecks were few and far between."

Jennifer's interest was really piqued then. "Honestly? Which rolling pin is it, Aunt Bessie?"

"I'll bring it out."

Jennifer hefted the slim stick, feeling the smoothness of the shank, and rubbed her fingers over the button-like ends. It was smaller in diameter than most of the rolling pins in Aunt Bessie's collection, and there were no distinct handles like the modern day ones had. There did, however, appear to be an old knick in one of the ends, worn smooth now with time.

"That's where a Johnny Reb bullet hit while Papa was carrying it in his knapsack. It saved his life!"

Jennifer was impresed. "How did he use this without handles?"

Bessie showed Jennifer how to roll the stick with the flat of her palms. "Papa taught me how, like this."

"And where did he get this pin?"

"He said he got it foraging in the kitchen of a Southern Plantation. It was light enough to carry in his knapsack. Would you like to read some of his letters?"

"Would I ever! You said he baked pies? Isn't that rather odd for a man to take up woman's work?"

"Papa was an excellent cook. He was very resourceful, and if it meant he could fill his stomach, or earn extra money to send to Mama and the children, there was no question whether it was woman's work or not. You'll find out when you read his journal and letters. He was remarkable."

"Then I see where you get it from, Aunt Bessie. You are remarkable, too."

Bessie laughed and waved the compliment off. She then disappeared into her bedroom, emerging a short time later, carrying a wooden box.

"It's all in here. Some letters and journal pages are missing, but it still makes mighty interesting reading. Enjoy."

Later, in her bedroom, Jennifer carefully unfolded the first fragile paper and immediately became lost in Andrew Herrington's account of the Civil War, starting in late April, 1864.

Legend II
"Andrew"
Part I

There were times when Andrew Herrington questioned his own sanity, and this night was one of those times. It was now 2AM, and after traveling for two days on the train, eating only raw salt pork and bread, the 45th Illinois Volunteers arrived in Cairo, Illinois. They had slogged the last two miles through mud at least a foot deep to reach the camp where they would get their regimentals before marching on through Tennessee. By then they would be hot on the road to join General Sherman, somewhere in Georgia.

"What possessed me to volunteer?" Andrew muttered. "I could have stayed home with my dear family, those I love the most on this earth. Now, here I am, 500 miles away, in strange territory, with mud everywhere. If it weren't for the Great Cause, I would think I had gone daft!"

He threw his blankets down upon a few sticks to keep dry, and immediately fell into a deep sleep. Visions of his dear wife Marion danced through his dreams, and when he woke the next morning the dream had seemed so real he could not shake the feeling that she had visited him during the night. He vividly recalled her bright copper hair, strands of which, as usual, escaped the combs that held the mass in a big roll at the back of her petite head. Even the shading of her huge eyes was imbedded in his mind, as he remembered how subtle the color could change from green to blue.

Andrew marveled at how petite his wife had remained, even after giving birth to three daughters and two sons, the oldest being nine, and the youngest just a wee babe of six weeks. Despite himself, tears stung at his eyes as he thought of those precious souls at home, and he could not quell the urge to put his thoughts on paper. So he wrote a letter again, which he hoped to post before leaving Cairo. He knew letters would be his only link to those he loved and left, and vowed to write every day. How or when they would reach his beloved, he did not know, but that did not deter his effort.

Three weeks of extensive drills sped by, leaving the 45th a well disciplined regiment, ready to begin the long march to join the main Union Army at Atlanta, toward which General Sherman at this very moment was fighting his way. Very little time was left for leisure. However, Andrew took every spare moment to write a few lines in his journal, or in the letters he forwarded on to his wife. Once the long march was underway, the writing would be difficult.

May 20, 1864. Andrew described the march south through Tennessee and into Georgia, 10,000 men, four hundred teams of six or eight mules to the team, pulling wagons of provisions and artillery, stretching out ten miles long. Eight thousand head of cattle were herded along. Andrew had never seen such a sight as this. The countryside was deserted, and many small towns through which they traveled had been destroyed. Destruction and desolation were all around. Even farmlands had been laid to waste. Everywhere one looked, all that could be seen were wagons, cannons, and soldiers, marching—marching.

Tonight we camp on a beautiful tract of land, he wrote in the third week of May. *As we have no tents, we have to make them, and as soon as we arrived at our campsite we began taking down farm fences, even though they protected the fields of cotton and corn. They made fine tents and fires. This place we are at belongs to a Southern Widow, and our commanding General made his Headquarters in her lovely home. There was a very fine garden, but our troops made quick use of it all. The Widow says this is the third time it has been destroyed, poor lady.*

Andrew felt fine after the first long march, and considered himself fortunate that his health was good. Unable to keep up, hundreds of men had already fallen out, straggling behind, or were taken by ambulance wagon to the trains in the rear. Many men had thrown away their knapsacks and blankets already, finding them too burdensome to carry. Andrew kept all of his gear, including extra shirts, canteen, blankets, books, rations, and cooking utensils. He could not abide those lazy ones who abandoned their posessions, for surely in the days, weeks and months ahead, they would be in dire need of such supplies.

Another two weeks march brought them near Cartersville, Georgia, where, at least for awhile, the 45th would be stationed, guarding a fort and railroad bridge. It was here that Andrew decided to improve upon his meager two-man quarters, and set about making his little shanty the most comfortable in the whole camp. Somewhere in his foraging, he had found a little window, which, when installed, he could open and close, making this little shelter a top-rate accommodation.

Never one to sit with time on his hands, he fashioned a table, bench, some shelves, a cupboard, and a bedstead. His disdain for the lazy soldiers was evident, and he had a hard time holding his tongue when listening to the moaning and griping of those whose only task in life seemed to be how much they could complain about.

His tent-mate, Joseph Harder, returned from the afternoon railroad bridge guard duty. Far in the distance, the great boom-boom-boom of heavy cannons could be heard.

"How are the trains?" Andrew asked his companion. Every day, all day, trains chugged to the front lines loaded with supplies and came back loaded with the wounded.

Joseph shook his head. "Comin' back filled with terrible wounded. It's an awful sight, poor men. Legs an' arms gone. Bloody uniforms. Heads all bandaged up. Cryin' and pukin', rantin' and ravin' out of their heads. It's a sorrowful sight."

Repulsed by the thought, Andrew silently damned the war. *What cause could be so noble as to pit brother against brother, man against man, American against American? To inflict such carnage and destruction?* For over three years this war had been going on. Thousands on both sides had been killed. Tens of thousands wounded, forever changing not only their own lives, but the lives of all their loved ones as well—those who were sadly left behind. It would forever change the fabric of this great land.

"I heard that Lincoln has made a call for 400,000 more men. Who would volunteer if they knew the terrible consequences?"

Joseph shook his head once more, unable to venture an answer.

"Look, I found some peas and new potatoes this morning on forage duty. In fact, I was able to milk a cow, so we shall have a dish of creamed potatoes and peas to go with our pork tonight."

Joseph grunted his approval, brightening up a bit. "Better'n hard tack 'n salt pork—salt pork 'n hard tack every day."

"I thought you might be pleased," Andrew replied as he went about preparing the evening meal. It turned out that Andrew was a first rate cook. Soon there was such a delightful aroma coming from their cooking stove, that a small crowd of soldiers gathered about, their mouths watering for the victuals

"Sorry, lads, but you'll have to forage on your own. Not enough here to go around."

The men turned away in disappointment, heads hanging low, mumbling and shuffling their feet in the dust.

That evening, as the twilight lingered long over the Georgia landscape, Andrew took his usual swim in the river. He could hear the cannons still booming in the direction of Atlanta. Surely by now, Sherman should have captured the city. But Andrew's mind was on home and family, and he wondered what they were doing at this very moment on such a fine night. In his mind, he could picture Clara, their first-born, being her mother's good helper, scurrying to control the other children. Clara was the serious one, and had her mother's hair, the shade of a new copper penny. She seemed so grown up at nine years old, as she took on so many mature responsibilities around the house.

"Don't worry, Papa," she had reassured him before he left home. "I will take care of Mama and the family." He was so proud of his oldest daughter.

Andrew's eyes misted as he pictured each precious face in his mind. Little Jessie, eight, the mischievous little mouse! Her dark hair and eyes favored Andrew's own coloring. Then came Mary Ellen, six, a studious child who was anxious to be a school teacher even before she ever entered a class. Her medium brown hair framed a round little face full of freckles. Andrew loved her button nose.

Next came the boys. Tow-headed, four year old William, who could never sit still. *I'll always remember him racing from one interest to another, full of questions and nonstop chatter,* Andrew mused and smiled even though a tear caught in his eye. The lump in his throat grew larger when his thoughts turned to little George, the wee baby, just a scant six weeks old when Andrew had volunteered.

Poor Marion, she surely has her hands full, caring for those precious ones all by herself. She is so small and fragile, I don't know where she gathers the energy to tend the house, children, and big garden, too. Thank heaven the garden will give them food to preserve for the winter, and hopefully her uncle will butcher some meat for them when fall comes. Andrew's mind was racing.

Then a great hurting began in his chest, and he knew it was homesickness that had plagued him since he departed, over two months ago. Letters had come spasmodically, but he devoured each one like a starving man, and clung to every word like a person drowning would cling to a life preserver. Only today he had received the first letter from little Clara, and read each word with such anticipation that his eyes had misted over. He kissed the very paper she wrote on, precious now because her little hands had written the lines. Again a pang of longing tore through him, twisting his insides until he thought he would strangle.

"What am I doing here, hundreds of miles away from my loved ones? I belong there with them!" he whispered fiercely, as he emerged from the water and retrieved his clothing. For a flickering moment, he thought of hopping on one of those rail cars which was carrying the wounded north. Worse still, the terrible thought crossed his mind, that if he were to be wounded, perhaps he would be able to go home. Quickly he dismissed that idea—but, just maybe—?

PART II

They had now been in the Union Army for almost three months, and still Andrew and the others had yet to be paid. It worried him, for by now Marion would be sore to have money to survive. His wages were long overdue, and there simply had to be a way to make some extra money. If he waited for the government to pay back wages, he might be waiting for a long time.

One afternoon, Andrew was detailed to guard the forager teams, who by now had fanned out in a spreading arc of several miles wide to gather what they could muster. They took foodstuffs, animals, and every useful thing from the hapless southern farms and plantations.

During the forage, while he had temporarily lost sight of the team, it was Andrew's fortune to come upon a stately plantation house quite by accident, nestled among some huge live oak trees. He watched the house for some time, peering through thick tree branches, and then stealthily approached, wary of the fact that he and his regiment were now deep in Rebel territory.

He had become momentarily separated from the main forage team, as they were out of sight in a gully some yards off. Now Andrew found himself in a predicament. His duty was supposed to be guarding the foragers, yet before him lay the possibility of riches beyond comprehension. Still, there was great risk; the Rebels could be anywhere, lurking behind any bush, waiting to ambush the Yankee patrol.

The big house appeared totally untouched by the ravages of war and was so secluded that perhaps the army had yet to discover its treasures. Andrew wondered how it had escaped the devastation so far. Then, taking every precaution, he dismounted, tied his horse, and crept closer to the plantation house. He figured it to be at least twelve miles from their camp, and set in such a peaceful, serene setting that he could easily lose track of the fact that war even existed somewhere southeast of the place. It stood proud and silent, a bit of yesteryear that prevailed in spite of the great conflict.

For some time, Andrew studied the house, ever watchful for any movement or sign of life. From his hiding place he could see a well kept garden, leading him to believe that the place had not been abandoned. Where were those who should be taking care of this large place? There must be darkies to tend to the gardens and the huge wide-porched house, two stories tall. Four white columns graced the front, and tall shuttered windows kept watch over the property like sentinels. Carefully, Andrew stepped from the shadows and one step at a time approached the house, his finger still on the trigger of the rifle he held in front of him.

Nowhere was there a sound to be heard. Not the cluck of a chicken, the bark of a dog, nor even the twitter of a bird. It seemed eerie, and Andrew held his breath as he soundlessly mounted the front steps. His heart was beating hard, and he paused for a long moment, with his hand on the big door handle, not at all sure he had the courage to push it open. But it yielded easily to his touch, and he found himself standing in the darkened hallway, waiting for his eyes to adjust to the dimness. The faint aroma of old dried flowers, vintage leather, well-polished wood, and fireplace ashes greeted him.

He was unprepared for the magnificence of the place. To his left opened a huge dining room, splendid with a long mahogany table, surrounded by what seemed to be a dozen Chippendale chairs. Glints of light danced off priceless pieces of sterling silver bowls, candlesticks, and vases on the deeply carved hunt table. Silk draperies hung at the tall windows, softly coloring the room with green and gold.

On the right, an immense formal parlor stretched the length of the house. A pair of overstuffed green mohair couches flanked a big marble fireplace, and upholstered chairs were grouped in other seating areas. Carved mahogany tables held knick knacks, books, lamps of painted blown glass, and decanters filled with what appeared to be fine brandy.

Ahead of him wound a graceful stairway, curving up to the floor above. Each carved baluster supported the shiny, much polished banister, the likes of which Andrew had never seen. In his day, he had done a fair amount of woodworking, and had to admire the craftsman who had created this masterpiece. As he placed his hand upon the banister, he thought he heard a sound come from upstairs, and held his breath, afraid to breathe. There! Again, he heard a muffled noise originating from above.

It took him almost ten minutes to slowly creep up the stairs, pausing at every step. Again he heard that muffled sound, and as he reached the top step, he thought he detected a moan. The floor creaked as he crossed the hall, causing him to swear under his breath. Several doors leading to bedrooms stood open, and he could see empty beds and furniture in each one. The door at the end of the hallway stood only part way open. As he approached, his heart pounded in his ears.

Andrew drew to the doorjamb, his rifle in hand, and with one eye, peeked in, startled by a soft moan which came from within. He slowly pushed the door open with the rifle, and what greeted him took his breath away. The figure of a young woman lay upon a massive four poster bed, her black hair splayed upon the pillows in long ringlets, disarrayed and tangled. Her face was as ashen as the linens upon which she lay. From the looks of the disarranged bedding, he could tell she had obviously been thrashing about. The young woman's eyes were closed, her lips chapped from fever, and only upon hearing a moaning sound come from deep in her throat, did Andrew know this poor creature was alive.

Carefully leaning his rifle against a chair, he cautiously approached the bedside, but the woman remained motionless. Putting out a trembling hand to touch her forehead, he found the girl burning with fever. Covers were piled up to her chin, yet she shook with chills. Quickly, Andrew went down the stairs, two at a time, found the kitchen, and pumped a pail full of water from the cistern, returning to the room on the run.

He tore a cloth from a gown he found, and started bathing the girl's face. She did not seem to respond. Then, impatiently, he pulled back the hot covers from her body and gasped, as he discovered she had not a stitch of clothes on. Her small, round breasts rose and fell with every labored breath, and her porcelain white skin shown like a translucent statue. Shocked, Andrew could not take his eyes from the beauty he saw before him. She was maybe seventeen years old, and every bit of her screamed of genteel refinement. Her slender waist flared out to rounded hips, and her belly was flat, with just enough of a little rise below her navel to cause Andrew to feel a twinge in his loins. He stared at the sight far too long, drinking in every detail of her exquisite features, his mind whirling with unthinkable thoughts.

"Jesus!" he muttered.

With difficulty, Andrew tried to force his eyes away from the delightful sight, but he had been away from his own wife's charms for too many months, and now he had to draw upon every ounce of self-control he could muster to keep from touching. He wanted more than anything to let his fingers caress her softness, to cup the small breasts in his palms, as he gazed down at her loveliness, and—and even—.

NO! A voice inside him screamed, and he begged God to give him strength to resist the terrible temptation. Then he ripped a sheet from the bed, plunged it into the bucket, and wrapped the wet cloth around the girl in an effort to cool her body as quickly as possible.

"Come on, Miss," he muttered as he worked at bathing her face and lips. "Wake up, little lady."

The girl's eyelids fluttered, and slowly opened, taking a long moment to focus her deep green eyes. The dark circles under her sunken eyes testified to the fact that she was gravely ill. When the girl was finally able to look at Andrew, at first her stare was blank and unseeing. Then, as if in slow motion, he could see recognition begin to light in the depths of her eyes until her eyelids flew wide open. She struggled to try to back away, and a strangled scream rasped from her parched throat as she recognized his Yankee uniform. The look on her face was of sheer terror.

Andrew tried to calm her. "Hush, little lady, hush! Shhh. I will not harm you. You are burning up with fever. I'm trying to help you."

Once more she struggled, but her efforts to free herself from the folds of the wet sheet were useless. She found herself far too weak to do more than just whimper and fell back limp and exhausted.

"Be calm. I swear I will not harm you. Here, try to drink this. You are dehydrated."

He offered her a sip of water, and the gentleness with which he held her head soon gave the girl no cause to struggle any longer. Besides, she found she had no strength, and lay exhausted, unable to even raise a finger.

"Are you alone? Where are your people?" he asked, suspecting that someone might return at any moment.

"G—gone!" she barely managed to whisper through her cracked lips.

"Gone? Everyone is gone?"

She nodded by closing her eyes in the affirmative.

"Then you are here all by yourself? Why?"

The terror returned once more to the girl's face as she realized how vulnerable she was, helpless beyond belief, at the hands of the dreaded Yankee enemy.

Andrew had to bend close to hear as she hoarsely whispered "They—the Negroes, all stole away in the middle of the night, several days ago. They left me here, sick with swamp fever."

Her voice trailed off, and she began to weep, tears welling up to roll down her cheeks. She could not believe she was telling him this. Her fevered brain left her with jumbled thoughts and only a vague notion that there was a danger she could not pinpoint. She possessed no strength to resist, nor fight, nor escape.

"Please, I want to help you. You are very sick. I will not harm you, little lady. Please believe me." Andrew pleaded.

Her green eyes burned into his, wanting to believe his every word, struggling to comprehend, yet not quite sure she could trust him. He attempted to keep his gaze on her face, all the while acutely aware of how the wet sheet clung to the girl's every curve. He knew if he were to see her naked again, he would not have the will power to remain a gentleman.

"My name is Andrew Herrington. What is your name, Little Miss?"

Slowly, barely audible, she whispered, "Carrie... Carrie-Marie Walker." Her faint voice held a pure southern drawl, one of notable aristocracy, which did not escape Andrew's notice.

What little conversation they exchanged had already weakened the girl, and Andrew felt compelled to hurry.

"Let me see if I have any powders for your fever in my saddlebag, Miss Walker, you lay back and rest. I'll be right back."

As he raced down to his horse, he was visibly worried about the girl. Her fever was very high, and he could tell the sickness had taken a deep toll on her. He was not sure the cool bathing had helped. He could see she was too weak to move, and thoughts flew back and forth in his head of how he could help her. *Is there a way to take her back to camp? Not likely.* And he dare not let the others know she was here, for those seasoned, rough men would not have any qualms about remaining gentlemen, because they were not. Andrew shivered knowing what the fate of a beautiful, even if sick, young woman would be if the soldiers ever were to lay eyes upon her, and he was sickened at the thought.

He discovered he had no medical supplies with him, and returned to the house. Rummaging through the kitchen, he found nothing useful for his purposes now, for he needed laudanum or some fever powders from the apothecary back at camp. As he returned to her room, he found

Carrie-Marie's condition had worsened. She had lost consciousness again, and he tried again to rouse her. Once more he bathed her face and lips, and his heart was troubled at her plight.

"Carrie-Marie! Carrie-Marie! I will be back, I promise. Try to stay awake, Little Lady! I am coming back to help you."

She roused slightly, opening her eyes to mere slits, but Andrew did not like what he saw, for just in those few minutes he had been gone, he could see her failing dramatically. The fever raged, and she was slipping. She mouthed the words "Help me," as Andrew placed a gentle hand on her brow, brushing back the hair from her face, and met her eyes with kindness and compassion.

"Hang on, little Miss Walker. Hang on. I'll be back."

On his race out through the kitchen, he spied a wooden rolling pin resting on the table near the cold, black fireplace. It was a simple, slim, rounded piece of maple, worn smooth with countless years of working lard filled dough. The little knobs at the ends were very symmetrical, and Andrew figured how they must have used the device to flatten their dough by using the flat of their palms to rotate the pin. He took the rolling pin, a curious plan already forming in the back of his mind. But trying to save the girl's life was foremost in his thoughts at the moment.

As luck would have it, he waylaid the rest of the foragers in time to head them off before they discovered the Walker Plantation. Even though his mouth watered and stomach growled for the vegetables he knew were ripening in the plantation garden, he instinctively knew that he could not let the men in his regiment know of the existence of the plantation, nor that it housed a hapless, desperately sick young girl. He knew that the men would trash the beautiful furniture, and burn the house, and the thought pained him, for he appreciated all things that were beautiful. He shuddered at the thought of the crass men finding Carrie-Marie, knowing she would surely be ravaged by each and every one of those ruffians, and left to die. He would be powerless to stop them, for he was only one man, and he cursed the spoils of war.

PART III

Andrew could not sleep that night, for Carrie-Marie's haunting eyes and exquisite pale body were in his dreams. His intentions were to return somehow to the Walker Plantation the next day, to take life saving medical supplies to the young southern girl. But the Army had other plans in mind. At three AM the 45th was ordered to march in order to set up a new base camp twenty miles closer to Atlanta. Andrew had no choice but to strike camp and march with the others. He was wretched inside, knowing the helpless young woman lay dying alone, upstairs in the massive mahogany bed. Each step that he took put more distance between them, until he sadly realized he was beyond a point where he could help.

Being a devout Christian, it tore at his heart to know he could not save the poor girl. Part of him wanted to alert the commander, to leap upon the first cavalry horse he encountered, and fly to her side. He even seriously thought of stealing away, to gallop back to the plantation, but every step drummed into his mind the fact he could not return.

All day, Carrie-Marie's image haunted Andrew, as mile after mile, he trudged through the red dirt, shoulder to shoulder with the other foot soldiers. Her long raven black hair burned a picture in his mind, as he remembered how the mass of it had cascaded across the lace pillows. He recalled every detail of her exquisite face, the fine nose, tremulous lips, and great pain filled green eyes. And the image of her lean nakedness was imprinted in his memory like a hot ember into wood.

"God forgive me," he moaned to himself. "Forgive me for not going back to save her. And forgive me for the lustful thoughts I have had on my mind." Andrew tried to bring the memory of his beloved wife into focus,—tried to remember all her soft curves, but somehow the firm body of Carrie-Marie kept getting in the way. His loins began to ache with longing for the comfort of a woman, and he was appalled at how easily he had been sidetracked from thoughts of his dear wife. Thank God he had not acted upon temptation when it had presented itself yesterday, but how sad to think of the plight of the abandoned young woman.

His thoughts were so strong of Carrie-Marie, he felt she would surely respond to his prayers for her recovery, and that it would make a difference. "Get well, Carrie-Marie Walker. God keep you," he prayed as he marched. "God, save that lovely girl, and forgive me for turning my back upon her." Still, he was filled with agony.

When they reached the new camp site, Andrew threw himself into the task of fixing up the two man tent, hoping hard physical work would take the edge off his masculine need, and help bury the thoughts of Carrie-Marie. He wrestled with fence wood, scavenged from the countryside, and again fashioned some creature comforts. In unpacking, he discovered the rolling pin he had taken from the Walker Plantation, and he vowed to make use of it. At the same time, he tried to erase the thoughts of the doomed girl, but found it was not an easy task. She seemed to haunt his every waking hour, and he prayed for her more earnestly than ever.

Early the next morning, in the first graying of dawn, before the camp was even stirring, Andrew was scouring the surrounding forest for blackberries he knew should be ripe. Before breakfast, he had picked two pails full, and with sugar, lard and flour procured from the camp cooks he had befriended, he soon had his little oven busy baking pies. He used the rolling pin with ease, flattening the flaky crust with a professional flair, and soon turned out twenty of the sweet pastries. It took no urging from the troops to buy themselves a pie, when they discovered how tasty the treats were. Before he realized it, Andrew had himself a thriving side business, and turned out dozens and dozens of little pies, expanding to offering apple, and peach flavors as well. The sweet starved men were delighted to eat something other than hardtack and salt pork.

Andrew was thrilled that the extra income would be sent home to help his dear Marion with the finances. The only drawback was he would have to wait to collect the money later, after the government paid the troops all that was owed them. In the meantime, while they awaited the outcome of

General Sherman's advance upon Atlanta, Andrew kept up a steady supply of pies to the regiment, selling now mostly to the officers. He was making quite a reputation for himself. All the activity hardly lessened the anxiety he felt about the welfare of his family. Letters he received barely disguised the financial burden put upon his dependents.

Andrew wrote in his journal:

Chattahoochee Bridge, Georgia
July 31, 1864

My Dearest Wife,

We marched immediately after my last letter to you from the mountain to relieve three regiments at this bridge. Now 300 men take the place of 2000 who held the bridge before us. I do not know how long we shall remain here. It all depends on Sherman's success. There has been dreadful fierce fighting the last few days, some of the worst of the war. Thousands have been killed on both sides.

Many citizens come to the picket post to trade. They come from miles away bringing onions, potatoes, squash, sometimes butter. Mostly poor women and children. They want coffee, sugar, salt. Some poor old women have packed bags of apples, blackberries ten or fifteen miles in exchange for a handful of salt. The poor creatures have dirty-ragged little children tagging along, mostly with no shoes. All tell tales of having no food, the crops having been totally ruined by fire or foraging by us Yanks. It's a terribly sad place.

In his letters, Andrew did not mention finding the dying girl, for he could be nothing but honest, and would have certainly given all details, which at this time he would rather Marion did not know about. For this he constantly felt a series of guilt, about his momentary lapse of pure moral thoughts, and about the lack of his Christian duty to save the girl's life. It left him churning inside.

Andrew could not have known the trials that lay ahead. General Sherman's siege of Atlanta was lasting weeks. In the meantime, the Rebels captured Dalton, behind Sherman's lines, cutting off the Yankee Army's supplies. They made a great raid on the railroad, destroying five miles of strategic line which was the main line between Sherman's Army and the supplies coming from the north. The Confederates only held the area for three days, however, and then it was recaptured once more by the Union Army. The five miles of destroyed track were re-laid in half a day by hundreds of Yankees, industriously working so the trains could move once more. Not only did the Union Army have to fight its best to keep up the siege on Atlanta, but it had to fight to keep the possessions they already had.

"Atlanta is ours! Atlanta is ours!" The word spread like wildfire down the ranks. "The Rebs received the biggest whippin' they ever had!"

"Thank God," Andrew breathed, "This horrible conflict will soon be over, and we all will be on our way home."

The price of victory, however was steep. Since leaving Chattanooga, Sherman's Army had sustained the loss of 30,000 men, and the Confederates even more than that. The 45th, being in the rear, and along the railroad line, had a chance to witness the great losses. Thousands of the wounded and hundreds of prisoners were constantly being sent northward on trains, away from the battle.

Andrew recoiled at the sight of the wounded as they came in on the railcars. The Rebel prisoners were ragged and dirty, most even barefoot. Weariness showed in their haggard faces, and their eyes stared out of sunken pits like half-lit lanterns. Andrew could see the unwritten horror behind the blank stares of the defeated men, and pitied them, saying a silent prayer for them and their families.

Walking with the Chaplain among some of the 3,000 men who lay in rows on the ground with sheets and tents stretched over them for shade, Andrew struggled with the morality of war.

"Is it worth it, Chaplain?" he asked quietly. "Is this conflict worth all this?" he asked again, sweeping his arm to indicate the massive human suffering which lay all around them. The men were bandaged, bleeding, groaning in agony, and most were minus limbs which had been amputated.

"Sometimes, son, I wonder myself. With all our self-righteous motives, the freeing of the black men who would be captive slaves, on the surface would seem a worthy cause. But to what lengths must we stoop to attain the results?" The Chaplain, a kindly, gray-haired man with withering blue eyes, the looks of which told one that he had seen too much, shook his head as if to doubt his own conviction.

"Is God on our side, then?" Andrew ventured, stepping around the cots of wounded. He tried to rationalize the scene before him, steeling his emotions from the grim spectacle. The sight that greeted them was one of horrible wounds, missing limbs, bloody gashes bandaged with cloths that could not hold back the seeping pink tinge of blood. Andrew wanted to cup his hands to his ears to block out the moans, cries, and occasional screams which seemed to come from everywhere. Many were delirious, talking out of their heads, and thrashing about like puppets on strings.

"My lad," the Chaplain said, turning his sad eyes to meet Andrew's gaze, "God is also the God of the Confederates. How can He choose sides? Those men are just like us. They have families... wives, children... homes, farms, just like our soldiers do. And they are fighting to save their lands just as we would. Don't you think they believe that God is on their side, too?"

Andrew closed his eyes tightly, shaking his head, trying to shut out the scene, and struggled to understand. Perhaps he never would. More trains would come, bringing more maimed and wounded on the cars. More prisoners would come by the hundreds, and he could not stop it. But, for the first time, he began to doubt why he was there, and wondered if, indeed, he still had a noble cause to fill.

A few days later, on a day pass, he and Joseph went to Atlanta to see for themselves what the weeks of Sherman's siege had wrought. The ruins of large manufacturing buildings stood like skeletons, smoldering from the depths of the rubble. The two men could see where eighty railroad cars, loaded with guns, cannons, and ammunition had been burned, and lay destroyed in a tangle of metal. Andrew's heart lurched at the enormity of the destruction to the once beautiful city. The Union Army Commander had ordered the evacuation of all of the city's citizens who still remained, demanding they go either north or way south.

In response to that decree, the city was in utter chaos, as wagons, buggies, people on foot or pushing carts loaded with whatever the owners could carry, were all scurrying in every direction. Andrew and Joseph witnessed the panic and watched as it became more of a rout. The streets were clogged, and there were shouts and screams of angry residents attempting to seek the safety of the countryside.

"I've never seen anything like this," Andrew muttered as they attempted to make their way to the train depot. "The poor women and children."

At the station, Andrew's heart went out to a woman who was trying to keep herd on her three young children. She appeared to be in near hysterics, trying to cope with her baggage and the little ones at the same time. In a moment of compassion, he bought some gingerbread from a nearby vendor, and presented it to the children. The little ones only had some hard biscuits to eat. He thought of his own little ones at home, safe from all this strife, and his heart surged.

The woman, dressed in black taffeta, looked Andrew in the eye as she accepted the gift. "Thank you, Sir," she said shyly, taking the gingerbread and wrapping it in her kerchief. "My children are much obliged."

"I have five children of my own back home," he said, and his eyes mellowed as he silently sympathized with the poor creature. Obviously, she was a widow, and he wondered whose Yankee mini-ball had done the deed. He wondered how she would manage and where she and the little ones would go.

"Bless you, Sir. Bless your family. I pray they will all await your safe return to your homestead in good health."

He was struck by her heartfelt comments. "I—I wish I could help you in some way—," he trailed off, not knowing just what to say.

"We will manage, Sir. We will do fine. Thank you again, Sir, for your most kind generosity."

Andrew could not believe how proudly the woman had accepted his gift and admired the southern lady's resolve as he watched the party board the train. Strong, solid, polite, capable. She was all of those things, and Andrew would not soon forget the chance encounter. He would carry with him for a long time the look in her eyes: one of determination, strength, and southern pride, when her gaze had met his. He would long remember this chance link of one woman, to one man, one Yankee touching a Rebel. This was not something between the North and South though, this was between one human being, with the world crashing around her, and a compassionate Yankee soldier, doing his duty for his country. A soldier hundreds of miles away from his home, offering a simple gesture of kindness to the enemy.

PART IV

Without warning, on October 2nd, 1864, the 45th Illinois Volunteers found themselves surrounded by Rebels who had mounted a surprise move by circling behind Sherman's Atlanta bullwarks, and had come across the Chattahoochee River to the north, before Sherman could get his forces gathered. The Rebs destroyed twelve miles of railroad, Sherman's supply link to the North, and the 45th had left Marietta to go back to Kennesaw Mountain. There were skirmishes all around them, and Andrew could hear the "pop-pop-pop" of rifles on every side. The 45th and 32nd, though only numbering about 2000 men, were able to repulse the enemy four times, even though the Rebs were almost 40,000 strong.

"Angels must be ridin' on our shoulders," Joseph remarked as they dug in during a lull in the fighting.

Andrew nodded in agreement, thinking how strange it was that Joseph would be speaking of angels. Had the man invaded Andrew's dream last night? How did Joseph know that that was precisely what Andrew had dreamed about? The dream had stuck with him when he awoke, and, he for one, was not surprised by the Reb's attack, for he already had dreamed it. What did surprise him was that it was Carrie-Marie Walker who had invaded his slumber. Or was it that he had not really been asleep?

Something had roused him deep in the night, and Andrew woke to see the star's pebbled blanket stretch to the edges of the earth. Faint light glowed from their twinkling enough to make out ghostly shapes of the sleeping soldiers wrapped in their blankets. Somewhere, he heard the hoot of an owl, the faint snort of a horse, and other night noises, soft and serene. For once, the guns were silent, and only the snoring from the exhausted soldiers broke the night's quiet. Rising from his bed, Andrew quietly went to the edge of the trees which ringed their campsite, drawn there by he knew not what.

"Andrew!"

He thought he heard his name called, and whirled around, but could see nothing in the darkness.

"Andrew!" It was but a whisper, or was it the wind?

Andrew turned around again and suddenly went cold, as the goose flesh rose on his body. He blinked twice, not believing the sight that appeared before him. A woman with a hooded cape draped over white frills of a gown stood a few feet away. Long black hair cascaded around her shoulders, and her white face shown translucent in the night.

"Carrie-Marie!"

He reached for her, but she put her hands up in front of her, palms out, and he halted, puzzled. Instinctively he knew he must not touch her, even though she was smiling at him.

"Where did you come from?" he stammered.

"I came to warn you of danger ahead."

The voice was clear, yet Andrew did not know if his ears actually heard it, or if he heard it only in his mind. Still, he understood clearly.

"Keep careful watch, for your enemies are close," the voice continued. "There will be trickery. Be ever watchful. Do not let down your guard."

"But, Carrie-Marie, how did you get here?"

"I come from a place you do not know, and where you cannot follow now."

He could see her green eyes clearly, and the soft gentleness with which she gazed upon him struck him like a hammer blow. It twisted a knot in his chest, yet he felt a warm glow spread through his body.

"God be with you, Andrew Herrington." It was but a whisper, and she was gone, faded into the night.

Some would say it was a hallucination, brought on by the stress of months on the march, seeing carload after carload of combatants wounded and dying, gashed and bleeding, daily examples of man's inhumanity to fellow man. But the next day, hunkering down in a hastily prepared breastwork, Andrew could not get the vision out of his mind, and was confident that he had not just dreamed the whole thing. Just as Carrie-Marie had predicted, they were ambushed by a surprise attack.

There followed an intense skirmish, with very heavy fighting. Mini-balls were whizzing in every direction, and Andrew's ears rang with the noise of gunfire. Puffs of smoke belched from hundreds of rifles, and the stench of gunpowder was strong in his nostrils. Once he felt a blow at his back, as something tore into his knapsack, but he never stopped firing at the unseen enemy, aiming at the flashes coming from the Confederate line.

The attack was over in an instant, and once more the Union Army had repelled the Rebel attack. It was not until much later, as Andrew inspected the knapsack he wore, that he muttered, "I'll be damned!" He removed the rolling pin he had taken from the Walker Plantation to discover a fresh triangle of wood was missing from one button end, a casualty of the war.

"Stopped a Johnny Reb mini ball! I'll be damned!"

He wrote again to his wife:

October 13, 1864

My Darling:

I am alive and well. Thank God for His protective care. We had several skirmishes with the enemy when they swept around fourteen miles below us, before Sherman could get his forces from Atlanta. The Rebs burned miles of railroad. From atop Kennesaw Mountain at night, I could see twelve miles of burning railroad ties. The Rebs were tearing up the iron, putting it on top of the burning ties. We could see plain as day by the glare of the fires.

The next day I walked up to the top of the giant mountain. I saw General Sherman with his staff looking through telescopes at the two armies below. From the mountain, we could see all around for miles. Both Union and Rebel Armies could be seen with the naked eye. I saw cannon belch forth at Altoona, and the whole line of Rebs, and the three long lines of our army. It was a wondrous sight to see the two armies, and thousands of army wagons with their white canvas covers stretching away for miles. There are hundreds of cannon, and over 100,000 men on the move. I never expect to see another such sight.

And later:

Ackworth Georgia
October 26, 1864

My Dear Ones:

Communications are once more open, and we received a large mail. I have four of your dear letters, and I press them to my breast — the only way I can hold you. It worries me to hear that sweet Jessie has been ill. I could not bear it if we were to lose our child. My heart is heavy with worry. If only I could be there to help her regain her health. You, my dearest wife, have your hands full caring for the little ones. How strong you are! And how I admire your spunk in caring for the homestead and my dear children.

It is strange that the Rebel Army has moved to Blue Mountain, Alabama. Perhaps General Sherman has been a little out-generalled, but if the enemy makes a stand there, Sherman will surely whip them as only he can.

Kiss the sweet baby for me.
Andrew

Two weeks later, Andrew and Joseph, while camped near Atlanta, secured passes to enter the city once again, to see if they could buy bread. They found the bakers had all fled the city, but both men were not prepared for what they saw. Everything seemed in confusion. Those who remained were taking advantage of and collaborating with the enemy. They were charging outrageous prices for their services. Thirty five cents for a shave—$1.50 for a shampoo. But since both men had recently been paid their back wages, they decided to pay the $3.00 for the luxury of a hot bath in the bath house.

"Las' day, gentlemens... las' day." A Negro proclaimed. "Yu jes' gettin' in on time, fo' we is closin' de bath today an' leavin' befo' de Yankees burn de city. If'n yu all wants a bath, it'll be fo' dollars a piece."

The price had suddenly gone up, but both men forked over the money to enjoy a long soak in the deep tubs. After the grime of the battles and marching had been scrubbed off, Andrew felt renewed and almost human again.

Back out on the street, the pair found mounds of chairs, tables, fences, doors, and every burnable article imaginable piled up, waiting for the burning. What tugged at Andrew's heart the most was seeing children's toys amongst the rubble.

By eight o'clock that night, scores of lovely Atlanta buildings were on fire. And the following day, November 12th, Andrew noted in his journal, he took a last walk through the doomed city. Pioneer Corps were undermining all the large stone buildings, ready to blow them up as soon as Sherman started to move on his way to the seashore. The passenger depot on the railroad, though a magnificent structure, was piled high with Confederate government wagons, ready for the torch to set it on fire.

On November 14th, Atlanta was finally destroyed. Warehouses, factories, homes, and mercantile buildings, were all set on fire, and it seemed as though the whole world was ablaze. Flames reached to the heavens, and smoke billowed thick, while sparks flew, dancing on the winds that the fires themselves produced.

Andrew could not help the bad feeling in the pit of his stomach at such waste. Soon, the city was in total ruins, and his heart ached for the women and children, the destitute, and the starving families who had been forced to flee. Would the South ever be able to recapture to its former days of glory? Andrew doubted it ever could, and cursed, because the South had yet to learn the folly of its ways.

Long into the night, the fires raged. Even from his campsite, two miles away, he could hear the barrrooom! barrrooom! of huge explosives as one after another, the beautiful stone and brick buildings were blown out of existence. The angry red glow in the sky from the burning was seared forever into Andrew's mind, and as long as he lived, he would remember this horrible page of history-in-the-making, and regretfully recall his part in the whole thing.

And so, on November 15th, 1864, the march to Savannah began. The Union Army, under the command of General Sherman, was beginning to cut a sixty-mile-wide swath of total destruction across Georgia, burning railroads and whole towns along the way. Mills and cotton gins, farm houses and slave cabins, corn cribs and barns, all lay in smoldering ashes. Everything combustible was torched. Foraging teams gathered all edibles from miles around, and left piles of foodstuffs along the roadway for the soldiers who came behind to fill their haversacks. Chickens, sweet potatoes, pork, turkeys, geese, vegetables of all kinds, all were ripped from the land to feed the Union Army.

The suffering of the country families, where the Army swept through like a tornado, could not be described. The Yankees only stopped to rest when the teams of horses and mules finally gave out, having not rested for days. The railroads of Stone Mountain and Macon had been destroyed, ties burned, and rails thrown upon the fires until the middles glowed red hot. Then men grabbed each cool end, and rammed the rails around tree trunks, bending them into "Sherman's Hairpins," rendering them useless. The Confederates would have a hard time rebuilding the railroads, for they could never use the rails as they were until they were re-melted.

Andrew wrote in his journal by snatches and bits, when time allowed.

On November 18th, he wrote:

We passed through Jackson at 2 PM. This little southern village had been wholly plundered, strewn with papers of all descriptions, from a letter by a Negro, George Augustus, to his adored Selferine; to a large bill of sale from Mr. Ellijah Dobbins to a Mr. David Muggins for 250 slaves. We marched 15 miles today, tired and weary, to roll into our blankets with nothing more than coffee for dinner. Hadn't been down more than an hour when the orders came to march again. We rubbed our eyes, struck tents in a hurry, and heard the gentle whisper of 'Military Necessity,' and began to march again.

They arrived at camp about midnight, having marched for hours in the rain. Andrew and Joseph immediately rolled into their blankets and oil cloths, and tried to get some sleep. It rained all night, never letting up. Sore and weary, they struck camp at seven AM and marched again. Skirmishes to the right and left of them kept them nervous and on alert, but still the army pressed onward. This day, they marched thirteen miles in seventeen hours in the pouring rain. By now, their clothes and blankets were soaked... nothing but rain, rain, rain. Through mud puddle to mud puddle they slushed, trudging until their arms and legs ached with a weariness they did not think their bodies could endure.

The awful conditions of mud and rain soon bogged down teams of animals, until they were mired completely. Teamsters swore at the brutes, and used their whips to try to prod them out of the bogs, but the animals only rolled helplessly in the mire. One six mule team had fallen off a bridge into a narrow, deep gulch, the four head mules had gone down, but the wheelers were still hanging down by their traces, thrashing, when Andrew and Joseph came along. The wagon was too large to go down, so finally, the men could do nothing more but to cut the traces, allowing the poor mules to crash to their deaths below. The road was so swampy, that scores of cattle got mired, too, and could not get out. They were shot where they stood, poor brutes, and piled up by the hundreds, the army having to march over them to get through.

By now, the men had been on the march for seven days, and still the morning broke wet and miserable. The musty smell of earth, swollen with rainwater, hung heavy over the countryside, and became unbearable mixed with the odor of dead animals, and dung. Yet there was no let up of marching, for onward, onward the troops pressed.

Andrew had been too tired to write much in his journal, but the following day, November 22, 1864, he wrote:

The railroads are all still burning. It even snowed a little last night, and is freezing this evening. There is heavy cannonading since 4 PM. Fitpatrick is feigning fighting to give the army a chance to go around. I doubt if Sherman expects to lose much time in fighting, for he needs to get to Savannah as soon as possible to get communications open. We continue to march on like a whirlwind, though the men are bone-weary and dispirited with fatigue. Twenty ambulances just came in, loaded with wounded.

Wednesday, November 23rd:

The weather finally changed and it looks good ahead. Had a good dinner of chicken, sweet potatoes, honey and cornmeal. Foraging remains plentiful, and I finally had fixed up a fine place for sleeping. However, at 5 PM, orders came to march immediately, and we found it another 'Military Necessity,' so we packed up and started once more. After marching through a swamp for two hours, we finally relieved the 4th division, who had been burning the railroad all day, and we commenced burning at 9 PM. By midnight, we had burned three miles. The whole heavens are lit up by the burning railroad ties and campfires. It is freezing quite hard tonight. Expect to have a fight at the Oconee River tomorrow.

PART V

If Andrew thought reaching Savannah would be the end of their trails, he would be proven sorely wrong. As they approached the city, they were met by heavy resistance. Reb batteries mounted on flatcars shelled them as they crossed the railroad lines, and skirmishes broke out through the woods on all sides. But Sherman's forces were too strong, and the Rebs retreated to the trench works. The Union artillery batteries began a constant thunder, making the Reb's sandbags fly in all directions.

Sherman's Army had marched 305 miles from Atlanta in 25 days, and set up a line sixteen miles long from the Savannah River to the Ogeechee River. Their 24 pounders, now in place, were constantly bombarding the Rebel forces. Andrew could hear their own gunboats on the Ocheegee River. When he and the troops heard Rebel shells whistle overhead, they would duck their heads behind breastworks as soon as they saw smoke from the enemy cannons. Fortunately, most of the shells burst harmlessly a half mile away. At one point during a lull, Andrew looked through a field glass, and could see a Johnny Reb making mush and coffee.

Two weeks of bitter fighting ensued there before the Confederates abandoned Savannah, and Andrew and the Union Army at last reached the 'First City of the South.' One of the most beautiful of all southern cities, it was full of parks, fountains, and shade trees. Nearby, Fort McAllister was taken, and at long last communications were once more established with the North. Supplies began coming from the coast, and none too soon, for the foraging for food had come up dry. Nothing useful had been left by the army that had cut a swath through Georgia like a swarm of locusts, destroying everything in its path.

Andrew wrote home that they had destroyed 300 miles of railroad and towns, burnt hundreds of mill and cotton gins, drove the enemy from the navigable rivers, and lived from rich southern plantation cellars. "We have gutted this part of the Confederacy."

On December 24, 1864, he wrote:

It is Christmas Eve, and oh, how I long to be home to fill the stockings of the darling children this evening. I would fill them to the brim. And for my Dear Wife, I would give you the world if I could fit it into your stocking. If only I could walk through your door this very night to surprise you, I would be in heaven. To hold you and all my precious ones again to my heart will be my dream tonight. Will you come to me in my dreams, sweet Marion, and lie by my side? May I kiss your sweet lips, and brush back the hair from your brow? Oh, would it be so! God willing, it shall be the last Christmas we shall ever be apart.

A north wind had been blowing cold for several days, and a rare freeze soon had the soldiers chattering with cold. Andrew, for all the enthusiasm and patriotic fervor which had sustained him the past nine months and during the fierce march through Georgia, now found a sudden emptiness shroud him like a black cloak.

For the first time, he allowed the homesickness he had been masking to spill forth, and his gut ached with longing for his familiar home and loved ones.

Tonight, the night of all nights, when he shut his eyes, he could picture the decorated tree in the parlor of the home he shared with Marion and the children. The tree would be flickering with tiny candles on the branches, and the children, with sparkling wide eyes, would sit at its base, and gaze in awe at the magical sight. Christmas morning would dawn crisp and cold, with a fresh snow blanketing the landscape, clinging to tree branches, bending them low. Andrew could almost hear the delighted shouts of the children when they claimed their presents from under the tree.

Oh, to be home once more, to feel the warmth of a crackling fire, to experience the embrace of loving arms again. For the first time, Andrew felt the cold fingers of doubt creep into his soul, and wondered if he would ever see home again, and he was shaken to the core. Up to now, he considered himself invincible. Mini balls had whizzed harmlessly all about him for weeks, yet one had not even come close. But now, tonight, on Christmas Eve, he suddenly had doubts.

He doubted whether the war would ever end. Doubted whether he had the strength to push on. He doubted whether Sherman was right in following his relentless path of destruction through the helpless South.

In his make-shift shelter, Andrew blew out his candle, pulled his blanket snugly up to his chin, and tried to sleep. He was just one of tens of thousands of weary soldiers tired of the fighting... tired of marching... tired of war.

The Christmas Eve letter to his wife was the last Andrew would write for ten weeks, for Sherman's march through the Carolinas swept so swiftly, there was scant time for putting pen to paper. In the years to come, all he would remember of that campaign was a jumbled maze of hard marching, continuous fighting, and constant rain. Endless mud was everywhere, invading every pore, seeping into every crevice of clothing, and still the army marched on.

When night time came, and fighting ceased for the day, Andrew's ears still rang long into the night from the constant bombardment of artillery that shook the ground like an earthquake. He no longer could tell how many days or weeks they had been on the march. Endless miles of railroad were destroyed, and foodstuffs from foraging depleted the pantry of every household the Yankees came upon.

In March, 1865, several of the Union Army foragers were found dead by the hands of Rebel stragglers. Cards had been placed upon the dead men's chests, saying "Death to Foragers." This angered Sherman, and caused him to retaliate by executing one Reb prisoner for every Yankee killed after being caught. Man for man, that was the decree.

The first Rebel prisoner that Andrew witnessed meet that fate was an old gray haired man. The unfortunate, wrinkled old man had been a conscript, forced into Rebel service beyond his will, and now it was his bad luck that he had drawn the lot. It fell upon Andrew to guard the prisoner until his time for execution came.

The old man shook with emotion until his gray old locks trembled, and his beard quivered. Tears streamed down the man's face as his thin lips moved in prayer. Andrew heard the man's crackling voice plead with God to care for his wife and seven children, sending a jolt of dismay though Andrew's stomach. There knelt a Christian, in the enemy's army against his will, ready to die at the hands of the Yankees.

How could this be happening? Oh, God! Andrew thought. *This is not why we are fighting this war, is it? To kill a Christian man with a wife and seven children at home? The world has gone mad!* Andrew feared the same fate may befall him before this horrible conflict would end.

"God, I implore you to be a husband to my wife, a father to my children," the old man pleaded.

"God be with you, Sir," Andrew managed to say, and wanted desperately to be gone from this place, so he did not have to witness what was about to happen.

The old man was led to his doom by the Chaplain of the Wisconsin 31st. Andrew anguished at the scene before him, and whispered, "Angels of God, take this man's spirit to eternal rest," as the man was blindfolded, then eight bullets tore through his body. He slumped without a groan.

The sound of the volley echoed through Andrew's head with a start, and he watched the man slump in slow motion to the ground. Andrew saw what no one else could see, that the man slumped into the arms of a woman. Her black hair splayed around her shoulders, and her green eyes shown bright with compassion and love as she gently lowered the man's body to the ground. As she did so, she glanced over her shoulder, meeting Andrew's startled gaze, and he could see her eyes mellow in recognition, with such a look of grace and love, it shot through him like a bolt of lightning.

He blinked, unable to comprehend the vision before him. *Carrie-Marie... how did she...?* When he opened his eyes once more, he saw only the body of the old man lying on the ground, already looking empty, his spirit had been whisked away in a fleet moment. At the same time, Andrew felt a strange sense of peace, for in that instant, he understood about God's love and understanding. As he turned away, he seemed assured that through the horrors of this terrible conflict, no matter what lay ahead God would be there to those who believed.

Fayettsville, North Carolina
March 12, 1865

My Darling Wife,

Thank God I am in good health. Since last I wrote, we have marched 384 miles through the Carolinas. Wilmington and Charlotte have been forced to evacuate by Sherman's Great Move. Never did a General lead an army through the enemy's country such as Sherman has done. Large cities have been burned, and the whole country laid desolate. Scenes are written in my memory that can never be forgotten. May God forgive us for some of the wantonness and cruelties inflicted, especially on innocents.

Retaliation has commenced. It makes a man feel chilly to see a lot of men draw lots to see who will be shot. Such is war. It will soon be over for the South. They cannot hold on much longer.

I feel anxious about my darling wife and the little ones. I am very weary and have so much to tell when I return. I dream dreams so real, I feel I am actually home with you all once more. Were it only true! I know you need money, and I hope once we have a permanent base, we will be paid. As soon as we do, I will send you all the money I receive.

> *Kiss the darling children for me.*
> *Lovingly,*
> *Andrew*

What Andrew said in his letter about being in good health was true. On the outside, he had sustained no wounds to scar his body, but he did not tell her of the deep scarring he carried with him on the inside. For the rest of his life, he would never recover from the trauma of the battles and the total devastation of Sherman's March. He would carry emotional scars with him forever.

Andrew's hope for an end to the conflict finally came in April. It had been a year since he last laid eyes on his loved ones, a year that had hardened him. He was leaner than he had ever been, his muscles honed to a fine edge. However, any thoughts of ending the marching were soon dashed, when it was learned that Sherman's Great Army would proceed to Washington, where there would be a Grand Review of Grant's and the Union armies. It took twenty days to march from Raleigh, North Carolina to Washington DC.

The Grand March through the capital on May 24, 1865, was the most spectacular event Andrew would ever witness. Hundreds of thousands of hardened, seasoned soldiers marched in tightly regimental form through the city to accept adulation from the throngs of citizens lining the streets. Heroes of Shiloh, Missionary Ridge, Altoona, Kennesaw, Chattahoochee, Atlanta, and Savannah marched in jubilation down the broad streets.

Words from a fellow soldier's song, composed along the devastating sweep through the heart of the deep south came to Andrew's mind, and he hummed to himself as he marched.

> Sherman, he was sent by God
> (And it was God's decree)
> To lead the Yankees through the South
> And set the Negro free.
>
> And trample down the bastard flag,
> The hated stars and bars
> And hoist the flag of Liberty,
> The glorious stripes and stars.

Marion's letter of June 25th held startling news, and Andrew was anguished when he read it. He and the 45th were stuck forever, it seemed in Louisville, Kentucky, awaiting dismissal from the service, and the journey home.

Dearest Husband,

Pray God you will hurry home. Our dear little William has been desperately ill, as have all the children. But William and our sweet Clara are the worst. I have been sore put to tending them all, day and night, and now find my own self not feeling well.

Jessie, Mary Ellen, and baby George have recovered and are on the mend. But I worry about William. And Clara is worrisome, too, but in a different way, though she seems better this morning. At the height of her fever last night, she talked out of her head. Something about seeing a beautiful lady with long dark hair. I passed it off as the fever talking, but today as I questioned her, she kept insisting that a beautiful lady with black hair and kind green eyes visited her last night, and told Clara that she would get well, just before her fever broke.

Oh, Andrew, dearest, I fear our darling first born has been tetched by the fever, and if she continues to talk such nonsense about seeing a black haired lady, I shall not know what to do.

Marion

Andrew sat down suddenly, the letter still clasped in his hands. He read and re-read the part about Clara's visitor, and knew in his heart that the child's vision was real. God's angel, Carrie-

Marie, had come to heal his daughter! He trembled as the wonder of the thing sank in. *It hadn't been a dream those many months ago on the march, she had been real!* And he had not hallucinated at the old man's execution. Carrie-Marie... Angel Carrie-Marie had been there. The enormity sent goose bumps up his spine.

For a long time that evening, Andrew Herrington sat in his tent staring at the flickering flame of the lonely lamp which illuminated his quarters. All the flames of Atlanta and the Carolina's burned again in his memory. He would never be able to shut out the sight of the ruin, devastation, broken bodies, and dead men. It all lay just behind his eyes. At one point he glimpsed himself in the looking glass, and for the first time realized how drawn and thin his face appeared. The normal sparkle of his brown eyes had dimmed a bit, as if there was a thin curtain drawn across them to hide something... to hide the ravages of the war he had been a part of. That curtain would never again be parted, for there were many things he had witnessed which he would never be able to share with anyone, not even his dear Marion.

He felt every bit of his thirty two years of age, even though his body was now lean and hard, a product of marching more than a thousand miles. Was that a thin strand of silver just brushing his temples? What a strange thought. The lamp now flickered, and shadows danced against the canvas wall of his tent. For hours that night, Andrew lived and re-lived the months of rain and mud, of cannons exploding, and rifles hurtling their deadly ammunition to crash into flesh and bone.

Thank God he had escaped the bullets, but he would never escape the sights and sounds, and yes, even the smells of war. All those things were seared into his memory forever, like a hot branding iron into flesh. Would he ever be able to hold his loved ones in his arms again and not anguish over the poor souls of the South whose lives had been ripped apart by the devastation wrought by the Union Army? Guilt would ride with Andrew for the rest of his life, a demon which would haunt him till his grave.

July 9, 1865

My Dearest, most precious, Marion;

Tomorrow, the train leaves for Cairo, Illinois, and the North. I will have come full circle then in fifteen months. Fifteen months since last I felt the warmth of your embrace and saw the joy of your face. It might as well be fifteen years, for that is what the time apart feels like to me.

You have my letters, which gives you something of our sweep through the South, and I have much more to tell when next I see you. I cannot wait to gather you all in my arms, and only hope they are long enough to embrace you all in one sweep, for by now my precious children would have grown. I can picture each and every one, except perhaps the babe, for by now he will be on his feet and scooting about, getting into everything.

Clara, with your dear Mother's hair coloring, you must be quite the little lady by now. And Jessie, what mischief have you been into lately? Driving your sainted Mother to distraction, no doubt. Mary Ellen, how I long to kiss every freckle on your face!

William, I hear you have recovered fully from the Fever. You and I shall go fishing when I return, and pull in a fish so big that Mother will not have a pan to fit it. Sweet, toddling George, you will not know your Papa, but we will go horsey back riding on my shoulders. How I look forward to that!

And for your eyes alone, my Sweet Marion my arms ache to hold you, to pull you to me and feel the warmth of your body next to mine. I long to feel your breath, like a butterfly, tickle my neck, and my lips cannot wait until they claim your sweet mouth. And the Angels will be singing 'Glory To God!'

Your loving,
Andrew

Chapter 10

On Tuesday morning a big moving van pulled up to the house bright and early, even before Jennifer had had her second cup of coffee.

"Do you really think this is the right thing to do?" Aunt Bessie fretted.

"I think it is an excellent idea, Aunt Bessie. This way we'll have you all settled in your apartment before Saturday's auction."

"I don't know if I should have let Mr. Warren talk me into it," Bessie said, and Jennifer saw a frown on her aunt's face for the first time she could remember.

"Don't worry, Aunt Bessie, it will work out just fine. I think Ralph was right the other day at dinner when he offered to get you all settled early."

"But I don't have room for you to sleep in the apartment, Jennifer. And I don't want to leave you here by yourself."

"It's all settled, Aunt Bessie. I am going to remain here so I can keep my eye on things. And you will have a chance to get acquainted in your new place before I go back to Phoenix."

Reluctantly, Bessie finally agreed, and Jennifer could see a slight slump in her shoulders when the older woman resigned herself to the change in plans. While the movers packed the van with items to go to the apartment, Jennifer helped Bessie gather the last of her personal things and loaded them into the Plymouth.

"Be especially careful of this box," Bessie told her, handing her a container similar to one that would hold a bouquet of flowers, long and slender. "I won't let the movers touch this! It's very special."

Jennifer nodded, and packed it carefully in the auto between stacks of clothing which were on hangers. The box was very light weight, and stirred a bit of curiosity in the young woman's mind.

"And can we take this portrait ourselves? Will it fit in the car? I don't trust the movers much," Aunt Bessie said, indicating the picture of her as a young woman, which had hung in her bedroom.

"Of course, Aunt Bessie. Oh, my! It is just beautiful! Is this of you when you were young?"

Bessie nodded, and let her hands linger on the frame as she gazed at her own likeness for a long moment, taken back into the nostalgia of so long ago.

"How old were you there?"

"Oh, about twenty, I think."

"Will you tell me about it sometime?"

"Yes, Jennifer, Dear, when the time is right, I'll tell you.

Was I ever that young? Bessie wondered. *Or that pretty? How the years have flown. Where did they go? Well, can't worry about that now. I'll think about that later.*

By the end of the day, Aunt Bessie's apartment was settled. The pictures even got hung, and the bed freshly made. She and Jennifer made a trip to Penney's where they purchased curtains for the windows and a shower curtain for the bath. Bessie busily unpacked boxes of canned goods into the small pantry while Jennifer finished hanging the curtains at the kitchen window.

The biggest problem was finding room for her rolling pin collection, as Aunt Bessie was adamant to keep the lot. Kitchen counter space was limited, so Jennifer thought they could bring one more small cabinet from the house and squeeze it into the corner of the dining area. The rolling pins fit just perfectly there, and would be in full view to anyone sitting at the table.

"Now, Jennifer, dear, are you sure you will be all right at the house?"

"Of course, Aunt Bessie. And thank you for the use of the car. Will you need it tonight?"

"No, you take it. I have everything I need right here. I'll just finish putting clothes away tomorrow, and probably rearrange things in the kitchen."

"Well, call me if you need anything."

The last touch of light on that balmy evening hovered long in the western sky, as if to hold back the velvet curtain of darkness, reluctant to let the blackness overtake the land. The moon had not yet risen as Jennifer eased her aching limbs into the porch rocker, sipping from a bottle of soda she found in the fridge. She wondered how Aunt Bessie was able to breeze through such a long, hard day, seemingly unaffected by all the work. Jennifer was only thirty two, and already she could hardly wait to soak in a hot bath and slip into bed, for she ached in places she had forgotten about. She tilted her head back against the rocker, felt the day's tensions begin to recede, and let her mind go blank, as she closed her eyes.

"Hello, Jenny."

Jennifer's eyes flew open.

"I did not mean to startle you. May I come up?" Ralph Warren inquired, as he stood at the bottom of the porch steps.

"Of course," she muttered, and watched as he took a chair next to her.

"Big day?"

"Yes," she sighed. "A very big, hard day."

"Did Miss Bessie get moved then?"

Jennifer nodded. "Yes, she is all moved in to her apartment. By the way, thank you for providing the truck and movers. That was very generous of you. You did not have to do that, you know."

"It was little enough, since I could not help much with this broken arm." He lifted the cast slightly, indicating his injury.

"You need not think you had to help at all, Ralph. After all, she means nothing to you. I mean, you're not related or anything."

"True, but she is a nice lady. Everybody's Aunt... always helping out wherever there is a need. They call her the Angel of Waterville, you know."

"How would you know, Ralph? You two don't exactly run around in the same social circles."

Ralph ignored the sarcastic dig. "Her reputation seems to be widespread even in my so called circle."

They sat in silence for a moment, as darkness slowly enveloped them.

"What's eating you, Jenny? You seem bitter about something."

Jennifer thanked the darkness so she did not have to let him see how his very nearness upset her. She could not see his eyes, but knew he was looking at her, and wondered if somehow he had a magical way of being able to see in the dark. She could hear his breathing, slow and steady, and put both her hands on the rocker arms so she would not reach out to touch him, though she wanted to. She longed to feel his face, run her hands across his chest, encircle his waist.

"Jenny?"

"Nothing's wrong, Ralph. I'm just tired."

After another short silence, he said, "This is the first time we have been alone to talk, Jenny. It really is good to have you back. It's wonderful to see you again."

She was too bone-tired to launch into a long conversation, so she tried to bring the visit to a close. "Ralph, I'm really tired. I want to take a hot bath and get into bed. It was a very busy day, and I am bushed."

He ignored the chance to play on her words about taking a hot shower and hopping into bed. Any other day, with any other girl, his glib tongue would have already had him half way up the stairs.

"Okay," he conceded. "But I want to talk to you about the house. Will you have dinner with me tomorrow night?"

Jennifer, her head reeling with exhaustion, thought for a moment, wondering what he could have in mind, finally answered in the affirmative.

"Fine! I will pick you up at seven."

"Okay."

"'Til tomorrow, then." He rose and stepped off the porch. Turning, he repeated, "Seven. I'll pick you up at seven."

"Yes, seven."

To Jennifer, the following day seemed like it would never end. She ran a few errands for Aunt Bessie, and toward late afternoon had the older woman drop her off at the house so Bessie could have the car.

"I'll be all right, Aunt Bessie. Ralph Warren is picking me up to take me to dinner at seven. Do you mind?"

"Not at all, my dear. You have a good time. Call me tomorrow."

Like a schoolgirl, Jennifer was full of butterflies as she prepared for the evening. After bathing, and carefully applying a little makeup, she took a long time deciding what to wear. There was not much choice, for she had packed lightly for the trip, so she decided at last on a simple white skirt and aqua blue lightweight knit top. The color complemented her dark tan, and blond curls, which she ran her fingers through a couple of times. She decided her legs were tan enough to go without hose, so she slipped her feet into a pair of white sandals. Glancing one more time in the mirror, and satisfied with her image, she went downstairs to await Ralph's arrival.

When the phone rang, she skipped to answer. "Oh, Patty! How sweet of you to call. No, Aunt Bessie is at the new place. We got her all moved in and settled yesterday." Jennifer filled her in on all the details, and asked about the new adventure. To her surprise, she found Patty to be jubilantly happy, almost lyrical in her joy. She was bubbling over with descriptions of the new bookstore, and its future prospects.

"I'm so happy for you, Patty! You two will do just great. No, I don't think it will be necessary for you to come on Saturday for the auction. You go ahead and work on the new store. Gosh! I wish I could come see it before I go back. Oh, the doorbell is ringing. I've got to fly. Love and kisses! I'll call you later."

Ralph was stunned when she opened the door. Jennifer was a picture of radiance standing there, and his eyes took in the vision all at once. With a well trained glance, he noticed every curve from head to toe, and did the proverbial double take.

"Wow! Don't you look super!"

She smiled a little shyly, as her face flushed slightly.

"These are for you. May I?" He fumbled awkwardly, as he handed over a corsage, and attempted to pin it on her shoulder.

Jennifer laughed at his one handed attempt, and helped guide his fingers until the corsage was firmly in place. His face was leaning close to hers, and she found her hands were touching his big warm fist. She could feel the sinews moving, and thrilled at the strength of him. They lingered like that for a brief moment, then their eyes locked, and Jennifer's heart did a flip.

For a fleeting minute, she thought he was going to kiss her, but he slowly pulled away, his eyes still burning into hers. She finally dropped her gaze, afraid to see what deeper thoughts might lie behind those blue eyes of his. She feared he would be able to look into her very soul and find the truth there, and she did not want him to know how foolish she was to have such deep feelings for him after all these years. After all, here stood a man who was every inch a playboy, having dozens, if not more encounters with beautiful women from one end of the country to the other, if she could believe the gossip she had heard about him.

They dined that evening on the patio of The Club, which Jennifer had never been privileged to attend before. In the twilight, the golf course rolled away like an emerald carpet, perfectly manicured, and the view could have been a movie set. Ralph introduced her to several fellow members, and even seemed proud to do so, she thought in retrospect. His friends politely shook her hand, and she felt genuinely welcomed. At one point, out of the corner of her eye, she caught a thumbs-up sign come from a few single males at the bar, and smiled in spite of herself.

The two lingered, chatting over dessert and coffee, with nothing more than flickering candlelight illuminating their table. A single hurricane glass, ringed with fresh flowers, centered the table. Soft music wafted from the dance floor inside, and Jennifer could not remember ever spending a night in such wonderful, romantic surroundings.

When Ralph softly gazed at her during their conversations, she saw how the flame from the candle danced in his eyes, and how kindly the mellow half-light painted his face and dimple lines when he smiled at her. She felt the attraction grow stronger and could not fight it any more. *Was there a hint of real affection buried behind his smile?* Was the casual, chance touch of his hand on hers simply an accident, or was it a concentrated effort to reach for her? She pondered the thought.

Later, gliding across the dance floor comfortably nestled in Ralph's arms, Jennifer closed her eyes and let the emotion sink in deeply. He was such a smooth dancer, even with his arm in the cast, that she thought he must be a professional. The music was slow and romantic, and the lights were low. Everything about the evening, the food, the atmosphere, his touch, all swirled in heady exhilaration, and Jennifer seemed to float on a cloud.

At their table, they toasted each other with champagne, and Ralph brought up the idea that had been in the back of his mind.

"I want to ask your opinion about an idea I have."

At this point, Jennifer grew curious and focused her attention closely. At the same time, Ralph tried to ignore how beautiful she was, to keep from being distracted, but it was difficult, sitting across the table with the flickering candlelight sending little highlights glinting off her blond curls. *Have her eyes always been that shade of hazel, or were they changing moment to moment?* It was impossible to tell. But whatever color they were, it stirred a feeling from deep within him. And for once he lost the ability to flirt outrageously with her, as he had done with all the others he had ever gone out with. *Why is she different?*

Ralph tried to pinpoint the time when the change had come over him. What happened to that devil-may-care attitude which always seemed good for a laugh? How come he was suddenly so serious? Was the old fly-boy losing his touch? Whatever it was, it bothered him. Something was vastly different, and it had hit him like a Mack truck.

"What idea, Ralph?" Jennifer was saying.

He snapped back to the present, cleared his throat and began, "I have an idea for the house. I am thinking of turning it into an Inn. It has five bedrooms upstairs, and with a little upgrading by adding bathrooms, it could be a wonderful place."

"Really?" Jennifer had not given any thought about what would happen to the house after the auction.

"I need your help, Jenny. I want you to design the inside. I mean, pick out wallpaper, and furniture, and everything! I am sure you could turn it into a charming, delightful place, where people would love to spend a few days."

She was surprised at the concept, and hesitated for a long time, not knowing what to say. It was apparent that Ralph was enthused.

"I know with your love of art and sense of colors, you could do a marvelous job. You did major in Interior Design didn't you? What do you say?"

Later they talked long into the night as they strolled along the river path in the moonlight. They could hear the river gurgling on its journey downstream in the background; for now it was simply a wide, darkened swath meandering beside them. Ralph's ideas gushed from his lips like the flow of the river, and like an excited child, he described how he wanted to turn the carriage house in the back of the property into cozy living quarters. He would make one of the downstairs rooms into a wonderful library, and pictured the big parlor fitted with comfortable couches grouped around the huge old fireplace. The porch would become a grand meeting place for the guests, to while away lazy hours, and the gardens would be the talk of the town.

As he talked, Jennifer started to picture the concept, and then she, too, grew excited.

"I know Aunt Bessie's desire is that someone keep the house restored to its original design. Her father built it in the year she was born. 1872, I think she said."

"Yes, that's my idea, Jenny! To keep it decorated in that sort of Victorian style, but with the modern conveniences. Will you help, Jenny?"

"Of course, Ralph," She replied, agreeing in an instant, for now she was completely engrossed in the idea of remodeling Aunt Bessie's great house. She began to dream about how it could be decorated. Soon she was excitedly adding ideas of her own.

It was very late when they arrived back at the old stone house, and they parted at the door.

"Tomorrow, I'll pick you up at nine, and we'll drive into the country to hit some antique stores I know about. Oh, Jenny! I'm really enthused about this project!"

On the spur of the moment, Jennifer said, "Come early for coffee."

"Thanks, Jenny. You're a sweetheart."

He bent down, kissed her on the forehead and was gone.

Chapter 11

After getting but a few hours sleep, Jennifer was up at dawn's first light. She had so many visions and ideas already swirling in her head about the house, she wanted to jot them down on paper so as not to lose the thoughts. Gray light found her prowling the rooms, cocking her head this way and that, visioning, dreaming, planning. After much searching, she found a measuring stick, and measured each room, noting window and door placement, closets, architectural features, stairways, and where the plumbing was placed. By the time Ralph arrived at eight, she had floor plans already drawn up. He was duly impressed.

"Jenny, you must have worked all night on this!"

"Not quite, but almost," she grinned.

He put his arm around her shoulder, giving her a squeeze, and flashed a wide grin. As he sat at the table with the plans spread before him, Jennifer poured coffee. She leaned over his shoulder, pointing out different possibilities on the plans, feeling the warmth of his body close to her. Her face almost brushed his cheek, and she laid a soft hand upon his shoulder. Ralph was acutely aware of her fragrance, a hint of jasmine, and wanted to drink in every waft of sweetness till his head spun. He could feel her breath on his neck, and felt his skin prickle with goose bumps.

It would be easy to turn his head just slightly and meet her lips, but somehow he forced his concentration back to the plans. Ralph knew instinctively that to make a move too quickly would send Jennifer flying away, and that was not what he wanted. In fact, he did not know exactly what he wanted, but it was not a quick hop in the sack. Any other day, with any other woman that would have been the case, but not here, not now, not with Jenny. Deep within him, he felt a different stirring and it puzzled him, for he had never experienced such a strong, strange emotion before.

Internally, he seemed to have changed ever since Jenny had come back into his life. While he struggled with understanding why he felt distressed when he thought about some of his activities over the years, a certain feeling of guilt hovered in the back of his mind, and he came to the slow realization of how stupid his actions actually had been, especially where women were concerned.

Suddenly he wanted to live up to a higher standard. Somehow the fact that Jenny, who he had always thought of as having a sweet, innocent spirit, was now back in his life, made it clear and gave him reason to shape into the person he desired to become.

She did not have to lecture him, nor preach to him, for her very presence was inspiration enough for him to recognize how he should shed his old character, bury the past and look to a brighter, more positive future.

It was as if a great weight had been lifted from him, and his own spirit soared with a fresh, exhilarating feeling. He felt free now, to fly as high as if he were in his plane, banking and turning, climbing to the heights.

Ralph's red '61 Thunderbird convertible cruised down the back country roads with ease, past fields of tall, ripening corn, and grain already golden. The morning sun glinted off neat farm buildings, whose tall silos stood like sentinels beside the barns, and a freshness in the air gave a hint that fall was but a few weeks away. Jennifer leaned her head against the back of the seat, closed her eyes and let the sun bathe her face. The warmth was like a kiss from the gods, and the breeze crossed her cheeks with the softness of chiffon.

It was a perfect day. The sky clear and deep blue, nary a cloud to mar its beauty. Exhilaration rushed through Jennifer, and she drew a deep breath, as if ridding herself of some invisible chains. For the time being, she forgot about her troubles with Don, the business, and the duties waiting for her back in Phoenix, and let herself flow with the joy of the day. A half-smile of contentment spread on her lips, and when Ralph glanced over at her, it warmed his heart to see her so relaxed and content. If he had not had his left arm in a cast, he would have reached over and held her fingers with the hand that was now on the wheel.

Momentarily he considered steering with his knee so he could do just that, but thought better of the idea. In his younger years, he had done such stupid things, which now seemed silly and foolish. He wondered what was wrong with him, what had happened to the daring kid he once was. He had noticed a sudden change in himself ever since Jennifer came back into his life. There was a seriousness, a certain maturity that now claimed him, and he was puzzled over the very idea.

They found a great old brass bed at a tumble-down country barn which had been converted into an antique shop, and arranged to have it delivered later. Jennifer still had difficulty relating to the "old junk," as she called it, and wished Patty were with them, since her cousin had a much better eye for those things than she did. Ralph, however, surprised her with his knowledge, and she quickly learned what to be looking for. Before the day was over, she became a good, discerning antique shopper, and it pleased him to find she was starting to pick out some fine things she knew would go well in the house.

At one of the shops, Jennifer picked up an old, wooden rolling pin, which had faded light green handles. After hearing all the stories Aunt Bessie had related, it made her wonder about the previous owner of this old pin. *Had someone used it during the depression days to help feed their family when most everyone was out of work and there was scarcely enough to eat? Was it used by a mother who lost a son in the war? Perhaps it belonged to a grandmother, who rolled out cookies for her grandchildren. What struggles and heartbreaks did the family who used this go through in their lives?* Somehow, Jennifer felt connected to the past and the unknown person who had possessed this pin.

"What do you want with that?" Ralph asked, curious that she was interested in an ordinary old kitchen utensil.

"Nothing, really. It's just that Aunt Bessie collects rolling pins, and she has told me several stories about the various owners of the ones she has. Some are pretty special. Maybe I'll tell you about them sometime."

They lunched at a quaint little roadside inn, a romantic place, if one were so inclined. Seated at a tiny table for two by the window, Jennifer was lost in thought as she gazed out through the lace curtain. The countryside brought back all the memories of her childhood, and she suddenly realized that the eleven years she had been away had almost disappeared, she was so at home here. It was easy to forget about Arizona, Don, and the girls. She even forgot what her own house looked like and almost forgot the reason she went to the southwest in the first place——to bear her first born and only child. Ralph's child.

She wondered how he would react if he knew the truth, that she never did have the abortion, but carried to full term, delivering a son. His son. *Would it make any difference to him or would he shrug it off? Would he be furious that I never told him about the baby? The baby—he would be ten now, half grown. Who had adopted him? What did they name him? What color were his eyes—his hair?*

A sudden frown creased her forehead, and she bent over as a stabbing pain crossed her middle. After all these years, it still physically hurt, losing him, that tiny bit of humanity torn from her, but to whom she was forever linked.

Ralph became alarmed as he sat across the table from her and saw her wince. "What is it, Jenny? Are you ill?"

She shook her head, straightened up, and forced a smile. "Nothing. I'm okay."

"Surely it is something. Are you feeling all right?"

"I'm fine, really I am." She tried desperately to shake the memory and changed the subject. "Tell me about your exciting life as a pilot, Ralph."

"Oh, it's really not as glamorous as they would have you believe. Rather routine, I would say. Sort of like driving a big bus. People get on, get seated, and then I steer them across the country, where we land, and they get off. Then another bunch gets on, and we fly back. Back and forth, back and forth, looking down at the same landmarks, over and over. Really dull!"

Jennifer laughed. "Somehow, I don't quite believe you! What about all the exotic places you get to see? What about all the interesting people you meet, especially the young ladies? All the stewardesses are as pretty as models. Certainly you must have met someone with whom you could settle down. Aren't you the marrying type?"

He chuckled. "Oh, I'm the marrying type, all right but I'm having too much fun this way." He paused. "Besides, I just haven't met the one who measures up."

"Measures up to what?"

He took a deep breath and let it out slowly. "To someone I knew a long time ago."

Suddenly he became very serious, aware that the 'someone' he was referring to was sitting across from him right now.

"Oh? What happened?"

"The Korean War got in the way."

"So you fill your days and nights with the—the floozies, huh?" She could not help but put that dig in.

"What are you referring to?"

"Patty and I happened to be on the River Queen the other night when you and your girlfriends whizzed by in the speedboat. The night you broke your arm. I recognized you on the water skis, even in the dark."

"Oh, those girls were just out having a good time. It was my foolish mistake about the arm. I missed the dock. Finish your iced tea, I've got something to show you."

Several hours, many laughs, and a few antique shops later, Ralph pulled the T-Bird down a gravel country lane, winding down the narrow way under big old oak trees to ultimately emerge into a clearing. Ahead shimmered the waters of a large lake. The late afternoon sun glinted across the wide body of water, and Jennifer could see the dark shoreline opposite, with a line of trees hugging the banks.

"I'll help you in," Ralph said as he untied a rowboat which was moored along a wooden pier. He hoisted a picnic basket into the boat, which surprised her. She had no idea he had stowed it in the trunk of the T-Bird.

"You'll have to row, 'cause I can only use one arm. If I did it then all we would do is end up going around in a circle!" He grinned a boyish grin, and his sky blue eyes sparkled.

Jennifer giggled as she hopped into the boat, put the oars in the locks, and skillfully headed the bow out into the water.

"Where are we going?"

"Just head for that island over there." He pointed to a dark mound about three quarters of a mile out.

"I didn't know you were so good at this," he said, admiring her skill and watching as she pulled back on the oars.

She braced her feet against the ribs on the bottom of the boat with each stroke she took, sending her thigh muscles rippling under her tan. Her white shorts made her legs look extra dark, bronzed by years in the Arizona sun. The young woman's slender arms flexed as she worked, belying the strength she possessed. Ralph found the view enthralling.

"Do you love him, Jenny?" he asked, his eyes centering upon the wedding ring she wore.

"Who?"

"The man you are married to. Tell me about him."

"That's a silly question, don't you think? Of course I love him," Jennifer answered routinely, yet wondered how she could have so totally put Don out of her mind. She guessed it was because they had been at opposite ends of the stick, and had had such disagreements about having a child together. The tension she had left in Arizona had been thick enough to cut with a knife, and she had to admit that things were far from perfect and tranquil at home. She had hoped that her short trip to Wisconsin would have given Don a little breathing room, and afford him time to think it over, perhaps even change his mind about not wanting her to get pregnant.

Ralph persisted. "You don't talk much about him. What's his name? And how long have you been married?"

"His name is Don. And we were married six years last May." She kept a steady rhythm on the oars.

"And no children?"

"He has two daughters by his first wife. They live with us."

"Somehow, I never pictured you marrying a divorced man."

Jennifer took her time answering, keeping up a steady stroke, and glanced over her shoulder to be sure she was lining up with the island.

"His wife died in childbirth with the youngest daughter."

"Oh, sorry. I didn't realize."

"I don't think Don ever got over it, really. Melissa, that's the youngest, is twenty-two now, and Colleen is twenty-four."

"He's a good deal older than you, then?"

"Don is forty-seven." She wanted to add that he does not want to father any more children, either, but bit her tongue and remained silent.

Ralph helped Jennifer beach the boat when they reached the island, and took her arm as they scrambled over some rocks. It was she who steadied him, for his balance was not good with one arm in a sling, and the other carrying the picnic basket. He was glad for the support at times. Following a single trail, they wound up a steady incline under the branches of large shade trees, where it was already dark and cool under the dense overhang.

Jennifer could glimpse the golden rays of the setting sun every few yards as it filtered through the leaves, etching each one with a gilded edge. Then they reached an opening upon a bluff at the highest point of the island where they could view the entire lake and shoreline. She could make out a red dot where the T-Bird was parked on the distant shore.

"This is what I wanted to show you, Jenny." Ralph said, and the expression on his face was one of serene pride. "This is where I want to build a cabin. A real log cabin. Isn't it a great spot?"

"It's beautiful, Ralph," Jennifer almost whispered. Somehow the setting seemed reverently sacred, as she drank in the exquisite panorama.

"They call this Blackhawk Isle. Legend has it that during the Blackhawk wars, this was the hiding place of the Chief himself. There is a cave down the side of this bluff which is blackened by the very smoke of his Indian campfires. It is said that sometimes, when the winds are just right, you can hear the sorrowful moaning of Blackhawk's widow as she waits for his return."

There was no sound then except for the twitter of birds and the rustle of leaves in the breeze. Even so, Jennifer shivered slightly at the thought of the long lost lovers, and could picture Blackhawk's woman waiting and watching for her warrior's return. Now, the sun was casting long rays across the water and shown for a brief moment upon the couple as they stood transfixed by the sight.

"Look!" Ralph said, turning his gaze toward the south.

"Oh! Wow!" Jennifer breathed in astonishment, for taking up almost half of the southern sky, a huge, solitary thunderhead billowed like a massive mound of cotton, already tinged pink, peach, and gold from the setting sun. Its reflection on the lake surface was a jumble of colors, tinting the ripples of water like a kaleidoscope. It was a sight so spectacular that neither had seen before, nor were they ever likely to see again in their lifetime.

The two of them stood mesmerized and watched for a full twenty minutes as the dramatic colors of the tremendous thunderhead changed and deepened into rose, then purple. Every now and then, they could see a jab of lightning streak from the cloud, but it was so far away, they could not hear the thunder.

"Oh, Ralph," Jennifer whispered, reaching for his hand to clasp in hers without realizing she had done so. "It is the most beautiful sight I have ever seen."

"Quite a spectacle, isn't it?" he said in a subdued voice, drinking in the scene to sear into his memory, wishing he had brought his camera. Her hand in his did not go unnoticed, and he felt warmed by her touch, unwilling to let go.

Even after the last kiss of the sun had faded, the cloud remained illuminated until only the faintest touch of lavender remained in the long twilight. Reluctant to tear themselves away from the vision they had witnessed, the two finally turned their attention to gathering some firewood, and soon had a campfire going. Like magic, Ralph produced fried chicken, salad, and biscuits from his cooler, a bottle of wine, and some sweet corn which they roasted over the fire.

"You amaze me, Ralph," Jennifer mumbled as she wolfed down the meal, suddenly ravenously hungry in the fresh night air. There was something about the smell of wood smoke and musty forest that triggered a pioneer instinct buried deep inside her, and she was content and relaxed.

"How's that?"

"I mean, here you are, a worldly, savvy playboy, if I may call you that, and I would not guess that you could like roughing it here in the woods, so far from your creature comforts."

"Maybe you don't know me at all, Jenny."

"Maybe not," she murmured.

She was beginning to realize that perhaps she had him all wrong, for now she was seeing a side of him that she had not known existed. A serious, contemplative side which was bringing out his deeper feelings. There was a depth of substance to his character that went far beyond the light hearted, devil-may-care persona she had known a decade earlier. Being with him last night and the entire day today was proving to be an eye opener for her.

They lingered over the last of the wine, full and relaxed, watching the embers of the fire glow red and orange, staring unconsciously as an occasional finger of flame would come to life, sputter, and then recede. Neither spoke, for each was lost in a private daydream. From time to time, their eyes would meet, and it was Ralph's smoldering gaze that rivaled the campfire, causing Jennifer to drop her eyes, afraid he might see her true feelings for him buried in their depths.

And here, in the solitude of this forest island, far from the life she knew in the Southwest, Jennifer found herself with her emotions shattered, her defenses evaporating like vapor in the wind. Her head was trying to tell her that she could not betray Don, but at this time, her heart threatened to overtake her head, and she struggled to gain a balance.

"Don't you think we should get back to the car?" Jennifer eventually asked, becoming slightly concerned at how dark it had become.

Ralph shook his head, "The moon should be up in a couple of hours, then we will have better light to find our way back."

Chapter 12

The last words had hardly left Ralph's mouth when there was a great flash of light, followed almost simultaneously by a tremendous crack of thunder, startling them so they both jumped. Another crashing boom repeated, and suddenly, the heavens were filled with lightning cracking and ripping the sky in every direction. A blast of wind tore through the trees, bringing torrents of slicing rain. Ralph grabbed Jenny's arm and started to run.

"Come on!" he yelled, but the wind ripped the words out of his mouth.

"Where?" Jennifer screamed.

"To the cave!"

Already the rocks were slick, and the gale soaked the pair through in an instant. Flashes of lightning enabled Ralph to find his way to the path leading to the cave, but it was treacherously slippery, and the two slipped and slid down the slope. Once Ralph let out a yelp of pain as he had to use his broken arm to break a fall when he tripped over a jutting rock. Jennifer twisted an ankle as she ran, unable to see where to step, yet Ralph pulled her on.

The wind whipped viciously, sending debris hurtling sideways, and it slashed at the pair as they ran. One more flash of lightning tore the top to a tree off, sending a large branch to the ground almost in front of them. The sound of the storm was deafening, and the very atmosphere seemed charged with electricity, making the hair on their arms stand straight up.

At last, Ralph found the entrance to the cave and pushed Jennifer in, then threw himself in after her, where they both collapsed onto the dirt floor. Fortunately, the cave was deep enough to be fairly dry, and they huddled against the back wall while the storm raged on outside. Every lightning flash showed the rain still being whipped by the wind, slicing almost horizontally, deluging the vegetation with silver sheets, slashing as if some huge hand were cracking a whip. Every so often, a fine mist would whirl into the cave and touch them both as they huddled with their backs against the far wall.

"I'm freezing!" Jennifer yelled above the storm as she hugged her bare legs and shook, cursing the fact she had decided on wearing shorts that day. Little help they were, for now her legs were scratched in several places, and bruised in others. The yellow top she wore was soaked and clung to her body in a wet, cold mass.

Ralph fared no better, his khakis were wet through and through, and his polo shirt was drenched. Nevertheless, he pulled Jennifer close, and tried to warm her with his body. His broken arm ached miserably, and at times, he even bit his lip to help relieve the pain. That's what he deserved for flailing the arm around so much while he ran. If they had heeded the warning about the approaching storm, they could have easily gained the safety of the cave without the treacherous downhill run, and getting soaked in the process. A little too late to think of that now.

He could feel Jenny shiver as her body pressed against his side, and he tightened his arm around her, pulling her even more closely to him. She felt good there, and even with the height of the storm raging outside, he was aware of the feeling stirring inside him. "Oh, Jenny," he breathed to himself. "My little Jenny!"

"How is your arm?" Jennifer shouted into his ear above the sound of the storm.

"I know it's there. It hurts!"

"I'm so sorry," she replied, hollering so he could hear. Then she wrapped her arms about his waist, trying to keep warm. She could feel his chest move with every breath, and when she laid her head against him, she could hear the thud-dud of his heartbeat.

"You okay?" Ralph asked, his lips against her ear.

She nodded her head. "Yes... I'm okay."

The storm continued to rage and crash, whip and slash, for almost half an hour before finally letting up. By now the temperature had dropped, and the fresh smell of rain-washed woods wafted into the shelter of the cave... a pungent blend of wet bark, leaves, and moss. Even when the storm abated, Jennifer did not move from her place. She leaned against Ralph and his arm still held her tightly, reluctant to let her go. He rested his cheek against her curly head, and drank in the scent of her, as the faint aroma of her jasmine cologne reached his nostrils.

It was suddenly quiet, the storm having moved on as abruptly as it had come, and only the cool, refreshing air left behind was proof of the violence that had just recently taken place outside the cave. Jennifer was aware that all she had to do was tilt her head and her lips would find Ralph's, yet she hesitated. Tears began to sting the backs of her eyes until she could hold back no longer. All the frustrations of her last few years with Don, the struggles with the business, Ralph uncannily coming back into her life once more, and her recognition that she was still in love with him, now poured out. She was helpless to stop the tears, and a soft sob escaped her lips as she clung desperately to Ralph's chest.

"What is it, Jenny? Were you frightened?"

The sobs strangled her, and she could not speak.

"Oh, Jenny, sweet Jenny," Ralph whispered, and turning her cheek with his fingertips, kissed her forehead. His lips kissed their way down across her cheek, edging ever so slowly until they closed in on the softness of her mouth, and found her lips trembling. He could taste the salty tears, as his kisses, first soft and warm, turned intense and urgent.

Jennifer was powerless to resist any longer, and throwing her arms around his neck, returned his kisses with a fervor that surprised him. It caused him to pull back, not sure of going into this dangerous territory.

"Jenny?" He questioned her sudden gestures, unsure of how to proceed for fear of ruining what he was beginning to hope beyond hope would be her honest reaction to him.

"Oh, Ralph," she sobbed, hardly able to speak. "Ralph, I love you! I have always loved you, all these years!" Her body shook in his arms.

Ralph's head reeled, and he wondered if he had heard her correctly as he pinched his eyes shut. He had not expected this turn of events, and he tried to clear his own feelings. All the years that had gone by... the war in Korea, his return to civilian life, the women, the parties, the wild life he had led, he now realized had just been an excuse to cover up his real emotions. It struck him like a hammer blow.

Long ago he had locked the love for one girl in his heart, burying it so deeply, that even he had not admitted it to himself. Could it be true? Was this actually happening? Or was he dreaming? Now, after what seemed like a whole lifetime, Jennifer had come back into his life, and was here in his arms, for real.

"Jenny, Sweetie, don't cry. We're safe."

Why in the world did he say that? Already he was kicking himself for such a stupid remark. Why couldn't he just admit to her the truth, that he loved her too? What was keeping him tongue-tied? Then he kissed her again, this time letting his emotions get more aggressive, and his kiss was rough, wanting to possess all of her.

Jennifer stiffened and pulled away, furious with herself for confessing her love for him. She knew it was the wrong decision, and now hated herself for giving in to his kisses. She was aware of what kind of man he was... a playboy who would probably never be able to love only one woman. But what did it matter? She was a married woman and had no right to be in love with someone else. Her life was in Arizona with the man she had wed, and his life and struggles had become hers, for better or for worse.

Jennifer's tears continued to well and splash down her cheeks, and she was miserable, attempting to shut down her feelings for Ralph with the hopelessness of it all. How in the world could she deny those feelings now? For the love had been there for years, smoldering like the dying embers of a fire. It had refused to be extinguished, no matter how long the separation. No matter what circumstances had ebbed and flowed in her life. She was in love with him... a deep undying love that was a once-in-a-lifetime love. A love that swelled and grew to completely overtake her very being.

"Jenny, I've never gotten over you, all these years," Ralph whispered, his lips brushing her ear. "Now you've come back to me."

He found her mouth once more, and kissed her with a long, sensuous kiss, sending Jennifer's senses reeling into the bottomless pit of passion. She met his kiss with her own wild needs, and this time abandoned all efforts to resist, allowing her heart to rule, surrendering her very soul to this long lost love. She let his kisses crush recklessly against her mouth, and thrilled at the very touch of him until she tingled from head to foot.

They forgot the storm that had forced them to this refuge. In the blackness of Blackhawk's Cave, they forgot the chill of the night... forgot the world... forgot the day, for they were both on fire now. The passion that they both had buried years before rose to a feverish pitch until they lay exhausted in each other's arms, whispering endearments when dawn's light eventually edged into their sanctuary.

Ralph's finger was tracing Jennifer's cheek as she lay cradled upon his chest in the first light of day. Their night of passion seemed like a dream when the sun's golden light peeked into the cave as they met the reality of a new day. Jennifer lifted her face and found Ralph's lips once more, kissing him softly, feeling his warm breath against her cheek, as if to reassure herself that it had not been a dream. She knew it was real when he returned her kiss, and his hand caressed every curve of her body. The passion began to rise once more, but this time Jennifer pulled abruptly away and stood up.

"We can't do this, Ralph," she said, her voice husky, still drowsy from sleep.

"What's wrong, Jenny?"

"This is wrong. We were wrong. Last night was wrong. I'm married, Ralph, very married, and this will lead to nothing but heartache."

"Let's not even think that far ahead, Jenny. Let's enjoy the moment. You and I are here, alive at this time... together on this little island in the middle of a lake in Wisconsin. We have a little world all our own here."

He reached for her, and enfolded her gently into his arms.

"Here we are, just you and I, Jenny, just like it was years ago. Just the two of us." His voice was mellow, emotional in her ear.

But there isn't just two of us, she wanted to scream. *There's another life out there somewhere, a young boy, ten years old. A boy who is part of both of us. Lost now, forever!* She wanted to blurt out the whole story, to tell him that he had fathered a son with her. She was almost going to open her mouth to tell him when he leaned down to kiss her, but she turned her head away.

"What's this? Are you suddenly getting righteous and noble... and faithful? You weren't very faithful last night! In fact, you were very, very unfaithful, my dear." His voice sounded bitter.

Jennifer's face turned red with the recollection of their fierce, passionate love making just hours before. She was hurt by the sarcastic tone of his voice as he reminded her of their indiscretion.

"I'm sorry about that. Sorrier than you could ever know! I'm sorry I let my feelings rule. I should never have let his happen, and I regret it terribly!"

"But you said you loved me, Jenny. You had always loved me."

"I do love you, Ralph, with all my heart. I tried to deny it... fought against it, but I am weak. I love you, and my heart is breaking. But I am married. I cannot go against my wedding vows, to toss them out as if they never existed," she stated emphatically, angry and ashamed of herself for giving in to her passion. Tears began to well in her eyes, and she continued bitterly, "Besides, this is nothing more than one more conquest for you, isn't it, Ralph? One more time to score and add notches to your bedpost! Just another one night stand."

Her words whipped him like a cat-o-nine-tails, ripping at the depths of him, shredding as surely as if blows had actually been struck. God, how he loved her... but the words would not come out. Why couldn't he form those three simple words? Why did his glib tongue fail him now? It should be an easy matter to just tell her what his heart knew to be true... that he actually was in love with her too, and had been all these years. Tell her that the strangling, longing, yearning feeling inside him was his love for her. Instead, he stood mute, letting her rake him up one side and down the other, becoming furious as she spoke.

"Are you finished?" he flashed, when she stopped for breath.

"Quite! Quite finished!" she spat out, spinning on her heel, heading up the trail away from the cave. Ralph stormed after her.

Jennifer rowed the boat back in silence, thankful that the night's storm had not torn the rowboat from its mooring. She would have hated the thought of having to swim back to the car, but that would have left Ralph stranded on the island, unable to swim with the cast on his arm. As she pulled on the oars, she pictured him in the water, with the weight of the cast pulling him down to drown. That would have been no loss to her now, she was thinking viciously. She was still furious. At him, at herself, at the circumstance, at her heart for loving him so.

Jackie Gould

Chapter 13

On Saturday, a huge crowd was on hand for the auction, and Aunt Bessie was busy flitting here and there, chatting excitedly with old acquaintances and neighbors. The weather held good. In fact, fresh from the recent storm, the sun now sparkled upon the furniture and goods set out for the auction. There was a carnival atmosphere as people followed the auctioneer from item to item, and Jennifer searched the crowd, looking for Ralph's face, surprised to find he was not there. She thought he might attend in the interest of the house he had purchased from Aunt Bessie, but as the day wore on, he failed to show up, and she found herself disappointed in spite of how she had felt yesterday when they parted.

They had each smoldered silently in their own corner of the car during the ride home from the lake. An icy shroud hung over the T-Bird while they had driven back, and Ralph had kept his eyes directly on the road ahead, never once glancing Jennifer's way. She, in turn, only occasionally peeked at his profile, which she found cold and stern. She noted his jaw had been set tightly, and her own mood had been one of angry frustration. Not a word was spoken when he had dropped her off at the old house. She remembered slamming the car door hard, stomping up the steps and slamming the front door shut, too.

Now, one by one, the auction items were sold, and the sound of the auctioneer's rapid chant echoed through the late summer's day. Jennifer kept an eye on Aunt Bessie, wondering if this dispersal of her family heirlooms would affect her, for it was sad to see all these old possessions go. However, Bessie was holding up well.

Curiously, a lot of the items were being bid upon by the same two people, and the bidding was fast and furious. Prices escalated, with items sometimes going for far more than Jennifer thought they were worth. The larger items were held until the last, and the crowd, except for a few curious hangers-on, had dwindled, leaving only a handful of serious bidders.

As Jennifer kept a careful eye on Aunt Bessie, the late afternoon sun slanted far to the west, throwing long shadows across the nearly empty lawn, and the last of the big furniture was auctioned. Surely the emotional day must be taking a toll on the older woman, Jennifer thought, but the amazing lady seemed as strong as ever, nodding approvingly as each piece was gaveled sold.

There was no doubt Aunt Bessie was pleased with the results, and at the very end, as the last trucks were pulling away, she congratulated the auctioneer for his good work.

"Looks like you made out real good, Miss Herrington," he said, as he conferred with the cashier. "We'll have your check ready in a few minutes."

"You did a splendid job, Herb. Thanks to you, it went very well."

He grinned as he scratched his balding head. "I can't figure it, though," he drawled, mopping his brow with a blue checked handkerchief. "Those last two bidders at the end were both buying for the same man, yet they bid each other up! Doesn't make any sense to me."

"What do you mean, Herb?"

"Well, the two guys were hired by Ralph Warren to bid for him. They were competing with each other, which resulted in Mr. Warren bidding against himself!"

Jennifer was stunned upon hearing that news. Then it dawned on her. If Ralph really had wanted to, he could have made an offer on the furniture days ago before the auction. But knowing that Aunt Bessie needed cash, he made sure the bids were high. So he ended up with the things he wanted to keep for the house, and saw to it that the older woman was well paid for them to boot.

Despite the animosity which now seemed to lie between them, Jennifer suddenly found a new admiration for Ralph for that gesture. Now a longing started to gnaw away at her, and she wished she could at least speak to him. Their silent return from the lake yesterday morning now began to appear to be nothing more than a silly teenage maneuver on her part. She had been in one of "those" moods, and had lashed out unduly at Ralph, which did not befit her at all.

"I just want to take a minute to go through the house one last time, if you don't mind, dear," Aunt Bessie was saying. "I hand over the keys tomorrow."

"Of course."

"It seems so different and lonely now," the woman mused, as their steps echoed through the vast emptiness. "This is where Papa spent his last years, almost blind, before he died," she said, motioning to a room off the parlor. "I took care of him for years after Mama passed away. It seems strange that all my brothers and sisters are gone now, and I'm still here. The last one. Now there is nothing left, not even the old family home."

Jennifer thought Aunt Bessie was about to cry, but the woman straightened her shoulders and turned to leave, toughening herself to accept the inevitable.

"Let's go, dear. Get your things. You can bunk with me tonight."

"Oh, Aunt Bessie, I don't want to be a bother. Just drop me off at the motel. I can take a room there."

"Nonsense! You and I need to visit some more before you leave for home. You have to leave soon, right?"

"I'm supposed to go tomorrow and catch a late flight out of Chicago."

"I do wish you could stay longer, dear. We've been so busy, we haven't had a good chance to really talk."

Later that evening, after dinner in the apartment, the two had a good girl-talk. Jennifer bared her heart to her Aunt about her disappointment in her marriage, and she confessed the burning love she had carried for years for someone she could never have. She did not name him by name, however, nor mention that Ralph lived right here in Waterville, and was now the new owner of Aunt Bessie's house.

At that point, Aunt Bessie disappeared into her bedroom for a moment, returning with the long, mysterious, lightweight box which Jennifer had carefully transported to the apartment for her.

She put it in the girl's lap, and invited her to open the box.

"I want you to have this, my dear."

"What is it?"

"Open it up and I will tell you about it."

Cautiously, Jennifer unwrapped the tissues which surrounded a fragile object, finally to expose a fine, cobalt blue, hand-blown glass rolling pin. She sucked in her breath in surprise. Obviously this was highly treasured, and fairly shimmered in Jennifer's hands. She could see through the pin, and noted how the color shaded from light to dark in places, and marveled at the richness of the glass.

It was the most beautiful thing Jennifer had ever seen, and she could see how precious and special the piece was by the gleam in Aunt Bessie's eyes as she gazed with obvious pride and love at the old rolling pin. The pin was tied at the ends by an old pink ribbon. Three hand painted flowers of white and pink decorated the shaft, though they were now somewhat faded with age, and there were some almost unintelligible letters on the other side.

"Oh," Jennifer whispered, "Where did you get such a beautiful rolling pin, Aunt Bessie?"

"It was a gift, my dear, from someone very special, a long time ago. It is a nineteenth century commemorative rolling pin, manufactured in England, I was told."

There was a certain softness that crossed the older woman's face at that point. A pensive, thoughtful, almost angelic look that Jennifer could not help but notice.

"It is the loveliest thing I have ever seen! How exquisite! And it is so old! How amazing that it has not been broken over so many years. Do I have to beg you to tell me about this story?" Jennifer grinned.

"No," Bessie laughed. "Now is the time for you to know about this special rolling pin. This most precious gift. My treasure. I want you to have this, Jennifer."

"But, Aunt Bessie, if this means so much to you, why do you want to part with it?"

"Because, my dear, I have searched for years for the proper person to hand this down to, and you are that person. You'll understand when I tell you how I got the pin. You, of all people, will understand, and I think treasure it also."

Legend III
"Bessie"
Part 1

"Nonsense!" Bessie's sister Jessie had written to her when Bessie attempted to decline her sister's invitation to visit Chicago in the summer of 1893. Just twenty-one, Bessie had tried to use the excuse that Papa would be all alone since Mama had died three years earlier. Besides, all the other siblings had long since scattered, leaving her the only one who remained at the homestead in Waterville.

"Papa is capable of taking care of himself for a few weeks," Jessie wrote. "You deserve to see the sights. Who knows? Perhaps you will like the city so well, you might consider making it a permanent change!"

Bessie had to admit that the idea did seem intriguing and exciting, since Jessie had insisted that her youngest sister journey to the big city that year to attend the World's Columbian Exposition. "A marvelously wonderful event, not to be missed," is the way she put it.

Bessie envied her older sister's courage and spunk, to live in a big city all alone, supporting herself. But then, Jessie had always been such an adventurer, trying daring new ideas, places and experiences. Young Bessie was well aware that it had pained her dear, departed mother to think that Jessie had chosen a life the older woman thought was "wildly Bohemian." Their mother had been aghast that Jessie had rejected marriage in favor of a career in the big city.

Now, as Bessie alighted from the passenger train, she was sure she had made a big mistake by coming to Chicago. Papa had been poorly when she had left home, however, she had engaged a woman to stay with him while she was away. It seemed Papa never had recovered from Mama's passing, and had withdrawn into himself even more than before. Bessie knew that the effects of his Civil War experiences took a far greater toll upon her Papa than anyone would admit. He seldom talked about those experiences, but underneath she sensed that it ate away at him like a cancer, slowly destroying the essence of him. She vowed to make her visit short so she could hasten back to Waterville. She was needed there.

There was such a crush of people hurrying and scurrying, Bessie felt quite alone at the train station. Ladies skimmed along the walkways in smartly attired, long skirted fashions which Bessie had not yet seen in her rural community. The gentlemen all were handsomely decked out in clean pressed suits, starched white collars and wore stiff Derby hats, adding a formality of sophistication to the scene which Bessie found attractive. It was quite a departure from the soft caps and more boxy style jackets that the men wore in small towns like Waterville. Bessie wondered how Papa would look dressed in a slim-fit, modern suit, sporting a Derby hat such as the ones she was watching bob up and down on the passengers' hurried way.

"Bessie! Darling sister!" Jessie gushed as she embraced the younger girl. Actually, Bessie was the taller of the two, however, they shared the same shade of dark brown hair. Sixteen years separated them in age, still she and Jessie bore a startling resemblance to each other. Except, Jessie's eyes were brown, like her father's, and Bessie's were the color of a bright summer sky.

"Oh, I'm so happy to see you, Jessie!"

Despite her valiant effort to the contrary, Bessie found her eyes misting with emotion as she returned her sister's embrace and kisses.

"Dear sister, I cannot believe it has been three years since last I have laid eyes upon you. Let me look at you."

Jessie backed Bessie up at arm's length, and cast an approving eye. "My! But you have grown into such a beauty!"

Bessie blushed, lowering her eyes, embarrassed by her sister's compliment, for she had never thought of herself as anything but most ordinary in the looks department. She certainly felt gangly, because she was taller than most other young women. Plain. That is how she would describe herself, with a nose that was a little too short, and just slightly turned up at the end. Thick, dark brows framed her blazing blue eyes with a graceful arch, and her dark lashes, full and long, added a depth to the eye color that was sometimes startling. Her skin was smooth and creamy, with just a hint of pink in her cheeks, and was her most positive feature, Bessie thought.

"Dearest sister, I would like to introduce you to my friend, Mr. Wheeler Aubrey. Wheeler, this is my little sister, Bessie."

Bessie found herself shaking hands with a tall, sophisticated looking gentleman, who, upon doffing his Derby, revealed blond, silky-soft hair which matched his meticulously manicured mustache. He slowly brushed her finger tips with his lips, while never taking his eyes from hers, and mumbled a greeting. Bessie nodded, shyly, sliding her fingers from his grasp, noting that he had held her hand just a bit too long. Perhaps she was not accustomed to the protocol of big city manners. She vowed she would learn, however, not wanting to appear to be just a naive country girl, easily swayed by the attentions of a handsome man.

During the hansom cab ride through the city, Bessie could not help but be impressed, for building upon tall building stood massively at attention, flanking the streets which were laid in a conservative grid pattern. She had never before seen any building taller than four stories, and she craned her neck to see the tops of these multi-story monoliths. Everywhere there was hustle and bustle, with men and women scurrying to the shops or to the office. Horse drawn street cars were loaded with passengers hurrying on and off at various stops.

"Tomorrow, we are going shopping," Jessie announced after supper. "You just must get some new clothes, Bessie. After all, you are in Chicago now, and we shall bring you up to date with the latest in fashions. Oh, I have so much to show you!"

They were in Jessie's three room flat, which was generously and comfortably furnished, as Bessie unpacked her grip.

"Jessie, how can you afford such a lovely place?"

"I'm a working woman now, remember? Besides, I have just been promoted to head the Lady's Ready Made Dress Department at Carson's. The first such position for a woman, I might add. Gentlemen have always been head of departments until my promotion. I must admit, it is hard to overcome the resentment of most males, and if I didn't have some pretty tough skin to ward off the nasty remarks, I would never survive. But you know me! Always cheerful, always the survivor of the many skirmishes of the minds. Some men are just so old fashioned in their thinking. Why do they fail to see that women must take their rightful place beside the men in the business world?"

That thought was a little beyond Bessie's comprehension, for she had no desire to compete in what she considered the traditional man's world of commerce and economics. No, she would be utterly content to marry, raise a family like the women in her family had done for generations.

That was not to say that she wanted to be downtrodden or abused by a man, but rather, she desired to be his helpmate, his partner, sharing his life as an equal, just as her mother and father had done. After all, Bessie had strength and love enough to conquer almost any task. Her father had taught her that, thank goodness. In fact, there wasn't much that she could not tackle and finish, if need be.

That evening, Jessie introduced her sister to some of the "Bohemian" way of life, which their mother had taken such an aversion to, when they attended a nearby coffee house, where Bessie met several of Jessie's friends. There were ongoing lively discussions of theatre and art, poetry and literature, which caused Bessie to decide that it was not as bad as her mother had envisioned. She was, however, too uninformed about the latest theatre presentations to add much to the conversation. Instead, she sat back and absorbed the spirited exchange of ideas, admiring how at ease her sister seemed as Jessie kept up a knowledgeable interchange with the men of the group. Wheeler Aubrey also sat quietly, occasionally letting his gaze drift Bessie's way.

"The great joy of living in the city," Jessie explained later, "is that there is so much culture here. There is the theatre, opera, ballet, art, and all kinds of museums. Everything is here, and I want you to experience it all, Bessie!"

"Do you go alone to these events?"

"Sometimes. It's perfectly safe and proper, Bessie. A lot of working girls fill their evenings that way. After all, they are modern and independent, and are earning their own money. But that's what Wheeler is for. He's my companion."

Bessie wondered what Papa would have thought. "Are you serious about Mr. Aubrey?"

"He's just a good friend. I don't have time to get serious about any man. I have my career."

The shopping spree the following day was like a whirlwind to Bessie, for her sister took over entirely selecting for her a smart new traveling suit, and several skirts and waists, some of which were stunning light weight summer gowns. She convinced Bessie that the days of wearing bustles were coming to a close, and chose in their place the popular new "Gibson Girl" look. Those skirts were slimmer, and very flattering to the young woman's tall figure, flaring out toward the bottom of the skirt, molding around her hips nicely. The sleeves of the waists were big and puffy above the elbows, which Bessie thought was a bit extreme.

As she tried on hats, both women giggled like school girls, while attempting to make their selections.

"Jessie! You are insane!" Bessie laughed at one point at the outrageous enthusiasm of her sister.

Even though it took some getting used to about Jessie's flamboyant lifestyle, Bessie found her sister's light hearted approach to life to be invigorating, to say the least. Trying to be conservative, Bessie protested at the extravagant amount Jessie insisted upon spending for her clothing.

"I can't possibly afford these things, Jessie. You know how little I have to spend."

"But this is my treat to you, little sister. Heaven knows I have had scarce chance to spend much time with you. You have just grown up all by yourself, and now I can make up some of those lost years."

It was difficult for Bessie to realize the age difference between them, for Jessie seemed younger than her thirty-seven years. It did seem strange and uncommon, however, to have a women of her age unmarried—a spinster. But it looked for all the world as if Jessie had no intentions to stroll down the matrimonial path, since she had found too much contentment and fulfillment in her career. Bessie felt sorry that

Jessie had no prospects for the traditional life, positive that her sister was wrong in pursuing the single path.

"I haven't told you the most exciting news!" Jessie announced as they relaxed over a cup of tea that evening, weary from the long day of touring Chicago's top shops, and the department where Jessie was employed.

"And what, pray tell, is that, dear sister?"

"You'll never guess!"

By now, Bessie was becoming used to Jessie's dramatic flair, and waited patiently for her to continue, aware that no matter if it were simply that the sun would come up tomorrow, her sister would make a big production out of the event.

"William is going to join us for a few days!"

"Our brother, William?"

"Yes! Isn't that exciting? He is back from England, and in between assignments."

Bessie had not seen William since she turned fifteen, when her older brother had followed his dream and left home to sail the seas as an officer on merchant ships. From time to time, when his letters had arrived at home, she would eagerly devour the contents, anxious to hear about the foreign countries he visited in his travels. Bessie would spend hours daydreaming about his adventures, trying to picture the scenes his words painted as he wrote in his letters. Now he was actually going to be home! Home—if only Papa were here.

PART II

William did not arrive alone, however, the sisters discovered when Jessie answered the knock on her door a few days later. Instead of one man, handsomely outfitted in nautical garb, there were two figures in uniform standing in the hallway.

"Jessie! By God, it's good to see you! And could this be—little Bessie? Is this you?" William's strong voice boomed as he engulfed her in a bear hug before backing away to get a good look at her. As tall as she was, he was taller still, and looked down at her with smiling eyes as he shook his head in disbelief that the gangly girl he had left six years ago had grown into such a stately beauty.

"Forgive my lack of manners," he gestured to the other man who stood shyly behind him, holding his cap in his hand. "Ladies, I took the liberty to bring my friend and fellow shipmate along. Please, may I present my Chief Navigator, Jeremy Greene. Jeremy, these are my sisters, Jessie and Bessie Herrington."

Bessie extended her hand and smiled slightly, tilting her chin down so that she glanced shyly at him from beneath her lashes, and found she was looking at the most handsome face she had ever seen. Jeremy was ruggedly good looking, with a shock of sandy hair glinting copper in the gaslight of the apartment, and his smile almost made her knees weak. However, it was the man's eyes which instantly fascinated Bessie. They were a shade of hazel that had a depth beyond comprehension. She could read kindness in them, yet strength and resolve, and found herself staring so long into them that she had to drop her gaze in embarrassment. Color slowly rose from her neck to her cheeks, turning them a shade of pink beyond normal.

Jessie was chatting animatedly with William and with a wave of her arm bade both men to be seated. Meanwhile, Bessie sat demurely off to one side where she could observe her older brother and his friend without seeming to be obviously staring. She did not recognize what the feeling inside her was with which she was now dealing, ever since the door had opened, but she only knew that she was greatly attracted to Mr. Greene. There was a magnetism about the man which drew her to him like moths to light. He was reserved and somewhat shy, yet she could tell by watching the expression in his eyes that he was happy for his friend to be reunited with his sisters.

"Bessie, be a dear and make some tea for our guests," Jessie said, and began to draw her brother's friend more into the conversation, inquiring about their recent travels to England. She was her usual vivacious self, laughing easily, and smiling at Jeremy Greene often with a flirtatious kind of ease.

"Jess, you haven't changed a bit!" William laughed, good naturedly. "Still keeping all the men in Chicago at bay, I see. And the right one has not come along yet?"

Jessie tossed her head and laughed. "William, you know very well that IF and WHEN I set my bonnet for a man, he will never have a chance!"

"How well I can imagine!" William murmured.

"Oh, forgive our banter, Mr. Greene, I fear I am embarrassing you by such talk," Jessie addressed her guest.

William was quick to respond. "Yes, Jeremy, you need to understand my sister, Jess. She has never been shy when it comes to speaking her mind. I'm afraid I should have warned you that she is no shrinking violet, and comes out with very frank conversations. Enough to make a grown man lose his voice."

Jeremy smiled, knowingly, and quietly shifted in his chair as he crossed his legs and gazed back at Jessie rather boldly. He had met a lot of women in his day, but never one quite as vivacious as this one. It intrigued him momentarily to find a woman who obviously was treading where few women had gone before. He was impressed by her apparent independence, not feeling any threat by her at all, as most men did who had crossed her path.

At that point, Bessie returned bearing a tray and was surprised when Jeremy jumped from his chair to help take the tray from her hands.

"Let me help you, Miss Herrington," he smiled, his voice like velvet, and his hand, warm and strong, accidentally enclosed her fingers as he took the tray from her. Bessie felt a tingle shoot through her body at his touch, and found herself bewildered by her reaction. Once more, she could feel the color rise to her cheeks.

"Thank you," she barely breathed, suddenly terribly shy and somewhat perplexed by how this man's proximity affected her. For once, she was tongue-tied and not her usual self. Her hand shook slightly as she poured the tea and handed him the cup and saucer. Again, his fingers brushed hers, and once more, like a bolt of lightning Bessie felt it go through her whole body. She sat down quickly on a chair close to William.

"How is Papa, Bessie?" her brother was asking, yet she barely heard him as she tried to concentrate on the teacup she held in her lap. He had to ask again.

"I think he is poorly, William. He has not been himself ever since Mama passed on." Her voice was small and worried.

"I plan to see him before I am due to go back to New York."

"New York? Oh, Will, you do get to see such marvelous sights!" Jessie burst out.

He grinned. "Now that's a place you should see, Jess. You would really fit right in. You should come back with us when Jeremy and I return. We've contracted out to a big clipper ship bound for San Francisco by way of around the horn."

New York, San Francisco, they might as well have been talking about the moon, Bessie thought. Such exotic, far away places were only names of dreams to her, as she tried to imagine what those cities were like. Well, she resolved, she would never see those places anyway, so why be concerned about them?

It was decided at dinner that evening that all of them would attend the World's Columbian Exhibition the following day. The Exhibition celebrated the 400th anniversary of Columbus' discovery of America. Jessie could only beg one more day off from her position at Carson's. Now, as they lingered over coffee and dessert in the restaurant, the foursome leaned forward to discuss their plans.

Bessie could see how interested Mr. Greene had become in her sister, as his attention seemed to hang totally on every word Jessie uttered. He laughed at her jokes, and seemed delighted in her conversation, admiring the way her eyes flashed with humor when she spoke. Occasionally, his gaze drifted to meet Bessie's, yet she warmed at each chance glance.

Bessie took the opportunity to study Jeremy's face closely, as he seemed to be enthralled with every word Jessie had to say, and a smile creased his cheeks from time to time. Bessie found herself increasingly attracted to him, more so as the evening wore on. At the same time, she found her heart sinking in disappointment that he appeared to pay so little attention her way.

The young woman was beginning to think perhaps Jessie may have found her man. At least, that is how Bessie perceived the situation. She was strengthened in that thought when William caught her eye and winked as he tilted his head toward the other pair, raising an eyebrow as he did so, and pursed his lips in a knowing smile.

Bessie lowered her eyes and swallowed hard, in her attempt to disguise her disappointment. But then, *what man would be interested in a too-tall young lady of plain face, who found it difficult to carry on an interesting conversation?* Bessie wondered. She bit her lip, and tried to force a smile, happy that Jessie might possibly become interested in a gentleman after all. She sighed deeply and sipped her coffee, turning her attention to Will.

"I do hope you will go visit Papa, Will. He misses all his children greatly," she whispered.

He replied in a subdued voice, "I wish I had seen Mother one more time before she died. Now, of all us Herrington children, you alone are the only one left at home. It's funny that we all left the homestead. Clara, married to the railroad man. Is she still living in Minnesota? What about Mary Ellen, still teaching up north?"

Bessie nodded. "And George is in Milwaukee, married with three children. He has a small bakery there."

"And you, Bessie? What do you want?"

"Oh, I don't know, Will. I have Papa to care for. He is really failing. Seems to be drifting in some sort of dreamland. Sometimes he talks out of his head about war, I think. Even though he was never wounded in the great confrontation, he was wounded in his spirit—and it is getting worse all the time."

"But that was almost thirty years ago, Bess. How can he still be living that long march?"

She shook her head sadly, and he could see how worried she was. He determined that, as much as he loved the sea, his next voyage would perhaps be his last for awhile. He could see he was needed at home. Poor Bessie did not have to be saddled with the full responsibility of caring for an aging parent alone.

The World's Colombian Exhibition proved to be a spectacle beyond Bessie's wildest imagination. There were wide avenues for pedestrians to walk, lined with great buildings constructed for the sole purpose of exhibiting new, exciting scientific inventions and displays.

The young woman was surprised that Jessie had brought Wheeler along, for somehow, Bessie had it in her mind that Jessie had set her sails, so to speak, for Jeremy Greene. But soon she found herself walking between Will and Jeremy, and began to relax and enjoy herself, shyly glancing at her brother's friend from the corner of her eye.

"Built by a man named G.W. Gale Ferris, from right here in Galesburg, Illinois," Will was saying, reading from an information brochure, as they craned their necks upward to see the monstrous wheel before them. It was the single most distinctive structure of all the dome-topped and columned buildings of the exhibition, and was named after its inventor, Ferris.

"Two hundred fifty feet tall—carrying thirty six cars, each holding sixty passengers!" Will continued to read, as they were awe struck by the huge Ferris Wheel.

"Come on, everyone, we're going on!" Jessie shouted, pulling on Wheeler's arm.

Bessie was reluctant to trust such a fragile looking contraption of steel girders and wires, the immensity of which she would never have believed, had she not seen it herself.

"Come on, Bessie," Will implored. "You can sit right between Jeremy and me, it will be great!"

She was still not convinced, even when they entered the cab, which was much like a trolley car, seating about thirty people on each side in rows of double seats.

"Here, sit next to the window, Bess," Will pointed out the seat.

But her eyes grew big, and she still shook her head and pulled back.

"Then you sit there, Jeremy," Will said, "and I will sit across from you."

With that, he shoved Bessie into a seat on the aisle next to Jeremy, and made himself comfortable across from them, facing the two, grinning all the while. Jessie and Wheeler were seated across the aisle, and Bessie could hear her sister's laughter.

As the car lifted off the ground, Bessie's heart began to race, and ever so slowly they began to rise above the throngs of people below. Her eyes widened as she could see above the treetops for the first time in her life. She had such a mixed feeling of sheer fright and exhilaration that she could not equate it to anything she had ever experienced before.

There was a gentle swaying of the car which was easily taken by the two men used to the roll of a ship at sea, but entirely frightening to Bessie, whose idea of stability was good old Mother Earth. She muffled a little cry as the car rocked, and without realizing, grabbed Jeremy Greene's thigh to steady herself. He good-naturedly put an arm across the back of her seat.

"Look, Miss Herrington, look at the view," he said, motioning toward the window. By now, Bessie had her finger tips at her mouth, and her eyes were huge with wonder, fright, and amazement.

"Look," he continued. "There is Lake Michigan, do you see?"

She leaned forward to look, peering across his chest, and he steadied her with an arm around her waist, pointing out various landmarks. He could feel the tension in her body slowly relax under his fingertips, and found her apparent innocence charming. Soon, she uttered little squeals of joy as she could make out boats on the water in the distance, and excitement replaced her fears. It was as if she were on a magic carpet, sailing above the rooftops.

"Oh, I have never been up so high!"

"Isn't it amazing?" Jeremy added, fully aware that her face was but a few inches from his own, and he could feel her breath against his cheek. "Would you care to change places now?"

Hesitantly, she nodded her head, and her eyes were shining as she slowly stood, accepting his hands for balance while they squeezed past each other. As they did so, the car swung slightly, putting Bessie off balance, and she leaned against him for a flustering moment, thankful for his steadying hand, before she safely took her place next to the window. From his new seat, Jeremy leaned close over her shoulder, still pointing out streets and turret topped buildings, street cars, and throngs of pedestrians as they soared above it all. He could detect a soft fragrance of lilac, and glanced at the young woman's porcelain smooth complexion, remembering how her long body had felt against him when they had exchanged places.

Bessie was almost the same height as he, only an inch or two shorter, yet Jeremy found it interesting to have a woman, tall as a man, be able to look him in the eye. So many women were small, and either too plump, or too scrawny. He admired how graceful her movements were, and found her perfectly proportioned even for her height.

Before the long ride was over, he noticed her shyness was slowly disappearing, and they were carrying on a friendly conversation, one in which she easily chatted with mature, sensible input. Jeremy found himself captivated by this young lady, for she was everything so many young women were not—bright, intelligent, sensitive, yet he could detect a strength that had yet to be tapped.

PART III

"Tell Papa I will come home soon," Bessie told William the following morning at the train depot as he was about to depart the city to travel to Waterville.

"And you look after my sister, will you Jeremy? I'm afraid to have her alone in the big city while Jessie is at work."

Jeremy had accompanied them to the train station, and now smiled and nodded, assuring

277

Will that he would, indeed, look after Bessie, and wished him well as he shook his friend's hand. When the train had pulled away, Jeremy turned, putting his hand beneath Bessie's elbow, and escorted her out into the warm summer day, ready to find a trolley to take them back to Jessie's apartment.

"Let's walk back," Bessie said.

"Of course, if that is what you would rather do," Jeremy replied, and glanced at her profile as he did so.

This time it was Bessie who tentatively put her hand in the crook of his arm, and they strolled toward Michigan Avenue.

"Tell me about yourself, Miss Herrington," Jeremy ventured, noting how easily she matched his gait, stride for stride.

"There is very little to tell, Mr. Greene. I fear I lead a very quiet, ordinary, small town life."

"Please call me Jeremy."

"If you wish, sir. Then, would you also please call me Bessie?"

She felt his other hand cover her fingers which were crooked in his arm, and give them a little squeeze.

"Bessie—that is such a fresh, lovely name."

She blushed. "I always rather thought that Mama and Papa had run out of names when I came along, so they just rhymed it with Jessie."

Jeremy laughed. "Somehow, I doubt that was the case. There is a difference in your ages, you and Jessie?" It was a half-question, half-statement.

"Yes. Papa had gone off to fight in the Civil War, and when he came back, with five children already straining the household, I fear they had little desire to add to the brood. I was born seven years after his return from the war, after Mama had lost two in between."

"I'm sorry to hear that, but I am delighted that YOU are here!"

Bessie felt color in her cheeks again, as she understood the deeper meaning of his honest remark.

"And your siblings are all long since scattered, I take it?"

She nodded and smiled. "I fear I am the baby of the group."

"You are nothing of the kind! You are a wonderful, mature young lady. I am sure your father must be very proud of you." Jeremy retorted, aware from his friend, Will, that their mother was no longer living.

"You flatter me too much, Jeremy."

They continued their stroll, and Bessie found herself telling of what she knew about her father's Civil War experiences, which greatly impressed Jeremy.

"Sherman's March To The Sea! What a spectacular piece of history in which to be involved. I should very much like to meet him one day."

"I'm afraid he does not like to talk much about it. However, I know he would be pleased to meet you, too, Jeremy."

During lunch in a small cafe, he told her of his love for the sea, and how he had met Will. The two men had become best of friends, he said, relating some of their adventures and voyages. All the while he was talking, Bessie concentrated on how the timbre of his voice thrilled her, and how his eyes flashed with sincere expressions as his gaze locked onto hers. He smiled often, softening the lines of his rugged face, mellowing his eyes even more as they bore deeply into Bessie's.

Jeremy's smile, his eyes, his voice, the gentleness of his actions and words permeated every cell of Bessie's being, and she discovered feelings inside her which were stirring for the first time in her life. She felt all warm and tingly, and wondered what it was. It felt good and right, and made her happy.

She found he was so easy to talk to that she forgot they had just recently met. Before long, Bessie felt she had known him for years. It was almost as if somewhere in the universe, two spirits, which had floated separately for eons, suddenly met—reuniting after an eternity to take up where they had left off. She felt a special bond with this man, like she had never known prior.

It was easy to accept Jeremy's hand as they left the cafe, while he pulled her arm into his, and his fingers remained, warm and thrilling upon hers. His arm pressed against Bessie's side, and she could feel the strength of him beneath the sleeve of his coat, again sending little jolts of excitement dancing through her body.

As for Jeremy, he knew he had never met anyone quite as innocent and charming as the girl he had on his arm right now. Not that he had not had his share of dalliances over his twenty-eight years. On the contrary, he had, and at one point even thought seriously about taking a wife, but, alas, the lady ran off with someone else while he was on the high seas.

But Bessie—now there was someone his very soul seemed to be melding to. She stirred in him his every masculine inclination, and he felt compelled to learn every little detail of her life— her wants, her wishes—her dreams. He was thinking of how she had felt as she had lurched against him yesterday on the Ferris Wheel, and his arm, which now innocently touched her side, reminded him of the encounter.

They came upon a millinery shoppe during their stroll, and Bessie suddenly stopped at the window, and a gasp escaped her lips as she stared at a hat that was on display. It was the most beautiful, most outrageous creation she had ever laid eyes upon. The huge brim was lined in tiers of very pink organdy ruffles, ending in a pile of matching pink lace and ostrich feathers high upon the crown. Huge pink fabric roses fastened one side of the brim up, allowing a swoop to the contour which would frame a lady's face in a most fascinating way.

"Oh," Bessie breathed, her mouth fairly drooping open. "It's beautiful! I have never seen such a beautiful hat in all my life! Isn't it beautiful, Jeremy?"

She still felt a bit uncomfortable calling him by his first name, somehow feeling that she was breaching the time-honored code of good manners.

The young man could see that her eyes were shining like a child's at Christmas. He grinned at her innocent exuberance and assured her he had never seen such a creation before. He could picture how lovely she would look with it upon her head, framing her dark curls and porcelain complexion.

"Let me buy it for you!"

"Oh, I could not let you do that," Bessie protested. "After all, Jeremy, we are so newly acquainted that it would not be appropriate." Yet her eyes were big as she turned once more to look into the window.

Jeremy watched the expression of Bessie's face, and smiled to himself to see such awe and longing in her gaze. His heart melted then, instantly recognizing that he was falling in love with her, as incongruous as it seemed, for he had only met her two days prior. And as sure as the sun sets in the west, he knew his own feelings, and his very being churned with a love that he could not quell. At this very instant, he wanted nothing more than to sweep this lovely creature into his arms. Yet he was aware that propriety ruled, and instead he just stood there and gazed at her, as the longing to hold her surged through him in waves—like the sea, crashing and churning.

Bessie turned from the window and happened to glance up into Jeremy's eyes. She was startled to see a strange look on his face that had not been there a moment before. His eyes were so mellow, and there was a look of—a look of—something! She tentatively smiled, and tried to act as if nothing happened, yet she knew something was very different.

"I want to see you in that hat, Bessie. It was created just for you. You MUST have it!"

"I couldn't—" her voice trailed off when their eyes met, and finally failed her totally, for the sensual look in his eyes sparked a deep surge in her heart and she was afraid to admit that her emotions for him were soaring.

"I could—I could—not accept such a wonderful gift," she whispered, never allowing her gaze to move from his.

For the longest moment the pair just stood there with their eyes locked onto each other, searching the depths of their souls, each helpless in the emotions that shot through them.

"But you shall—you must!" His deep voice was low and intense, and another long moment passed while they stood on Michigan Avenue in the middle of Chicago's bustling commerce area, staring at each other, while the crowds hurried by. It was as if the world had stopped and only the two of them were left on the planet, so intense was the exchange of unvoiced emotion. It was Bessie who lowered her eyes first, as color rose up from her neck to her cheeks, and she felt her face on fire.

Jeremy broke the spell, propelling her into the shoppe door, and addressed the flustered sales lady inside, who had witnessed the exchange beyond the window.

"Madam," he said, "we wish—that is, the lady wishes to purchase the exquisite hat you have on display in the window."

"Of course, Sir," she smiled knowingly, and sailed effortlessly across the shoppe's wooden floor to retrieve the prize, placing it into Bessie's shaking hands. "There is a looking glass on the counter, Madame."

Bessie carefully placed the hat on her head, adjusting it a couple of times before she was satisfied, and then turned so Jeremy could see her face. He was dumbstruck, for there could have been no lovelier a creature on the face of the earth than the one standing before him at that very moment. All he could do was suck in his breath and stare at the exquisite sight Bessie made as she held her head slightly aside, allowing the full sweep of the brim to totally surround her head. The hat sat cocked a little to one side, accenting the dark beauty of her brows and hair.

"Bessie," he managed to say, his voice cracking a bit, "you are the most beautiful creature I have ever laid eyes on!"

"Please, Jeremy, you are embarrassing me," she smiled, glancing nervously at the shoppe mistress, shyly dropping her eyes, and her cheeks turned the color of the hat.

"Would Madame care for the matching parasol to go with this?"

Bessie shook her head in a negative manner, but Jeremy stepped forward and emphatically agreed, whereby the sales lady produced a white lace parasol elaborately embellished with matching pink roses.

"There! That is perfect," Jeremy said, as Bessie put the open parasol over her shoulder and smiled shyly. He quickly paid the delighted sales lady and steered Bessie out the door onto Michigan Avenue, proudly pulling her hand into the crook of his arm. A horse drawn trolley went by, and he was pleased to see the stares of those on board as women whispered to each other.

"Jeremy, I should not have accepted such a gift, and cannot repay you for it," Bessie was trying to say, but he hushed her, leaning close to put a finger against her lips.

"Just to see you in this beautiful chapeau is payment enough for me," he uttered, and smiled at her with such delight that she knew he meant what he said.

Spying another shop across the street, he directed Bessie to cross with him. They entered a photography studio where Jeremy immediately engaged the startled shopkeeper behind the counter.

"Hurry up, man, get your equipment, lest you miss the greatest portrait you shall ever take!"

The photographer fumbled with his tripod, camera, and flash-pod, obviously nervous at Jeremy's insistent orders. Bessie was directed to sit on a bench in front of a dark canvas backdrop, and she could not help but laugh and make playful, self-conscious faces at Jeremy.

"Please, Madam," the photographer pleaded, "sit still."

Then he disappeared underneath a black cloth as Bessie turned her profile to him, trying to wipe the grin off her face. Just as she turned her head back to the camera, pooff! The powder flashed, catching her solemn profile three-quarters of the way turned, the pink hat curved perfectly to frame her face.

"Please turn to the camera, Madam," he instructed, setting up for another try.

Bessie obliged, attempting to hold an unnatural pose. This time she blinked at the flash. Slightly upset, the photographer suggested that Jeremy join the lady in a double portrait.

Jeremy declined. "I would not dare to ruin the lady's beauty," he said, smiling, and to himself added that there could never be anyone so lovely in all the world as the one who sat before him now.

Bessie glanced to her left at Jeremy, and let her shoulders relax. She simply gazed at him, and only a soft upturn of the corners of her mouth suggested the beginnings of a smile. Her eyes mellowed at his warm returning gaze, and she hid the wonder and questions beginning in her mind.

Pooff! The flash powder exploded again.

"Very good, Madam. Very good!"

"When may we see the results?" Jeremy asked.

"Give me three days, Sir. I shall have them ready for you in three days."

Jeremy vowed to return on Friday, and slipped the man a tip. "Take great care in your developing, my man, for you have a masterpiece here!"

Next, much to Bessie's surprise, it was back to the World's Colombian Exhibition. Jeremy was not about to let the opportunity slip by where he could proudly stroll arm in arm with the statuesque Bessie on his arm, to show her off to the widest audience. At first, she was self-conscious, but soon, bolstered by Jeremy's calm presence, she held her head high, and had a wide smile on her face. Heads turned to follow this beauty in the shocking pink hat. Surely it must be a celebrity of some kind, the tongues wagged, but none could recognize her.

The pair passed by the monstrous ferris wheel on the Midway Plaisance, and paused at the giant carousel. This was as equally magnificent as the ferris wheel, but in a lesser venue. The carousel was topped by a red and green canopy, and a steam calliope blared a variety of current tunes, setting an almost surreal scene by the little puffs of steam misting to obscure the gilded pipes. There, Jeremy lifted Bessie sidesaddle onto the back of one of the dozens of hand carved life-sized animals. It was a proud white stallion embellished with pink, gilt, and yellow flowers entwined in the flowing mane and tail. The steed's arching neck and flaring nostrils were almost realistic.

Dazzling gilt baroque carvings embellished flashing mirrors and the ornate carved wooden animals rose and fell in a rhythmic motion as the huge platform whirled around to the calliope music. Bessie was on the outside horse, and threw back her head, laughing like a delighted child as she rose and fell, up and down, up and down, each time, the sensation tickling her tummy. Jeremy stood by her side, holding on to her waist as they sped around the perimeter, grinning at her delight. People in the crowd gathered around the outside of the carousel to watch as the strikingly lovely girl in the huge pink hat sped past.

All the men in the audience envied the handsome man who accompanied her, and the ladies fairly swooned with longing to own the pink hat she wore. There was no question that Bessie was a true vision in white, sitting upon the white horse, and the pink of her hat blended with the floral decorations adorning the animal she rode, as if each had been made for the other. At one point, the poof of a camera's flash powder went off as they whirled around, and a photographer from a New York publication nodded in satisfaction, convinced he had captured the perfect picture for his rotogravure.

When the ride ended, Jeremy got a ticket again for them to remain on, and this time mounted the black horse next to Bessie's. They held hands then, stretching to reach as one rose up, and the other down. His eyes never left hers, as he watched her, memorizing every feature of her face, to burn into his mind every curve, every dimple, every whisp of hair. She returned his gaze with warmth in her eyes, and tried to read his thoughts, but could not. The ostrich feathers of her hat ruffled in the breeze as they whirled, and Jeremy's heart grew warm within him, as he remained holding her hand in his, thrilling at her touch.

All too soon, the ride ended once more, and this time he dismounted and lifted her off the white horse, which had stopped in the highest position. As Jeremy lifted her, Bessie fell against him, and he found his lips close to hers as she slid slowly to the ground. For a long moment, they looked into each other's eyes, while he continued to hold her close, and a thousand thoughts raced through each of their minds, until Bessie broke the spell when she felt a flush rise to her cheeks.

They paused at the next stand close to the carousel, and with the music of the steam calliope still fresh in their ears, blaring out "By the Light of the Silvery Moon," Jeremy stopped and purchased a beautiful, cobalt blue commemorative glass rolling pin. It was adorned with white and pink flowers, and small letters proclaimed "Remember Me." The object was tied with a pink moire, ribbon. He presented it to Bessie, saying "For you, my pink angel, to remember this day."

"Oh, Jeremy! It's beautiful! But I don't need a souvenir to remind me, I shall remember this day forever!"

There was a shy boldness to her statement, a hint of a promise for the future in her soft reply. "Thank you, thank you," she breathed.

Bessie was thrilled with the extravagantly beautiful rolling pin, and clutched it to her breast, afraid, almost, to hold it, for all its fragility, fearing she would break it by merely breathing. If Jeremy dared at that moment, he would have bent to kiss to kiss her lips, but chose instead to kiss her cheek, sending the blood to flush her face in a charming way, and she smiled broadly at him.

PART IV

Bessie was in such a state of excitement later that evening, that she could hardly contain herself, and wondered if she had dreamed the whole wonderful day. It was difficult to suppress her exuberance in front of Jessie, yet she hoped that her sister would not guess the object of her excitement.

"My gracious, Bessie, but you are in a rare mood this night. I haven't seen you look so happy and excited, forever, it seems. What brings this all about?"

Bessie blushed. "I had—just a fine day. I think I can be happy, can I not?"

"Of course, you silly! But something extraordinary must have occurred to trigger such a reaction. You look absolutely radiant!" Jessie mused, as they sat sipping after dinner coffee. She peered closely at her younger sister, surmising that a man must be involved, for Jessie's years of experience could lead to no other conclusion. Only the attention of a man could bring a glow to a girl's face such as Bessie now displayed, sitting there on the other side of the table. Even the subdued light of an oil lamp could not diminish the sparkle in her eyes, nor the color that flushed her face.

"Oh, all right," Bessie sighed, smiling broadly, sending a flash of white teeth Jessie's way. "I will show you."

She disappeared into another room, to reappear moments later wearing, at a jaunty angle, the pink creation that Jeremy had purchased for her. Jessie's jaw dropped open, and she gasped at the mound of pink organdy and lace which Bessie proudly wore. The girl's eyes fairly danced as she sought Jessie's reaction.

"Do you like it, Jess?"

For a moment, Jessie was speechless for this flamboyant creation was not what she would have expected her conservative sister to choose. Nonetheless, it seemed to fit her to a tee, framing her dark locks with an exquisite elegance that transformed her into an absolute beauty.

"Bessie," Jessie whispered in awe. "It is the most beautiful—you are—you are simply ravishing in that hat! Where did you—how—?"

"Sorry, Jess. My secret," Bessie smiled and popped open the parasol, casually cocking it over her shoulder. No amount of prodding could drag from Bessie's lips the origin of the hat, so Jessie finally gave up trying. It was not until days later that the woman put the pieces together. One thing Bessie did not reveal, however, was about the glass rolling pin, preferring to keep that as a treasure that only she and Jeremy shared.

The following day, after Jessie had left for her position at Carson's, Jeremy arrived at the flat precisely at nine, per their conversation the preceding afternoon. They were embarking upon an all day outing, which Jeremy promised would be a mystery. Regardless of how much she pleaded for him to tell her of his plans, he slyly refused to even give a hint.

He simply said, "Bessie, please wear the hat!" as they were about to leave.

"Don't you think it might be a bit too pretentious?"

"Not in the least. I want you to wear it every day we are together, everywhere! You are so beautiful, and it crowns your beauty like a tiara."

Bessie blushed again. "Please, Mr. Greene, you are embarrassing me."

"Mr. Greene? I thought you were to call me by my given name?"

"I'm sorry, Jeremy."

She returned shortly with the pink hat towering upon her dark tresses, the parasol tucked under her arm. Sunlight streaming through a window silhouetted her figure, and

Jeremy thought he was seeing an ethereal vision emerge from a mist. His heart skipped a beat at the sight of her, and he loved her more at that instant than he ever thought possible.

Yes, he was in love—wildly in love—deeply in love, not only because she was such a stunning beauty on the outside, but, more importantly, she was beautiful in her inner essence. The pure innocence of this young woman's soul, her compassion, her quiet strength, all delightfully combined to send him to the heights of love that knew no bounds, until he felt his chest was almost bursting.

The day turned out to be like no other. A deliciously warm summer day, with azure blue skies, and a soft breeze that stirred the leaves of the trees in little flutters. Jeremy had chosen to hire a rowboat on the large lagoon in the park, and they spent hours slowly drifting along the darkened waters, chatting and laughing. Bessie sat in the stern of the boat, the skirts of her summer dress spreading about her ankles, shading the pink hat with her parasol. They took turns reading from a little book of poetry, each falling deeper and deeper in love with the other, all the while.

From time to time, she trailed her fingers in the placid water, and once playfully flicked some droplets at Jeremy, laughing as she did so. As he dodged the sprinkles, and smiled broadly back at her, Bessie knew by the warm look in his eyes that she had fallen desperately in love with this man, whom she had known for such a short time. As for Jeremy, he could not believe his good fortune, discovering the love he now felt for his Angel in Pink, as he called her.

> Awake, my soul! Not only passive praise
> Thou knowest not alone these swelling tears,
> Mute thanks, and secret ecstasy. Awake,
> Voice of sweet song! Awake, my heart, awake!

Jeremy read to her, as they drifted lazily along, his deep voice resonant in the stillness of the lagoon, oblivious of all the other boaters, aware only of each other. A pair of white swans rode the gentle swells, effortlessly gliding with but a push of one webbed foot at a time, arching their graceful necks, eyeing the couple with an almost knowing look. Little noises of songbirds twittering in the trees were as a soft symphony accompaniment to the poetry Jeremy read.

> A wind came up out of the sea
> And said, 'Oh, mists, make room for me!',
> It hailed the ships and cried, 'Sail on,

Ye mariners! The night is gone!

Bessie's heart filled her breast with a spreading glow of warmth and tingling, as she listened to Jeremy's low, soft voice rise and fall as he read various verses from the little book. From time to time, their eyes met, and Bessie dared hope that what she saw so deep in his mellowing eyes upon hers was a kindle of love, a spark, a wish, a dream.

> She wept with pity and delight --
> She blushed with love, and virgin shame,
> And like a murmur of a dream,
> I heard her breathe my name.

Jeremy continued as they reclined at water's edge on the shore, under the graceful trailing branches of a weeping willow tree. There they had consumed the edibles from the wicker basket Jeremy had so thoughtfully provided. He was coatless, and had rolled up the sleeves of his shirt to mid-arm, as he continued to read.

> Twas partly love, partly fear,
> And partly 'twas a bashful art,
> That I might rather feel, than see,
> The swelling of her heart.

He stopped then, and gazed with unflinching eyes at Bessie, who sat with her back resting against the trunk of the willow tree, letting Jeremy's words sink into her soul. She had removed the pink hat, and stray locks of her dark hair softly brushed her face. Jeremy was propped upon one elbow, close to her side, as he read, and was near enough to smell the faint lilac scent of her cologne. A gentle breeze fluttered the folds of her sheer skirt against his arm, like the touch of an angel's wing, sending gooseflesh along the length of his body.

"Bessie," he breathed, and tentatively put his hand at the back of her head, and slowly, gently, drew her face to his. "Bessie." It was a sigh, which she barely heard. He saw her lips tremble as they neared his, and cautiously, she allowed him to kiss her cheek, shyly averting her lips. Yet she did not pull away, and he gradually kissed her cheek again, and again, each time edging his lips closer to her own, until they finally engulfed her tremulous mouth, and his kiss was like fire.

Bessie put a shy hand upon his shoulder, and tilted her head once more, to accept another kiss from him, this time boldly kissing him back, throwing caution and impropriety to the winds. Jeremy's very touch sent her heart beating wildly, and she felt a deep surging within her. She could feel the intensity of his mouth as it encircled her full lips, and thrilled at the warmth of him. She felt the masculine whiskers of his mustache as his mouth worked against hers, and she then put both arms around his neck, shamelessly returning his passionate kisses with a desire of her own.

As he held her close, with his mouth against her ear, he whispered, "Bessie, I love you!"

The very feel of him crushing her to his chest sent her senses reeling, and Bessie clutched him, never wishing to let him go. Tears welled in her eyes, and she struggled to speak, her voice cracking with emotion, as every inch of her burst with the sensation of love.

"I love you, too, Jeremy," she breathed, "I love you Oh! I love you!"

"Bessie, my angel—my love—my Angel in Pink!"

He pulled back, cupped her face in his hands, and looked deeply into her tear moistened eyes. Then he brought her lips to his once more, and kissed her long, with a sensuousness that sent Bessie spinning. His lips were warm, working, tasting the sweetness of her mouth.

Later, the golden shafts of the low afternoon sun glinted upon the waters, shimmering on tiny ripples as Jeremy slowly pulled on the oars to send their boat silently back into the lagoon. Bessie watched as the oars dipped into the water, leaving little whirlpools at each stroke, and felt her heart swirl in its own whirlpool of newly discovered love. When he lifted the oars, the sun caught small droplets glistening off the paddles like shimmering garlands of gold.

Bessie would remember forever the sights, the sounds, the smells of this day, and wished with all her heart it would never end. Basking in the glow of new-found love heightened her every sense. Sounds were more melodious, and she clearly heard the sweet calling of early evening birds. It was as though they were singing just for her, swelling her heart with love. The trees were the color of precious emeralds, sparkling with clarity, shape, and form. She noticed that the late sun played like the glow of a magic lantern upon Jeremy's face, accenting his angular features, and glinted copper off his hatless head.

He smiled a secret smile at her, and winked.

"Read to me, my Angel," his voice was low and dreamy, sending her thrilling again at the thought of his love.

Bessie opened the book at random. "Thomas Moore—" she quoted,

She is far from the land where her young hero sleeps.

And lovers around her are sighing;
But coldly she turns from their gaze and weeps,
For her heart in his grave is lying.
Oh! make her a grave where the sunbeams rest,
When they promise a glorious 'morrow;
They'll shine o'er her sleep like a smile from the west,
From her own loved island of sorrow.

Bessie's eyes welled at the words of the star-crossed lovers, and she felt a lump in her throat, constricting it tightly, as she pictured the sorrow of the young maiden. Jeremy was touched by her tenderness, and urged her to read another.

"From Shakespeare,"

How sweet the moonlight sleeps upon this bank?
Here we will sit, and let the sounds of music
Creep into our ears: soft stillness, and the night,
Become the touches of sweet harmony.

Bessie's voice was like a musical bell to Jeremy's ears, and he savored each line she quoted, never taking his eyes from her face. With each stroke of the oars, his love for her deepened until he was bursting from within. Bessie, my Angel, Bessie, the oars seemed to whisper in their rhythmic cadence as they dipped in and out of the water.

"Here's one you'll like," Bessie said as she flipped through the pages. "It's called 'The Phantom Ship,' by Elizabeth Oakes Smith," and she began reciting verse after verse, ending with

> And many a hearty seaman,
> who fears storm nor fight,
> Yet trembles when the Phantom Ship
> drives past his watch at night
> For it augers death and danger:
> it bades a watery grave,
> With seaweeds for his pillow --
> for his shroud a wandering wave.

A sudden chill sent a shiver through Bessie as she read the last words, as if a prophecy had been spoken, and a premonition shuddered through her. She closed the book, unable to look at Jeremy, for her eyes were dim with tears. *Jeremy, my love no, not you, Jeremy, not you. Not a watery grave for you.* It was a prayer, silent upon her lips—a wish—a hope—a command.

Chapter 14

Jennifer sat in stunned silence, waiting for her Aunt to continue. "What happened, Aunt Bessie?" she asked in a faint whisper.

The older woman shook herself back to the present, a tear glistening in her old eyes, shining behind her glasses.

"We had five wonderful days together. Then Will returned, and both he and Jeremy headed for New York. Jeremy asked me to meet him in San Francisco in six months when their ship was due to arrive from its journey around the horn. He told me that he would then claim me as his bride, and he would quit the sea forever."

"And did you go to San Francisco?"

Bessie nodded. "As it turned out, Jessie had an opportunity to manage a department in a new Carson's store that was opening in the city, and she begged me to travel with her. I struggled with the thought for a long time, wondering if I should follow my heart's desire, or stay with my responsibility in Waterville. It was a hard decision, for I knew that father needed me. But circumstances finally allowed me to follow my heart, when a cousin of mine agreed to look after Papa. So I wrote to Jeremy before he sailed and said I would be waiting for him in San Francisco."

There was such a long silence, that Jennifer grew concerned. She never saw such an expression on the woman's face before, and suddenly, Aunt Bessie looked old, tired, and dejected.

"Before I left Waterville, a big package arrived by Railway Express from Chicago. It was the hand-tinted portrait that had been taken—you know, the one in the big pink hat. It was the exposure where I had just glanced over at Jeremy and saw love and admiration in his eyes as he gazed back at me. Jeremy had instructed the photographer to send the portrait to me. He sent a note along with it."

With that, Aunt Bessie fumbled in her pocket, and brought out an old folded piece of yellowed paper. She tried to read it out loud, but could not, for the tears in her eyes fogged her vision. She then handed it to Jennifer with trembling fingers, and the young woman began to read out loud:

"My Angel in Pink," it began. "Hold this portrait for me until I return to you in California. Then, *we* shall hang it on the wall of *our* home so it can be seen from every room! I have a miniature of the same to carry next to my heart. It will forever remind me of our love. I love you, Bessie, as no one has ever loved before, nor can ever love again.

What we share is of eternity—at one with the stars—the moon—the heavens!"

Jennifer hesitated momentarily before continuing.

"I shall fly to you as I sail on the Clipper Ship, my Angel, catching the swiftest of winds, knowing that you will be awaiting my arrival in San Francisco. Oh, then to hold you, and to kiss you once again will be my dream. For me, please be wearing the pink hat and hold dear the glass rolling pin. Do not allow it to break, because it symbolizes our love for each other. It reminds me of how we met at the Chicago World's Colombian Exhibition, and the carousel ride, when I first knew I loved you. I loved you then. I love you now. I will love you tomorrow and all the tomorrows to come. You are my angel, my Angel in Pink—my life, my love—my hopes, my dreams—my forever." It was signed Jeremy.

Jennifer had to wipe a tear from the corner of her own eye as she finished and returned the note to her Aunt Bessie. She waited patiently for the older woman to complete her story.

"I waited and waited," Bessie whispered hoarsely. "Every day, I wore the pink hat, and went to the wharf, hoping his ship would arrive. It never did. Months went by, even long after the Clipper he and Will were on was scheduled to arrive. Finally, the shipping line, which owned the ship, pronounced that it had officially been lost at sea, presumably the victim of a violent storm, probably around the horn. All hands were pronounced lost."

"Oh, Aunt Bessie!"

Bessie sighed deeply, a sob caught in her throat. "He was the one true love of my life, Jennifer. My eternity. I could never love another." Her voice sounded broken.

"And of course, your brother, William perished also?"

"Yes, Dear. Little did I know when I read that poem of the Phantom ship that it was an omen. Yet, somehow, I knew deep in my heart that tragedy lay ahead."

"And then you returned to Wisconsin?"

"Only after several years. I stayed in San Francisco until, unfortunately, more tragedy occurred with the Earthquake that hit in 1906. My dear sister, Jessie, died in the quake, and I was left with only rubble for a home. I don't know how, but the portrait, and the glass rolling pin survived the quake. The pink hat did not."

Then, with nothing for her there, Bessie had returned to Waterville, and taken over the care of her ailing father, who by that time was going blind. She became his right hand, his angel of mercy, devoting herself to him around the clock. After his passing at age eighty-eight, she was determined to spend her life, not in grief and self pity for what might have been, but in service to anyone who needed her helping hand. She had known the highest form of love, and it miraculously opened her heart and soul to the greater things in life's scheme.

Bessie became known as the Angel of Waterville to everyone in that small community, lending a tireless hand to those who could not do for themselves, even anonymously at times, funding needs from her own meager savings.

"I wanted you to know dear, that at one time, I too was young. I, too, knew the joy of being in love. I don't want you to only know me as an old lady, I want you to remember me as I once was. Young and vital—alive, and bursting with the miracle of love."

With a lump in her throat, Jennifer bent to embrace her aunt. She found the older woman suddenly weakened and frail, as if all the strength that she possessed had been drained from her body.

"Whatever it is that is troubling you now, Jennifer, follow your heart!" Bessie said as she looked her grand-niece knowingly in the eye. "Follow your heart! For, even though the days ahead may be many, the future could spring a surprise or two, and the days for true love can be cut short in a fleeting moment. When you live as long as I have, you will realize how time flies by so swiftly. Follow your heart, Dear, wherever it takes you, for you may never have another chance at what you have today. The future may be like a robber in the dark, stealing away your love like a mysterious thief. It is never wrong to love—take it while you can. Follow your heart, dear."

The following day, after Jennifer had said a tearful good-bye to her Aunt Bessie, she headed for the bus depot at The Dairyland, laden with her suitcase and the box containing the fragile blue glass rolling pin. Despite Jennifer's protestations, Aunt Bessie had insisted that the girl take the pin, whispering to her to remember the love that it represented. Jennifer promised to guard it always, and assured her aunt that she would never forget the story of Jeremy Greene.

To her surprise, Ralph Warren was waiting at The Dairyland Cafe.

"I thought I might find you here," he said, reaching to take the suitcase from her hand. He put it in the back seat of the '61 T-Bird.

"What are you doing?" Jennifer demanded, disturbed at his actions.

"I want you to stay, Jenny."

"I can't, Ralph. I have a flight to catch at O'Hare this evening."

"But you haven't finished your job."

"What job?"

"About the Herrington Inn."

Jennifer frowned, still not following him.

"You know, Aunt Bessie's house. You promised to help with the decorating, remember?"

"Yes, Ralph, I did, but that can be months, or years away yet, after you get all the remodeling done." Her voice was cool and distant.

"Then at least let me drive you down to Chicago to the airport. Please, Jenny. We need to talk."

Reluctantly, Jennifer climbed into the passenger side of the T-Bird, holding Aunt Bessie's rolling pin box on her lap. The top was up on the convertible now, for clouds were rolling in, promising rain. It occurred to her on the way to the airport that she had arrived in such weather just a couple of weeks ago. Somehow, the young woman felt her life had changed upside down in those two short weeks. All the comfortable routine that she had known now seemed scrambled and disjointed.

She tried to picture Donald, and her life in Phoenix, but just could not get the picture in her mind, nor reconcile the fact she would be returning to pick up her life there as she had known it. *How could she pick it up as if nothing had happened here? EVERYTHING had happened here in Wisconsin! Nothing was the same.* It was as if she were leading two lives, and the two could not be melded.

"What time is your flight?" Ralph was asking, as he drove down the freeway through the rolling farmland.

"Six forty-five," she answered, acutely aware of his warm presence beside her. He was driving with his right hand on the steering wheel, the left still encased in the cast. She wanted to reach out to touch his arm, to feel the muscles and sinews that worked as he drove, longing to feel the flesh of him—even feel his arms around her.

"Jenny, you will be coming back, won't you?"

"I don't know, Ralph."

"But I need you, Jenny!" Because he couldn't live without her, he wanted to shout.

"You don't need me, Ralph. Anybody can pull that Inn together." *Try one of your bimbos*, she thought viciously. *Why does he have to be so damned handsome?* she wondered, glancing at his profile, studying it to blaze it into her memory for all time.

"No, Jenny. It's your touch that will make it. You have a great talent, you know."

They drove on in silence for awhile, the low gray clouds echoing Jennifer's mood. Soon Ralph had to turn on the windshield wipers, and Jennifer mentally hummed a sad song to the slap-slap-slap beat of the wipers.

"Jenny, I can't lose you now, after all these years, not after just finding you again. Please!" He pleaded as they were about to part at the terminal.

The loudspeaker announced the boarding of her flight, and she rose to go through the gate. Ralph grabbed her, whirling her to him.

"Jenny, whatever is bothering you, if I have said anything—done anything, please! I am sorry!"

Her eyes filled with tears, and she felt as if she were being strangled. The love of her heart—the love of her life—was standing there before her. All the hopes, the dreams, the yearning she once had, and still had, were wrapped into the man who was pleading with her, trying to detain her one more minute. Soon she would be gone, and her heart ached already for the loss, for what might have been.

"Good-bye, Ralph," she whispered through her tears.

He tilted her chin up, and kissed her, trying to hold back the choking in his own throat. His lips were warm and hard against hers, moving, tasting. She broke away then, and turned to go. He held on to her arm, whirling her forcibly around once again, and gathered her in his arms.

"Jenny! Jenny, my God! Don't go! I love you!" he said, his voice low and resonant.

She looked at him, startled, wondering if she had heard him correctly. Did he really say the words she had been longing to hear for years? *Could it be? Did he say he loved me?*

"I've always loved you, Jenny, always! My God! Don't leave—don't leave me! Stay with me!" He was in anguish now, writhing inside with the knowledge that she was about to walk out of his life forever.

Tears welled in her eyes, and she let them roll down her cheeks. She slowly shook her head and barely squeaked, "I can't. I must go."

"Jenny! I love you!" he breathed, and kissed her salty lips for the last time.

She whirled away quickly and almost ran down the ramp, turning at the door to the jetway, trying to stem the sobs that wracked her body. Ralph was looking at her with a pathetic, lost expression, pain clearly visible in his eyes, and his shoulders sagged dejectedly. For a moment she thought about turning back, but instead, mouthed the words, "I love you," blew a kiss with her fingertips, then disappeared into the plane.

Chapter 15

On a cold December day, almost three years later, Jennifer was putting the final touches on the holiday decorations of the Pink Angel Inn, the name by which the old Herrington house was now known. A crisp, gray and white cut-out sign out front proclaimed the name proudly and swung in the harsh wind swirling snow across the front lawn, coating everything in blankets of white. Inside, she stepped back from the fireplace mantle in the parlor, satisfied that the garland of greens hung just right, and straightened the last ribbon that fastened the end.

A huge, glittering tree standing in one corner was festooned with gold and burgundy decorations, matching the Victorian wallpaper in the formal room. Everywhere, candles and greens, shiny ornaments, ribbons, and pine cones added particular warmth to the charming decor that Jennifer had painstakingly spent months achieving, capturing the essence and romance of the old house.

The long awaited first guests were due to arrive on the 24th, just two days away, for the official Grand Opening of the Pink Angel Inn, named for the portrait of Bessie Herrington, which now hung predominantly in the entry hall. Bessie's haunting beauty, in the towering 1890's hat, was sure to be a point of conversation among the guests as the printed color brochures were already suggesting. An air of mystery was written in the publicity text. It hinted at love found and love lost.

Jennifer paused in the hallway and adjusted the portrait slightly, cocking her head to be sure the picture was hanging straight. A soft portrait light lit the picture to bring out its most vivid colors. A small engraved brass plate attached to the elaborate frame was inscribed simply, "Pink Angel" in discreet script lettering.

Underneath the portrait, mounted in its own protective acrylic box, was the cobalt blue glass rolling pin, Jeremy's parting gift to Bessie so many years ago. Now it had its own place of honor along with the owner's beautiful portrait.

"I'm sorry you won't be here, Aunt Bessie," Jennifer said to no one, for on this day she was alone in the house. "You would have loved how the house turned out."

She fondly remembered how strong and vibrant her Aunt had been, and could hardly believe that more than a year had passed since her death. Now she would be remembered far into the future with the opening of her homestead, named after Jeremy's pet name for her. Jennifer was pleased that the romantic legend of Bessie and Jeremy's love story would live on in the Pink Angel Bed and Breakfast Inn. Already, publicity about the pair had provoked unusual interest, including interviews by the editors of the travel sections of the *Chicago Tribune* and the *Milwaukee Journal*.

The dining room had already been set up with three tables, laden with crackling white starched linens, polished silver, and sparkling crystal. All was in readiness for the guests, and Jennifer breathed a sigh of relief, looking forward to tomorrow, which promised to be a day of relaxation after her weeks and months of intense work. She had tended to all the minute details of turning the big old house into the sparklingly decorative restoration it had become.

It had literally taken years to remodel the house and acquire all the antique furnishings which embellished it. Five upstairs bedrooms had been carefully restored to their original 1800's decor. Fine wood armoires, big old wood or brass beds, tables and comfortable chairs for lounging or reading graced each room. The color schemes were derived from numerous hand-stitched old quilts, which were used as wall hangings, bed toppers, or simply folded, warm and inviting, on shelves in the armoires.

Red and white, blue, yellow, and green distinguished the various guest rooms. The largest bedroom, facing the street and encompassing the rounded turret section of the house, was designated the "Pink Angel Suite." Jennifer had turned that room into a fairy tale of pink velvet, and swathed it in sheer pink fabric, floral wallpaper, lace and ribbons. It was a romantic haven to rival the best anywhere.

She had opted to use several smaller tables in the formal dining room, making it more intimate for the guests, instead of one massive table. Jennifer planned to use the library off the main parlor as a place for informal coffees and teas, with cozy seating arrangements before a marble fireplace. Overstuffed chairs and loveseats were arranged in the parlor for intimate seating where guests could sit and simply relax and read, or chat in small groups.

Jennifer jumped as the telephone rang, startling her back to the present.

"Mrs. Warren?" the caller began.

"Yes, this is Mrs. Warren."

"I'm sorry to bother you, Mrs. Warren," The voice on the other end sounded hesitant and serious. "This is Hugh Lyon from Lyon's Aviation. Ralph's charter flight is overdue, and I don't want to worry you, but it seems we have lost contact. He did not clear the check point."

Jennifer sat down suddenly, all the blood draining from her face, and she felt faint.

"You all right, Mrs. Warren?"

"Yes, Hugh," she managed to say. "But I'm afraid you have wrong information. Ralph was scheduled on his routine American Airlines flight out of Chicago this morning."

Hardly able to disguise the concern in his voice, Hugh Lyon continued, "He had a charter flight from Madison to Duluth, taking some emergency medical equipment to the hospital up there."

"But when he left this morning, he was going on his regular commercial route out of Chicago. You must be mistaken!" Jennifer insisted.

"When he got here to fly his private plane down to O'Hare, he checked with the airline and switched flights with another pilot so he could surprise you and be home for Christmas Eve. I guess he didn't tell you. While he was here, this emergency came up, and he volunteered to fly the equipment up in his plane. He must not have let you know about the switch."

Jennifer was numb, barely hearing or understanding the man on the other end of the line.

"We know Ralph left Duluth on the return flight, but there was some bad weather around

Lake Superior, and the tower lost contact twenty minutes out."

He could hear a choking sound on the other end of the line. "Mrs. Warren? Now, don't worry. It is possible he just ran into some little trouble, like maybe his radio quit, or something. Maybe he had to make an emergency landing. They have sent out a search plane already."

"Do you think so, Hugh?"

"Of course, Mrs. Warren. I'll keep you informed as soon as I hear anything."

"Thank you," Jennifer said faintly, hardly able to speak. She was strangling—trembling—suddenly nauseous. Her legs gave way, and she sank to the floor.

"Ralph! It cannot end like this!" Jennifer cried, "not after the events of the last three years. No— not now! I'm not ready—I'm not ready to lose you," she sobbed.

So much had transpired in those three short years, that it all seemed like a jumble in her mind. Jennifer had tried to blot out the horrible memories of her return to Phoenix where she had found Don in a state of despair. Business reversals had sent him into a deep depression. Despite months of therapy, counseling and medications, and trying everything she could do to help, nothing worked.

She had tried to keep the business afloat, tried in vain to help her husband's depression, even at the risk of her own health, and it became almost too much to bear. She also tried to overcome the horrid, lonely yearning of her own heart at the loss of her ties to her first love. Even though she had not had any contact with Ralph after she left Wisconsin, in her heart he was vividly alive, and she relived his parting words over and over, when he told her that he loved her.

Somehow, it had soothed her to know that finally Ralph had admitted his love for her. Even though she could not, and would not act upon her desires, it was enough that she knew he loved her, too. Instead, Jennifer chose to bury all the impulses and threw herself into the duties of her marriage commitment to Donald and their life together.

The crowning blow had come at dawn one morning when she discovered Don, lifeless, in his car, a revolver beside him. How she had survived the next few months, she could not even remember. Everything blurred together, and thankfully, shock of the tragedy erased the details from her memory. Jennifer had her own sense of guilt that she had not been able to rouse Don from his depression, and even though she knew better, somehow she thought that it had been all her fault.

When several months after his death, a call had come telling of Aunt Bessie passing away, and that she, Jennifer, had been designated as the Executrix of the estate, she moved back to Waterville for good. There, she put Don's suicide and her life in Arizona completely behind her. Don's two girls were already on their own, and had given her their blessings on the move.

Ralph had been there, waiting for her, as she had hoped he would be, never having dated anyone else from the time she had left. He could not, he had told her, for his heart was always with her and always would be, come what may. No matter if he had lost her forever, no one else could possibly take her place. He had relegated himself to permanent bachelorhood, vowing he would remain faithful to her memory for the rest of his life.

Even after Jennifer returned to Waterville, they had taken up their lives together very slowly, making sure that what they had together was pure love, though each knew it could be no other. It was not until August, two years to the day of the thunderstorm on Blackhawk's Isle, that they were married on the very spot. Patty and James had come from Iowa to attend them as they repeated their vows that summer day, under the gazebo which Ralph had built on the bluff above the cave.

A crisp sun sparkled off the ripples on the lake that day, dappling across the lawn in front of the new log cabin Ralph had built on the highest point of the isle. Down below, his rented seaplane bobbed at its mooring place next to the wooden pier at the bottom of a long staircase. Ralph had flown the four of them and the minister in at noon for the four o'clock ceremony.

Jennifer had dressed in soft yellow, with a wreath of yellow and white flowers woven into her hair as she stood beside Ralph under the flower-decked gazebo. He had stood proud, tall and slim at her side, dressed in dark trousers and the white, short sleeved Captain's airline uniform shirt which Jennifer insisted he wear. She liked to see him in uniform, never tiring of how handsome he appeared.

After the vows, the champagne toast, and the wedding dinner of steaks grilled on the charcoal grill, Ralph had ferried Patty, James, and the minister back to the river outside of town, where the had left their automobiles. While he did so, Jennifer had changed into slacks and a tee-shirt. As she brushed her hair, she heard the soft throb of the seaplane motors in the distance and ran down the stair steps to the pier. She watched as Ralph settled the craft gently down onto the water, sending a rooster tail of spray to sparkle gold in the late afternoon sun as he taxied to the pier.

"Welcome home, Captain Warren," Jennifer smiled, as she embraced her new husband. They went up the steps arm-in-arm.

"Thank you, Mrs. Warren. Mrs. Warren! Do you know how great that sounds?" he said and stopped to kiss her.

When they approached the cabin, he lifted her into his arms to carry her in the front door.

"Wait," she said. "Put me down."

"Jenny, what are you up to?"

She took hold of his hand and led him down the path on the side of the bluff to the entrance of the cave.

"Now you can carry me," she grinned.

His eyes mellowed and crinkled at the corners as he smiled at her, then lifted her into his arms. "You remembered," he said as he gave her a long kiss.

She nodded. "I want our first night together to be here, where we made love all night so long ago. This time, I even brought down some creature comforts. Blankets and pillows!"

"Jenny, oh, my sweet Jenny!" He kissed her then until she felt on fire and carried her into the cave, laying her gently upon the blanket she had spread.

Outside, the twilight wind moaned, or was it the soft, yearning wail of Blackhawk's widow?

Chapter 16

Now, as Jennifer sat in the waning winter afternoon watching the snow swirl outside the Pink Angel Inn, alone and frightened, she prayed. Prayed that Ralph had been able to land safely. Prayed that he had not crashed, or was not injured, or—worse. Tears continued to roll unchecked down her cheeks, and she tried valiantly to keep a hopeful heart, but she was losing the battle. Not knowing was the worst.

It was dark when a knock came at the door, and Jennifer braced herself as she opened the old leaded-glass door and stared at the man bundled into a big winter coat standing before her. Snowflakes clung to his hat and shoulders.

"Mrs. Warren? I'm Hugh Lyon."

"Please come in." Jennifer felt her knees weaken as she ushered the man into the soft light of the parlor.

He thoughtfully stamped the snow from his boots in the hallway before entering and took a seat in a chair where he sat awkwardly on the edge, twirling his hat in his hands.

"May I get you some tea or coffee?" she inquired, surprisingly calm, even though she knew why the man was here. Instinctively, she tried to ward off what she suspected was coming, attempting to prolong the inevitable.

Hugh Lyon shook his head. "No, thank you Mrs. Warren," and cleared his throat. He took a deep breath. "Mrs. Warren," he began, his voice husky. "We had a telephone call from the Duluth Airport."

Jennifer gripped he arms of the chair she was sitting in and felt a wave of lightheadedness sweep over her.

Hugh Lyon continued, gently. "A search plane found what they believe is the plane on the ice in Lake Superior off the Apostle Islands."

Jennifer's heart went as cold as the ice of the lake, and she felt the blood rush away from her head. She turned ashen white, and every bit of her froze.

Hugh continued, "Just before dark, it was. It appeared the plane has burned. I'm sorry, Mrs. Warren—I'm so sorry!" His voice cracked, and he wanted to reach out to the poor figure sitting before him.

Jennifer buried her face in her hands, and a sob escaped her lips. Hugh Lyon knelt on one knee in front of her, putting a comforting hand on her shoulder.

"I've known Ralph for years, Mrs. Warren. He's always kept his private plane at our aviation field. He was a good pilot—the best! He flew this mercy mission because that's the kind of guy he was. Someone was in desperate need of the special medical equipment, and Ralph never thought twice. 'I'll go,' he said, 'I'll go—'"

Jennifer nodded, still unable to speak, for the tears caught in her throat were strangling her. She barely heard what Hugh was saying.

"As soon as it is light enough, they will send out a recovery team tomorrow morning."

Jennifer heard the words as if she were a million miles away. *Recovery team—recovery of—what?* she wondered.

"Can I call someone? Can I get something for you?" he solicitously asked.

Jennifer shook her head.

"Let me get my wife, Lucy, to come stay with you."

"No," Jennifer managed to say. "No, thank you, Hugh. I'll be okay. Really. I want to be alone now. I would prefer to be alone." She said in a bare whisper.

He turned to leave. "Are you sure?"

"Yes, and thank you." Tears glistened in her eyes as she looked blankly at the man.

"As soon as I hear anything, I'll let you know." He turned to go to the door, and his heart went out to the pathetic little figure that huddled in the chair by the fireplace.

Jennifer allowed the sobs to come after Hugh Lyon had closed the door. Great, wracking sobs, that shook her until she collapsed onto the floor.

"Ralph—my love—my life! We have just begun. Oh, this is too soon—too soon!" she sobbed and buried her head in her arms. A great aching filled her, and she felt as if the very life of her had been ripped away. How could the hopes and dreams of all the tomorrows to come be dashed in one minute? Now instead of anticipating a future life together, there would only be memories. Memories of too short a time together—memories of hopes for a future that would never be.

"Oh, God!" she anguished. "Oh, God!"

A long time later, and somewhat more composed, when for the moment no more tears could come, Jennifer wandered through the house, pacing with nowhere to turn. A huge, gaping emptiness yawned inside her, and she moved like a zombie, unknowing, unseeing. Finally she ended up on her knees before the Christmas tree which stood in the grand parlor. In the hall, a grandfather clock struck ten as she watched the colored lights of the tree cast shadows like a rainbow on the walls and ceiling. Somewhere, a radio she had left on still wafted Christmas music to echo through the lonely house, and Jennifer felt her heart could break no further as waves of agony washed her through and through.

Everything reminded her of him, for his touch was throughout the house: the little spot on the ceiling where his paint brush accidentally missed, the replaced leg on a wingback chair. Even the aroma of pipe tobacco coming from the pipe stand where, occasionally, Ralph would sit contentedly to puff upon his favorite pipe, now sent stinging waves of despair through Jennifer's body.

"Oh, Ralph, my love," Jennifer whispered through the ache in her throat. She picked up a small, wrapped gift box that had lain beneath the tree, and fingered the bright ribbon attached. "Now you will never know."

Tears welled again and blurred her vision as she clutched the little box to her chest. "You will never be able to open this little gift to discover the surprise inside. I will never be able to see your eyes grow big with wonder when you see its contents." She sobbed again and again.

"My love, you never knew that years ago you and I had a son, and now you will never know that the precious little booties inside this box are to announce the child that I carry within me. You'll never see, nor hold our baby. Our baby, Ralph. You will never know that you are to become a daddy."

Jennifer rocked back and forth on her knees, still clutching the Christmas wrapped gift to her breast, while the sobs kept coming. Earlier this week the doctor had confirmed that she was eight weeks pregnant, and she had been so excited to tell Ralph. But, instead, she had decided to wrap the booties as a Christmas surprise for him to open Christmas morning. How she had looked forward to that surprise! He would have been thrilled, for they already had talked of starting a family.

"I'm forty, Jenny, for God's sake!" he had said not long ago. "Let's get on the ball. I want to see my kids grow up before I am too old."

Now, he would never get that chance, and Jenny's heart was breaking. She wandered into the kitchen to brew a cup of tea, for the winter chill had crept into the old house, "a little around the edges," as Aunt Bessie would have said. As she waited for the water to boil, Jennifer absentmindedly ran her fingers across the various rolling pins. Aunt Bessie's rolling pins which now hung individually along one kitchen wall as a focal point, thanks to Ralph's ingenuity.

These pins were sure to spark some interest to the Inn's guests in the days ahead. The legend of "The Pink Angel" would grow to be a local curiosity, Jennifer wisely surmised, and she would be proven to be right in years to come. Now, she recalled some of the stories connected to the keepsakes and wondered where the angels were which had been so much a part of Aunt Bessie's stories. Jennifer needed an angel right this very moment, more than ever before. An angel to help her through the rough days and months that lie ahead.

With a mug of hot tea in her hand, she again found herself in front of Bessie's portrait in the hall. Tears still welled in her eyes and sobs still caught in her throat as she gazed up at the likeness. With a trembling finger, she tentatively traced the face on the portrait.

"He's gone, Aunt Bessie. Just like your Jeremy. You told me to follow my heart and I did, but it has lead to only heartbreak and sorrow, just like you."

Immediately, Jennifer could feel the pain that her Aunt Bessie must have gone through. A terrible, ripping apart, as if some huge part of her had been torn from her body. She felt the emptiness, the despair, the total crushing darkness, and she wept achingly for her aunt's loss, too. She wept for her own loss, for Bessie's loss, and all the losses that anyone had ever experienced, for it seemed all romances ultimately ended in tragedy and emptiness. It crossed her mind that every love story would eventually end in loss, for no matter how many years together, one of the partners usually preceded the other in death. But normally not so young, Jennifer thought bitterly. "Not yet—we haven't had our time together, Ralph. Please, God, not yet!" she whispered.

"How can I get through this, Aunt Bessie?" Jennifer addressed the portrait. "How did you cope? How did you survive, when you must have wanted to throw yourself into the Pacific Ocean to drown, too, when you lost your love? Right this moment, all I want to do is walk out that front door, without my coat and just keep walking in the snow—to the river, or somewhere to be buried in a snowdrift to die, too!"

"Where are your angels now, Aunt Bessie? I need them. I need an angel—" she burst into tears again, clouding her vision until she could no longer see Bessie's face, nor the blue glass rolling pin.

The phone rang again. This time, Jennifer brushed her eyes with a shaking hand, lifted up the receiver and glanced at the grandfather clock in the hall. It had just struck ten-thirty. At this hour, the call could only be bad news.

"Hello," she said shakily, trying to control her voice.

The line had a fair amount of static, and the voice on the other end was faint and hard to hear.

"Mrs. Warren? This is Sheriff Olson of Bayview County."

There was such a long silence that Jennifer slid to the floor and sat propped against the wall, steeling herself for the news to come, struggling to keep conscious. This was it—this was the awful moment, the dreaded instant that she wanted to ward off.

Please, God, let it be yesterday. Let this terrible day never have happened.

Let it be yesterday, when Ralph was here, alive, loving, excited about the opening of the Inn. Let it be last night when she was safe in his arms as they cuddled together under the warm comforter of their bed in the stunning afterglow of their lovemaking.

She could picture him, even this morning, as he had left early to fly down to O'Hare to connect with his American Airlines flight. He had turned back at the door to give her a long, searching, loving glance, and had come back into the room to embrace her once more. She could still feel the strength of his arms as he had held her tight. The sensation of his kiss was still warm upon her lips. She could remember the clean scent of him—and now—now it was all gone—crushing the very life out of her.

"Mrs. Warren?" the voice on the phone repeated.

"Yes, I'm here." Her voice trembled, and she shook so violently that she had to use both hands to hold the receiver to her ear.

"Someone here wants to talk to you," the voice said.

There was a moment of silence while the telephone obviously changed hands.

"Jenny?—Jenny?" Ralph's voice was strong and anxious.

She could not speak because tears of shock and joy choked her, and Jennifer stifled a scream.

"Jenny! Are you there?"

"Yes—yes—. Oh, Ralph, is it you?" She burst out sobbing and laughing all at once.

"You'll never believe what happened," he shouted over the phone. "I belly landed the old bird on the ice. Damn near hit a fisherman's shanty. Well, I scrambled out, and then the damned thing blew up!"

"Oh, God, Ralph, my love—Are you all right?"

"I'm fine, Sweetheart. Got a bump on my head. But, Jenny, the strangest thing happened! I was in a whiteout blizzard. Didn't know where I was or which direction to turn, when, like magic, this guy appeared out of nowhere in the snow—with a dog team and sled, of all things! Well, he wrapped me up in some blankets, whisked me across the ice and dropped me off right in front of the Sheriff's Office.

When I turned around, to thank him, the man was gone! There was no trace of him or the team. No tracks or anything! The Sheriff said he had not seen anyone in hours. It was weird, Jenny!"

Jenny had a hunch and it made her heart skip a beat. "What did he look like, my love?"

"Well, it was strange. The guy had sort of sandy hair and a reddish mustache. He was wearing what appeared to be an old fashioned naval uniform. Now that I think of it, he wasn't even dressed very warmly. But his hazel eyes were what I remember most. They had such a penetrating, yet kind look in them."

"Ralph, darling! I love you!" Jennifer shouted into the receiver. She already knew who Ralph's angel was, and someday, she would be able to explain to him that Aunt Bessie's Jeremy was there with him.

"Jenny, I love you—I adore you! Sweetheart, somehow, some way, I'll find a way to get there. I promise I'll be home for Christmas Eve!"

Tears still glistened in Jennifer's eyes as she hung up the phone, and her legs still shook, but this time from relief. She turned her gaze to the Christmas tree and saw the precious little package nestled underneath which held their future. The little box represented their world, their tomorrow, their legacy. The second chance at what had so rudely been stripped from them years before.

"Hurry home, my love," Jennifer whispered, and her heart soared. "Hurry home!"

Also from the author of
Of Angels and Rolling Pins...

The obscure origins of an ancestor inspired Jackie Gould to write this thrilling tale of adventure and romance on the colonial frontier, her second novel based on family history. In 1754, Nathan Herington sails west from London, falling for the beautiful, young Elizabeth Wood along the way. Before Nathan can win Elizabeth's heart, he must contend with hostile Indians, volatile English-French relations, and the strange and dangerous wilderness out of which he must try to make his home. The details of human drama are carefully captured on a canvas of vibrant history in this blood-stirring, heart-breaking story.

ISBN 0-9788283-0-5; 363 pages; $12.95

To order, call Acacia Publishing toll-free: 866-265-4553
www.acaciapublishing.com

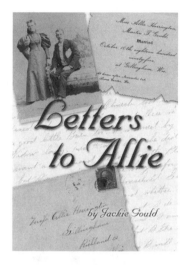

In the archives of the Gould family lie fading letters telling a story of forbidden love. As Jackie Gould read these letters from her Grandfather Martin to his future bride, Allie, their story came vividly to life. The author quotes from Martin's letters written in 1895 and fleshes out the lovers' tale from the artfully imagined perspective of Allie to transport us to an era of simplicity and strict social mores. One hundred years later, their story is a testament of the sustaining quality of love.

ISBN 0-9762224-0-X; 178 pages; $10.95
To order, call Acacia Publishing toll-free: 866-265-4553
www.acaciapublishing.com